Meant to Be Mine

Also by Hannah Orenstein

Head Over Heels

Love at First Like

Playing with Matches

Meant to Be Mine

Hannah Orenstein

ATRIA PAPERBACK
New York London Toronto Sydney New Delhi

An Imprint of Simon & Schuster, Inc.
1230 Avenue of the Americas
New York, NY 10020

First Atria Paperback edition June 2022

ATRIA PAPERBACK and colophon are trademarks of Simon & Schuster, Inc.

Interior design by Erika R. Genova

Manufactured in the United States of America

1 3 5 7 9 10 8 6 4 2

Library of Congress Cataloging-in-Publication Data

Names: Orenstein, Hannah, author. | Olson, Kaitlin, editor.
Title: Meant to be mine / Hannah Orenstein.
Description: First Atria Books trade paperback edition. | New York : Atria Books, 2022.
Identifiers: LCCN 2021030427 (print) | LCCN 2021030428 (ebook) |
ISBN 9781982175252 (paperback) | ISBN 9781982175276 (ebook)
Classification: LCC PS3615.R4645 M43 2022 (print) | LCC PS3615.R4645 (ebook) | DDC 813/.6—dc23
LC record available at https://lccn.loc.gov/2021030427
LC ebook record available at https://lccn.loc.gov/2021030428

ISBN 978-1-9821-7525-2
ISBN 978-1-9821-7527-6 (ebook)

In memory of my grandparents:

Jerry and Eleanor Hart

Rose and Fred Orenstein

I couldn't have done this without all their love.

one

The minute the cab door slams shut behind me at JFK, the hair on my arms stands on end and my heart beats double-time. My palms are coated in sweat, and not just because it's a sweltering day in late June. I wipe my hands on my vintage white Levi's, grip the handle of my suitcase, and take in the travelers pulling luggage out of taxis and steering kids through the airport's revolving door. I don't know exactly what I'm looking for, but I'm banking on the hope that I'll know it when I see it.

I take my sweet time entering my name and flight number into the kiosk's touch screen, hoping to meet someone, until I feel someone's presence a polite few feet behind me. As the machine prints out my boarding pass, I sneak a glance over my shoulder. I was right—there *is* a man there. Holding hands with another man. I offer a self-conscious smile.

"Sorry, almost done," I promise.

Going through security takes ten times longer than the Zara checkout line on a Saturday afternoon. But I don't mind the wait today. My flight isn't for another two hours, and I can use this idle time to scope out attractive people who happen to be passing through Terminal 5 on the morning of Friday, June 24, 2022.

My eyes skim over the couples and families ahead of me, pausing at the men who appear to be alone or traveling with friends. Near the front, there's a group of bleary-eyed frat bros. Too young. Further down the line, a man in a tie-dyed tank top and bun totes a hiking backpack (not my type), and another in a T-shirt and headphones nods vacantly along to a beat. I watch him for a moment until he reaches up to adjust an earbud, revealing a wedding band. Everyone shuffles through the line until, eventually, I make it to the TSA officer. He looks like he's my age. Crooked nose, white teeth, no ring. I hand him my boarding pass and driver's license. He studies my picture—taken around the time I graduated from the Fashion Institute of Technology, in the thick of my retro phase: heavy on the eyeliner, hair teased sky-high—and flicks his dark eyes up to meet mine. I wait for a spark, a sign, *something*.

"You're all set." He hands the materials back to me, gesturing for the person behind me to step forward. "Next!"

None of this is my typical experience. I usually skid into the airport with less than an hour to spare, late from packing, overthinking, and re-packing. But this is *the day*. My day. I've been fantasizing about it for nearly half my life.

I heave a sigh. For all the countless times I've imagined today, I never considered how it would test my patience. I've waited thirteen years for my life to change, but a minute longer might break me.

My nerves are thanks to my grandmother Gloria. She always insisted that my twin sister, Rae, and I call her Gloria, not Grandma, because she refuses to feel old. (Two technicalities: One, her real name is actually Gladys, but nobody's dared call her that since she was old enough to jettison that clunker. And two, she is ninety years old.) In 1955, straight out of secretarial school, she got a splashy job working at an ad agency in Manhattan. She adored it—not only the gig, which gave her work assisting important people and a salary of $92 per week, but the lifestyle: date nights with ad men at shows on Broadway, beautiful restaurants and boutiques on Madison Avenue, pocket money to buy pearls at Fortunoff, cigarettes on Central Park benches, city air. A life completely different from the one she grew up with across the East River in Brooklyn. If she got married, she'd be expected to get pregnant and give up working. So, she broke off one engagement to a nice but boring lawyer, then broke off a second one to a handsome but bland doctor. And then it happened.

The vision came to her on a lunch break with her fellow secretaries. She was enjoying a pastrami sandwich on rye and listening to Annette Lyons gossip when her vision blurred. She felt dizzy and warm, like she was floating in a hot bath: disorienting, but not unpleasant. She saw herself—not as she was, sitting in the red vinyl deli booth in her favorite cardigan trimmed with rhinestone buttons—but holding hands with a man, looking deliriously happy. She couldn't see his face. Then the voice came, soft at first, then loud and full of static, like a blaring radio tuned to the wrong frequency. *June 1, 1958*. She didn't know why, but she was certain that was the date she would meet the man she was meant to be with. As quickly as the feeling came on, it vanished.

Sure enough, three months later on June 1, she met Raymond Meyer at her friend Janet Weisberger's dinner party. They were married within the year. *He* was a man worth giving up a job for, Gloria said. They bought an apartment on the Upper East Side within walking distance of Central Park, and he truly didn't mind that she preferred to spend her days strolling Museum Mile and reading in cafés to keeping the house and preparing hot dinners. She felt vindicated that she had held out for a husband who was smitten with her exactly the way she was. He never wanted to tamp down her sharp tongue or her creative mind.

If the vision had only happened once, she might have written it off as a coincidence. But the images kept coming: she forecasted her brothers and sister meeting their matches, and then a handful of cousins, and her own daughter and son, and then my sister, Rae, and then me.

Gloria has seen it all coming: Her sixty-four-year-old aunt finding true romance with the woman who moved in next door after decades of an unhappy marriage to a man; my cousin Evan kissing a girl on the playground in preschool and marrying her twenty years later; even Rae meeting her boyfriend—soon-to-be fiancé—during her freshman year of college. She's never been wrong.

Today, Friday, June 24, 2022, is my day. Gloria has known the date since I was a little girl, but didn't reveal it until I was sixteen and completely crushed that Kyle Washington asked Michaela Francis to homecoming instead of me. She wanted me to know life had more in store for me than just a date to a high school dance. I've imagined this day in countless ways over the years: At sixteen, I fantasized about bumping into a beautiful French man on the Pont des Arts, the love lock bridge in Paris; at twenty-two, I dreamed about styling a cover shoot for a magazine and falling for whichever heartthrob celebrity's pants I was cuffing; at twenty-five, I got honest with myself and figured I'd probably swipe across my future husband on a dating app. But now, at twenty-nine, it seems none of those scenarios was right.

It was only last month that Rae's boyfriend, Max, asked our family to secretly fly to Maine to watch him propose. He wanted to ask on Clifton College's campus, where they first met, in front of both their families. (He's a sap like that.) But his choice of today means half my day will be spent traveling. I doubt he realized his proposal would overlap with the biggest day of my life, and I didn't want to put a damper on his plans, especially given how long they'd been in motion—he and my twin sister have been together for eleven years, after all. And anyway, fate doesn't care if I'm in an airport or 30,000 feet up: it'll find me no matter what.

After I run my baggage through the scanners and slip my purple, block-heeled sandals back on, I take a long, slow stroll toward Gate 53, stopping every chance I get. I dip into Starbucks to order a cappuccino, buy *Vogue* and *New York* magazine at Hudson News, browse the racks of "I ♥ NY" T-shirts at a gift shop. I scan for eligible bachelors, but each store is frustratingly empty. It turns out, 9 a.m. on a weekday isn't a popular time to travel. I briefly consider sitting down at the darkened bar to order a drink. Don't people always hit on each other at airport bars? But I'd hope my destined date doesn't imbibe before noon.

I futz with my cuticles—a nervous habit I have no right to indulge in, considering what portion of my income I spend on maintaining a flawless red manicure. I need to relax. But I can't.

I duck into a restroom to touch up my hair and face. The heat has made my hot roller curls fall flat. I revive them with a mini comb and a travel-sized bottle of hairspray I keep tucked in my purse. It's moments like these that make me grateful to be a stylist who's picked up a few tips and tricks from hair gurus and makeup artists on photoshoots over the years.

I swipe on a heavy coat of lip balm and reapply red lipstick on top of it. (All you need to know about MAC's Ruby Woo red is that Rihanna swears by it, and I hope that explains why I've worn it every day for the past ten years.) I dab a rollerball of Tom Ford Tobacco Vanille on my inner wrists. Gloria would approve. She's always reminiscing about the days when air travel was considered the height of glamour.

I took great care in choosing my outfit today. Since I didn't know what kind of person I'd meet—what he'd like best—I had no choice but to dress to my own tastes. I knew this would be the right move: Grandpa Ray loved Gloria exactly as she was, too. I have on my favorite jeans, a sweetly feminine blouse, my black leather jacket that feels like a second skin, a printed silk scarf swirled with red to match my lips and nails, and Gloria's own pearl bracelet, the one she had given me on my eighteenth birthday.

The woman washing her hands in the adjacent sink eyes me curiously. She's dressed casually in leggings and a T-shirt; her face is bare and her hair is in a lopsided ponytail.

"Hot date?" she asks, grinning.

I can't help but beam. "Something like that, yeah."

I finally take a seat at Gate 53. My knee bounces as I open the family group text, catching up on the chatter. Our parents secretly traveled from Westchester and New York City to Maine already. Rae thinks she's there to visit friends who settled down in Portland.

Has it happened yet???? Rae wrote in our group chat with Shireen, our best friend since we were babies in playgroup together.

As inseparable kids, we called ourselves the triplets. Shireen always felt more like family than a friend; we were constantly helping ourselves to snacks straight out of each other's kitchens. Even after we scattered to different colleges, the three of us reunited for a study abroad semester in Paris (Rae had wanted to go to Buenos Aires, but Shireen wanted to practice her French and I wanted to live in the fashion capital of the world—we out-voted her two to one). These days, Shireen works in the New York office of a French executive search company. She's the only friend we've told about Gloria's gift.

Wishing you good luck, not that you need it. Whoever this man is doesn't know how ridiculously lucky he is to have you in his life.

Ahhhhhhhhh

How are you feeling?!

Nervous. No sightings yet.

He'll show up. And if not, *I'll* marry you.

We've had this contingency plan in place ever since the Kyle Washington fiasco. She was dumped by Isaac Berman the same week.

Love you.

She shoots back a flurry of heart emojis as the gate agent makes an announcement that passengers in my section of the plane can begin boarding. I take a final look around the waiting area. There are families who look like they're heading off to summer camp, couples with sunglasses perched atop their heads for vacation, and a smattering of women (not for me) and older men (again, no). If there are no real prospects for me here, maybe that means my match lives in Maine. Wouldn't it be awful if I bumped into a coed at Clifton and found out *that* is supposed to be my match? I don't have the patience to date a college student. I'd like kids in five years; we'd be on different time lines. And anyway, I like my outfit too much to risk splattering beer all over it.

There's another flicker of fear that's more painful to consider. Maybe there's nobody coming for me because I already met the love of my life—not earlier today, but three years ago, when I bumped into Jonah at The Strand, the famed bookstore near Union Square. We were both browsing for photography books: I was hunting down fashion photographer Richard Avedon's work and he was looking for inspiration for his own photography. Back then, I had a strict "no relationships" rule.

What was the point of getting too involved when I knew my soulmate was waiting just a few years down the road? But when he asked for my number, I gave it to him. I never meant to fall in love, but it happened anyway, in tantalizing increments: at the West Village wine bar where we had our first date; then outside that night, huddled under the awning of a bodega to kiss as rainwater soaked his oversized wool sweater; on long walks with his camera slung around his neck; in diners on Sundays as we split hefty omelets stuffed with lox. I couldn't tell Jonah about Gloria's prophecy. How was I supposed to tell my ultra-logical, atheist boyfriend who scoffed when I read my horoscope that I was destined to want someone else even more?

I forced myself to break up with him six months ago, thinking I'd have just enough time to heal before my date rolled around. If only I knew then how raw and shattered I'd still feel now. At my lowest points, I worry I was too superstitious, too quick to blindly believe in something close to magic. Too hasty in my decision to leave Jonah.

So, I have to have faith in the prophecy. I've given up too much *not* to believe in it. Gloria has never been wrong. I cling to her guidance even more closely than our other family members do. We're kindred spirits. My favorite childhood memories are of playing dress-up in her closet while she told stories about each piece: trying on long strands of turquoise beads that Grandpa Raymond bought her in Hawaii, shrugging on the fabulous sequined jacket she wore to Mom's second wedding, stepping into the too-big slingback pumps she wears to the ballet. She trusted me with the secret ingredient that makes her dirty martinis so spectacular (I'll never tell) and took me to Paris for a week in high school when Rae was busy with soccer camp. Gloria wouldn't mess up—not ever, and certainly not for me.

"This is the final boarding call for flight 1224 to Portland, Maine," the agent announces.

My chest feels tight as I roll my suitcase toward the gangway. The flight attendant scans my boarding pass. I walk down the narrow passage, step over the threshold onto the plane, and find my seat, 11A. The New York–Portland shuttle is small enough that there are only four seats per row. If nothing else is in my favor today so far, I'm grateful to at least have a window seat. Seeing my city from above always reminds me of how many joyful experiences I've crammed into a few small square miles.

I stow my carry-on in the overhead compartment, pull out a magazine, and rest my purse on the aisle seat next to me. Flipping through the pages will calm me down. I've barely made it past the ads and the editor's letter when I hear a deep voice.

"Excuse me, do you mind moving your purse? I believe this is my seat."

Ocean-blue eyes. High cheekbones. A mess of dark blond hair. I look up to find the most handsome man I've ever seen in my life—right on schedule.

two

The man standing in the aisle offers an apologetic smile, like he's sorry he has to cram all six-foot-plus of him into the narrow airplane seat next to me. I stash my purse under the seat in front of me.

"Thanks." His voice is rich, deep, and a little gritty.

"No problem," I manage to respond. I'm not usually the type to chat with strangers on planes, but today, I wouldn't dream of closing myself off to that possibility.

This is a man I would have noticed at the airport. He must have arrived just after me.

He has a straight nose, full lips, and his hair sticks up like he's run his hands through it a few too many times today. He reaches up to close the overhead compartment and a sliver of flat stomach peeks out from the hem of his black T-shirt. The edges of his tattoos creep down his wrists, jutting out from his denim jacket. I don't mean to gawk—I snap my gaze back to my magazine, but I can't focus on any of the words in front of me.

"That's this week's issue?" He nods at the cover of *New York* magazine.

I flip it shut. It's easier to make eye contact with the actress on the front instead of the man to my left, although I'm grateful he made the first move.

"Yeah."

"I'm in there, you know."

"Are you serious?"

He takes a casual sip from his water bottle. "Page forty-seven."

Who is this man? In all the various iterations I've dreamed up over the years, I never imagined my soulmate would look like he belongs on a Calvin Klein billboard in Times Square. I riffle through *New York* until I find the right page. There are thumbnail photos of a half dozen bands, each accompanied by a block of text about their upcoming gigs.

"Here?" I ask.

He taps a photo of four guys and a girl posing with a guitar and a drum kit. I look closer, and sure enough, there he is. According to the magazine, he's Theo Larsen, the frontman of an up-and-coming indie rock band called The Supersonics. They have a series of shows at venues around Manhattan and Brooklyn this summer, and they're working on a new album, out next year.

"Impressive," I say tightly.

I'm too nervous to gush. He's probably used to winning women over.

His modest smile is a little uneven. It's charming. "Thank you."

"What do you play?"

"I sing and play guitar."

That explains the voice.

"And I teach kids' music lessons on the side, too. We aren't selling out Madison Square Garden any time soon. But we perform at some amazing venues and we're getting press like this, so I'm psyched."

"That's awesome," I say, softened by his enthusiasm. The mental image of him helping tiny humans pick at a guitar is adorable. "I still kind of pinch myself when I see my work in magazines, too."

He snaps his fingers. "I thought I recognized you from this issue, too. The supermodel on page sixty-eight?"

He flashes me a playful grin and my breath catches. No wonder he gets invited to pose for magazines. That smile could sell out newsstands.

"No, not at all," I laugh. "I'm a stylist. I've worked on a few shoots for *New York* and I style some celebrities and regular folks, too, for red carpets and events."

"That's fantastic. And it explains all of this," he says, gesturing to my outfit.

His eyes flick ever so slightly up and down, like he notices more than just my clothes. I blush.

"All of what?"

"You look like the coolest person on the plane."

I'm conscious of how narrow the armrest is between us. His knee brushes against mine so subtly that I wouldn't have noticed were my senses not on such high alert. I smile to hide my butterflies.

"Professional hazard."

Whatever panic I had felt earlier at the airport has simmered into a giddy sense of ease. I like flirting with him.

He holds my gaze. "And what, may I ask, is the name of the coolest person on the plane?"

"Edie." I extend a hand.

His handshake is firm. I pray he can't feel my pulse racing.

"Theo. Pleasure to meet you."

Edie and Theo. Theo and Edie. I like the sound of that, like a creative power couple—maybe photographed by *New York* a few years down the road in our artfully decorated Brooklyn brownstone. The walls would be lined with framed shoots I've styled and The Supersonics' vinyl records, and a kid or two could toddle around in the OshKosh overalls I've always found so precious. My earliest attempts at styling were for my baby dolls, fussing over their clothes and pushing them in toy strollers as Mom and Gloria cooed over my efforts. I've always wanted to be a mom.

We're interrupted by the safety demonstration. The flight attendants sweep the cabin to ensure passengers have their seat belts fastened. The plane rumbles down the runway and takes off smoothly. I lace my fingers together and watch New York City grow miniature. Whenever Mom, Rae, and I fly anywhere, we hold hands for takeoff and landing; this doesn't feel the same on my own.

"I'm sure you'd like to get back to your magazine," Theo says politely. "I'll leave you to it."

He pulls a pair of headphones from the canvas backpack by his feet—real headphones, the kind that fit over his ears. They're cognac leather and look expensive, like what you'd buy if you really cared about audio quality. He thumbs through his phone to select a song.

I had been so immersed in our banter that it hadn't even occurred to me that it could end. From the moment he sat down, I assumed I knew what would unfold: We'd get to know each other over the duration of the hour-long flight, and right after landing, he'd ask for my number. We'd go on a date. Then another. And another. He'd tell me about his bandmates, his hidden talents, his go-to take-out spot, the TV show he can recite word for word thanks to so many repeat viewings, the existential questions that keep him up at night. There's an excitement in wanting to know everything about someone. Maybe I'll wind up discovering everything, bit by bit, over the next months and years and decades. But for now, a few more morsels of information will have to do. I have to keep the conversation going.

"You're not distracting me," I rush to say. I flip the magazine shut. "I like talking to you."

He stops scrolling and pulls the headphones an inch off one ear. He gives me a bemused look. "Yeah?"

I cast around for a subject. "So, are you from New York or Portland?"

He tugs the headphones down around his neck. "My family's in Maine, but I live in New York. For now, anyway."

I'm intrigued about where he'd want to go next, but asking feels inappropriate.

"I'm from New York, too. Well, originally, I'm from Westchester—I grew up in Mount Kisco. My mom and stepdad are still there."

This is more information than he probably cares to receive; I'm rambling because I'm nervous. But he listens and doesn't look bored, so I throw out another question.

"You're going home to see family?"

"It's my dad's sixtieth birthday. There's going to be a big party. You?"

"I'm going to surprise my twin sister."

She's usually the one to surprise *me*. She's always had more than enough energy for the two of us, pushing me into hiking trips and white-water rafting adventures, music festivals and sunrise silent raves. In return, I've convinced her (and Max) to live a mere three blocks from me in Brooklyn and introduced her to the best of our neighborhood. I'm not much of a cook, so I can raid her kitchen whenever I like—Max is a fantastic home chef. On the few occasions she has to wear something nicer than scrubs or sweats, I find her in my closet, sifting through my dresses like we're teens in adjoining bedrooms again. We call the stretch of Grand Street between us—packed with a bodega, a nail salon, a plant shop, a lingerie boutique, a dim sum restaurant, and a terribly delicious cocktail bar—our hallway.

"What's the surprise for?"

"Her boyfriend is finally proposing. The whole family's flying in to celebrate."

"Aw, that's sweet."

"They've been together for eleven years. College sweethearts."

Rae didn't want to get married until after she finished med school and got settled into her residency.

"Wow. It took her all these years to ultimately decide he was the one?"

I suppress a laugh. He couldn't be further from the truth. "Nah, they've been smitten since they met."

He whistles. His eye contact falters. "Well, that's very sweet. I'll keep that in mind as inspiration the next time I'm trudging through dating apps."

It's hard to imagine that someone like Theo would have a tough time dating.

"I've never really spent much time on the apps," I admit. I've never seen the point of putting myself through that if I know something good is guaranteed around the corner. "But I think the lesson I've learned from watching my sister's relationship is that sometimes, you just know when you've met someone special."

"Well, an early congrats to the happy couple." He lifts his water bottle like he's making a toast.

"I'll tell them you said so." If only he knew how serious I was. I pivot to a new subject to keep the conversation flowing. "Do you write your own songs?"

"Of course. No shade to musicians who perform covers, but I love the challenge of translating emotions into music and lyrics. I think I'm pretty good at it, too."

"What do you write songs about?"

"Well, *that's* a personal question, Edie." He raises an eyebrow and looks down at his lap, briefly flustered.

Did I cross a line? "It's too personal to ask about music you belt out onstage in public?" I ask, surprised.

He tilts his head like he's trying to figure out the best way to explain it. "People can read whatever they want into the lyrics, and they do. But they start off meaning a lot to me, and I'm not exactly in the habit of divulging *all* the messy details of my life to beautiful strangers I meet on planes." He holds my gaze steady as his words sink in.

"You're shameless," I accuse him. I can feel my cheeks turning Ruby Woo red.

He grins. "I have a song called 'Shameless,' believe it or not. It was the first song I ever wrote. I was sixteen and completely infatuated with my girlfriend at boarding school."

The prospect of *him*—this sexy, confident musician—being infatuated with anyone makes my stomach flip. It makes me wonder if, some day, he'll talk about me that way.

"Before I wrote music, I wrote—please don't roll your eyes at this—*poetry*. Really awful poetry," he continues. "One night, some guys and I got our hands on a bottle of coconut rum, and I wound up wasted in my underwear, reciting the sonnets—oh yeah, I wrote her sonnets—outside her dorm window. I got suspended from school for that."

"Because the poetry was so terrible," I joke.

He laughs. The sound lights up my insides like gold. I didn't mean to sass him like that; that kind of playful banter was a hallmark of my relationship with Jonah. I didn't realize until this moment how much I missed it.

"Because I broke about a thousand school rules—drinking, curfew, nudity—but yeah, probably that, too. I got sent home and wound up writing this song about being shamelessly in love," he explains, putting the phrase in air quotes. His blue eyes sparkle at the memory. "Of course, she dumped me over Facebook chat like a week later, but still."

I pretend to scrutinize the magazine in my lap. "It seems they forgot to publish that detail."

"Thank god for that." He shakes his head.

I actually read the clip in full now. One line in particular makes me perk up. "You're playing at Baby's All Right?"

"Yeah, and Mercury Lounge, Brooklyn Bowl, Rockwood Music Hall . . ."

"Baby's All Right is fantastic," I interrupt. "I live a few blocks away."

"In Williamsburg?"

I nod. "Yeah."

"I'm not far—Bushwick. But I'm in your neighborhood all the time. Maybe we've bumped into each other."

"No," I say, a little too confidently.

If we'd run into each other earlier, then today wouldn't be my day, or he wouldn't be my match.

"How can you be so sure?"

I shrug him off. "I'd remember someone like you, that's all."

He ruffles up his hair with his hand and grins down at his lap, like I've made him nervous. It's very endearing.

We spend the next hour or so talking about our corner of Brooklyn: shows we've seen at Baby's All Right, horror stories from our respective apartment hunts. Unbidden, I see flashes of what could be our future together: Saturday afternoons flicking through racks of thrifted clothing at L Train Vintage, singing along with the crowd at The Supersonics' gigs, regular trips to Portland together on flights just like this one to see his family. A big Brooklyn wedding in a converted warehouse, all exposed brick dripping with green vines and chandeliers. A rock star melting over a tiny toddler one day. I barely know him, but after a lifetime of wondering who my match would be, even the smallest morsels of information are intoxicating.

There's a *ding* over the loudspeaker. The pilot announces we're descending. It's not long until landing.

When we reach the gate, Theo stands and lets me out of the row before him.

"Ladies first," he says, helping me with my luggage.

He has one more minute to ask me for my number while we file out of the airplane. I know I could ask him, but I've always imagined my match sweeping me off my feet. I pictured him as someone forward, confident.

We make it into the airport. I feel rattled with nerves at the prospect of him following me to the exit, where my parents are waiting. But then, he waves—the most friend-zoned gesture known to man.

"It's been nice chatting with you, Edie," he says, walking toward the men's restroom.

I do a double take. This isn't how it's supposed to go.

"Wait, what?" I feel jolted out of a daydream.

Theo cocks his head. "Everything okay?"

Maybe I misread the entire situation. Hadn't he called me beautiful? Cool? Fantastic?

"Uh, yeah. Have a great visit with your family," I say lamely.

He gives me another wave and disappears inside the restroom.

For a moment, I feel stunned. Frozen to the spot. I check my phone's calendar to confirm that today is, indeed, Friday, June 24, 2022. It is—I have an all-day event titled, "THE DAY!!!" so I haven't gotten the date wrong. And it's not like Gloria can be wrong, either. As I make my way through the airport, past the signs for lighthouse sightseeing tours and local lobster restaurants, I know two things.

First, and most important, Theo Larsen may very well be the love of my life.

And second, I shouldn't have let him walk away.

three

My family is waiting for me at baggage claim. Mom lights up when she spots me; there's nothing more I want in this moment than to crumple into her arms so that she can hug me, stroke my hair, and reassure me that everything is going to work out.

She must know how I feel. Her date was August 27, 2000, the year she turned forty. She didn't believe in Gloria's powers, so she married her college boyfriend, Barry, shortly after graduation. But within weeks, she discovered he had a nasty temper and a terrible habit of lying about everything from his finances to his fidelity. So, she filed for divorce and, after her dad's death in 1992, decided she could make peace with being single if she could at least have a baby. Her long-time best friend Kevin donated sperm; one turkey baster and nine months later, Rae and I showed up. Sure enough, she and a stranger named Allen reached for the same *The Talented Mr. Ripley* VHS tape at Blockbuster on a Sunday night in 2000. He raised us like we were his own.

"Good to see you," Allen says, ruffling my hair in a dad-like way.

I instinctively pull back so he doesn't ruin the curls.

"She's all primped up for her big day," Mom warns him. "Don't mess it up."

She rolls her eyes affectionately and gives me a hug. If I had to guess, she probably met Allen while still wearing business-casual slacks and loafers straight from her accounting office, with her hair wound up in a claw clip. Not so romantic—and yet, obviously, it didn't matter.

Then there's Pops—Kevin—and his partner, Rocco. Gloria predicted their 2003 meet-cute at a karaoke bar, too. I dive into Pops' hug. We've never lived under the same roof, but Rae and I often went to Pops and Rocco's house for dinners and sleepovers. We're family. I get my strong eyebrows and round face from him. Rae inherited more of Mom's looks, down to the hazel flecks in her fierce brown eyes and her square chin.

Next, I spot Gloria. I bend to kiss her cheek, and she grabs my arm. She has regal posture, even in the uncomfortable airport chair, gripping the top of a glossy black cane with manicured hands. Her age shows in her white shock of hair and deeply lined face, but her eyes are still bright and sharp under the elegantly oversized glasses she's worn since the '70s. They gleam like the pearls around her neck.

"You'd wear open-toed shoes on a flight?" she asks, raising one disapproving eyebrow.

She has a thing about sandals. She thinks they're only appropriate on the beach.

"Easier to slip on and off at security."

"But bare feet on a dirty airport floor?" She grimaces.

"How's this—let's all do pedicures this weekend?"

I've never seen her nails without a shiny coat of pearlescent polish.

"If there's time, of course." She fingers the scarf around my neck. "Meet anyone special yet?"

"Maybe. I'll tell you all about it—but later," I promise. I don't want to dwell on Theo walking away. "Let's go surprise Rae. Max will kill us if we're late."

An hour later, the six of us are packed into a Clifton College sorority house bedroom, sitting three each on a pair of twin extra-long beds that belong to students here for summer classes. There's an Audrey Hepburn poster Scotch-taped to the door and a dresser drawer hanging open to reveal a sea of going-out tops. We snuck into the once-white shingled house quickly to avoid being caught by Rae, who's somewhere nearby amid the rolling green hills that make up campus.

We're here because this building's backyard abuts the frat house where Rae and Max met on September 26, 2011. He wanted to propose on the spot where they had their first conversation, a second-floor balcony. That's why we're camped out here—looking out this bedroom window, we can sneakily watch and take photos. The girls who live here—Addie and Vanessa—linger in the doorway, eager to watch this all go down.

Gloria looks at the decor with amusement. "You know, I paid forty dollars a semester for tuition when I was a student," she tells the girls.

Their jaws drop.

"Can we come in?" someone asks.

Addie and Vanessa part to usher in another group. I recognize Max's parents, Dale and Cindy, and his sister, Alana. They live in Illinois, so we aren't all together very often, but we've met a handful of times over the years—like when Max and Rae graduated from Clifton and when we all pitched in to help them move to the city. The two sets of families greet one another in a flurry of hugs. From here on out, we'll all be one big extended family.

"C'mere, c'mere." Mom beckons us all toward the window. "They'll be out there any second now!"

"Can one of you take the photos?" Cindy asks me and Alana. "I don't trust myself with this."

"On it." I position my phone by the window.

"Shhhh, here they come," Dale whispers.

A nervous hush falls over the room. Maine weather is temperamental, but Max and Rae got lucky with a beautiful day: fat white clouds hang in a bold blue sky, and the maple tree in the yard lends soft shade over the balcony. Max must have paid some college kids to clean it up because it actually looks nice. From what I remember of my Clifton visits, the balcony was covered in broken lawn furniture with Solo cups left out on the railing. But today, there's even a healthy-looking potted plant in one corner.

Rae opens the faded white door and steps outside. She's dressed for a casual day running around to see friends, not one of the most romantic moments of her life—shorts, a T-shirt, and sneakers, with her light brown hair pulled up in a high ponytail—but she isn't the type of person to care about that. Max follows her onto the deck and flashes a jittery, enthusiastic grin our way. Rae, oblivious, leans onto the railing, and looks around the yard.

"Boy, they cleaned up around here," she says.

I'm grateful we're within earshot.

"It's beautiful," Max agrees. "But I still have a soft spot for the first time we were out here."

"He doesn't look nervous," Dale whispers.

"He knows she'll say yes," Gloria murmurs.

Mom shushes all of them. "Quiet, I want to watch."

Rae gives him a nervous side-eye, like she's suddenly piecing together why they're standing there.

"Do you remember the night we met here?" Max asks.

"Oh my god," Rae says, giggling. "You're such a sap. Of course."

"I couldn't believe my luck that you approached me," Max recalls.

I can. Rae was initially crushed when Gloria predicted her date. She got her prophecy very young—she was just thirteen at the time, and the date was five years away, barely a month into her freshman year of college. She dreaded what the prediction would mean for her life's path, and it made her skeptical. She asked Gloria endless questions in an attempt to find a loophole to the magic. She was afraid that settling down young would be boring, that it'd curb her zest for chasing down adventures, or that it would affect her dream of going to medical school. Rae has been a fiery nightmare since infancy, when she began flinging herself out of the crib. The reveal of the prophecy only made her more intense. That's why she spent that first month at Clifton blatantly hitting on every man she saw. ("I have to cram an entire lifetime of sexual experiences into four-and-a-half weeks!" she moaned.)

Flirting with cute strangers was right up Rae's alley when she met Max. He never would've had the guts to make the first move on someone as vivacious as Rae.

"I had to bring you back here because there's something very important I need to ask you," he continues.

He presses a kiss to her temple and takes her by the hand, leading her a few steps away from the railing. This means I can get a better shot. I start snapping away.

Max swipes the ring box from his pocket and sinks down onto one knee. Rae claps her hands to her mouth. I'm surprised to feel a lump welling up in my throat as my vision goes blurry with tears.

"I've been a very lucky man to spend these past eleven years by your side. I love your endless energy, your fierce loyalty to the people you care about, and the way you've helped me grow into a better man," he says, pausing as his composure breaks.

Rae is already saying "yes" and nodding ferociously, which only makes Max laugh.

"I'm going to finish proposing to you now, if that's all right," he says, grinning and wiping the corners of his eyes beneath his glasses.

She doubles over to laugh and straightens up again, smoothing a hand over her hair.

"Sorry, yes, keep going."

Classic Rae.

"You make every single day an adventure. I want to have adventures with you for the rest of our lives. I love you. Rachel Amelia Meyer, my Rae of sunshine, will you marry me?"

"Yes, of course, oh my god, yes! Oh my god, oh my god."

He slips the ring I helped him pick out onto her finger, then shoots up to stand and kiss her. I snap another billion photos with the urgency of a fashion photographer attempting to nail the September cover of *Vogue*.

We all erupt into loud cheers. Rae stops kissing her new fiancé and turns to the source of the noise, shrieking when she sees us.

"What!" she screams. "What are you all doing here?"

She covers her face with her hands again, and even from across the yard, I can see her shake with happy sobs. Max wraps her up into a hug and she cries even harder.

"He nailed it," Pops says.

"Let's go," Mom says, misty-eyed.

We file out of the sorority house. Gloria ushers us all in front of her so she can take the stairs at her own pace.

"You catch up to them," she tells me. "I'm savoring my stroll through this beautiful house."

She's in amazing shape for ninety years old, but her high heels now have a permanent spot in the back of her closet, and she rarely travels other than to see family in Florida once a year. While most older Jewish New Yorkers wind up spending winters in Boca Raton, if not moving down south permanently, she's always balked at the idea of leaving Manhattan. She says too much sunshine makes you soft. But she wouldn't miss this moment.

The newly engaged lovebirds have made their way downstairs, too, and we meet in the middle of the lawn for a raucous group hug.

"I can't believe you're all here," Rae sputters.

The parents all take turns squeezing their kids and their future in-laws. I wait as patiently as I can, the grass tickling my ankles. Finally, when Rae is free, I fling myself at her, wrapping my arms around her and burying my face into her neck.

"I'm so happy for you," I say. "You and Max are going to have the best damn life together."

"I know." She sounds awestruck.

We've always known this. Gloria's prediction warps relationships in strange ways. There's no will-they-or-won't-they tension. Instead, it's *when* will they. *How* will they. There's no question of whether or not a couple will ignite sparks, or if they can succeed in making their relationship work. They will.

"I'm so happy, I could puke," she says. Her cheeks are flushed pink. "I knew this would be an amazing moment, but . . . it's even better than I expected."

A weird thrill washes over me: Will Rae and I switch places a few years from now when it's my turn to get engaged? Will Theo be the guy down on one knee? I cut myself off from this train of thought. This is Rae's moment—I don't need to dwell on myself right now.

Gloria interrupts our hug by asking to see Rae's ring. I guided Max toward a round-cut solitaire diamond in a low-profile, platinum setting that wouldn't snag on her latex gloves at work.

"I know you took an oath—do no harm, et cetera—but you could put an eye out with that thing," she says mischievously.

Rae squeals. "No! It's stunning."

Gloria taps her hand reassuringly. "It's a knockout. The boy's got good taste."

She grips my hand and whispers an aside to me so subtly, I could've missed it. "And I know where he gets his good taste from."

"She approves!" Rae calls over to Max.

He jogs over to give Gloria a hug. Max's own grandparents have been gone a long time, and so she's become something of a surrogate grandmother to him over the years. She calls him to hear about his work at the lab and trade recipes.

Cindy, Rocco, and Allen are already batting around wedding venue ideas, while Dale and Kevin kvell over Max's speech. Mom and Alana tag-team the task of organizing Rae and Max into position for a few more photos, and then just a few more, and then—wait—no, they promise, *these* are the last ones.

"Edie, we look great, right?" Rae asks, exasperated. "Back me up here."

"Mom, think you've gotten enough shots?" I ask.

"Oh, I know I'm going overboard," she sighs. "But what a special day."

Gloria smirks and glows with pride. "I told you it would be."

four

That evening, the eleven of us are clad in flimsy plastic bibs, tearing apart bright red lobsters at an outdoor seafood shack on the pier. The table is littered with decadent bowls of melted butter and tall glasses of local Allagash beer, and the briny scent of ocean water drifts through the warm summer night. This is already about a million times better than my last experience with lobster, when I styled a shoot for *Rolling Stone* starring a rapper who showed up four hours late and high with a posse of friends. In between shots, he'd wander off set to eat the lobster he had delivered, dripping crustacean innards and butter onto the Gucci pants on loan. It turns out it's easier to appreciate high-end seafood when you aren't nauseous with nerves.

Gloria nudges me. "So, when are you going to tell me about your fella?"

I snap off a claw. Juice spurts onto my plate.

"I didn't want to steal Rae's thunder," I explain.

She waves off my concern. "She's as happy as a clam."

Across the table, I can plainly see that she's right. Rae has pierced green, jiggling lobster guts with a tiny fork and is threatening to wiggle them onto Max's plate. He yelps in protest. They're breathless with laughter.

I'm suddenly shy. Telling Gloria about Theo would make it feel real. She'd know from the tone of my voice how I'm feeling, and she'd want each detail, including the fact that I'd watched, frozen, as he walked away. She cuts a piece of haddock—she doesn't eat lobster; it's not kosher—and watches me expectantly. I pull a tender piece of speckled meat from the claw and drag it slowly through the butter, considering what to say. Further down, a soft rock cover band is playing. The music and the din from the surrounding tables mask the sound of our conversation.

"I met a guy on the plane today," I explain. "His seat was next to mine, and we started talking, and I really hope he's the one for me. I got such a good feeling about him."

She nods approvingly. "Your *bashert*," she says, invoking the Yiddish term for *soulmate*.

"You think so?" I blurt out, desperate for some sign I'm on the right track. I'm grateful she's still around to discuss meeting my match; when she first predicted my date, I calculated what our respective ages would be, and I wasn't sure she would make it.

She hesitates. "Fate works in mysterious ways. But it's certainly possible he's the one. Today is your day, after all. Tell me about this young man."

"He's a musician, and he seemed funny, confident, charming," I recall, thinking over our banter from this morning. "I felt like I could be myself around him."

"Well, that sounds very nice," she says diplomatically before pivoting to the question never far from a grandparent's tongue. "Is he Jewish?"

Of course she asked. The tattoos, the Scandinavian last name—I doubt it.

"I don't think so."

"Well, you can't win 'em all," she tuts.

"I thought we clicked right away. But then we got off the plane and that was it. He didn't get my number or ask me out."

I can't believe I let my window of opportunity slip by. How stupid am I? Gloria sips from her martini glass—leave it to her to find a martini at a seafood shack on the water—and gives a mysterious smile.

"I can't tell you for certain what's going to happen. All I know is that today, you're supposed to meet someone. But if you liked this man, he's worth pursuing. Maybe you can be a modern woman and ask *him* out, hmm?"

She punctuates her words with a judgmental purse of her lips. I sink into an avalanche of self-loathing for not making my move earlier on the plane.

"I could," I admit. "That's just not how I always envisioned it happening."

"How old-fashioned," my ninety-year-old grandmother muses.

Ashamed, I pick at my cuticles. She bats at my hand for me to stop, then casts an appraising eye around the room. Waiters in red aprons bustle between tables, diners crack lobster claws, and people at the bar sip drinks while watching TV.

"Surely, there must be one or two gentlemen here who catch your eye. The day's not over yet."

It hadn't even occurred to me to keep looking once I met Theo.

"Why don't you go take a stroll and see who you meet?"

Her brown eyes glow mischievously. I guess it doesn't hurt to explore my options—and I'm not about to back down from a dare leveled by my grandmother. I untie my lobster bib, scoot my chair back, and pick up my purse.

"I'll be right back," I announce.

Our table is at the end of the dock, and I meander toward the bar at the front of the restaurant as slowly as I can stand, forcing myself to make meaningful eye contact with the men who aren't sitting with dates. Some don't notice me, while others flick their gaze to mine briefly before pulling it away. I'm fooling myself if I genuinely believe somebody would stand up from their dinner—while up to their elbows in lobster juice, no less—to run after a woman who happens to be passing by.

I make it to the bar, where there's more likely to be a single man sitting alone and unencumbered. There's an open stool between two thirtysomething men, and I force myself to move toward it before I lose my nerve. To my left, a dark-haired guy in glasses nurses a beer; to my right, a man with a shiny shaved head picks at a plate of French fries. Both stare at their phones.

Maybe a meet-cute would feel more plausible in another era. People must have been more open to striking up conversations with strangers before we all walked around with our faces buried in screens. I imagine possibility hung in the air more often back then—like you'd never be able to predict who you'd meet, what you'd learn, or where the night would take you. But maybe I'm romanticizing the past. What seems novel to me probably felt routine back then. And I've spent enough time in vintage store dressing rooms to know that garter belts and nylons meant no woman was ever comfortable enough to casually lounge around striking up conversations with random men. When Gloria was my age, it wasn't considered appropriate for women to even *be* in bars with men.

"Hey there, what can I get you?" the bartender asks.

"I . . ." I don't know what I'm doing here. I have no intention of ordering a drink. Neither of these men stoke my interest. I know there's more to chemistry than pure physical attraction, but I don't feel a pull toward them, the way I instantly felt with Theo. He has to be my person. I'm sure of it.

"Uh, I was looking for the bathroom?" I lie.

"Right behind you," she says, nodding to a door very visibly marked RESTROOM.

"Sorry, right, thanks."

I escape through the door and lean against the cool, white-tiled wall. I pull my phone out of my purse and Google The Supersonics. It takes all of ten seconds to find their Instagram, then a tagged photo of Theo, and then his personal account. I scroll through his pictures, careful not to graze my thumb against the screen and accidentally "like" anything. The most recent post is a flyer for the band's upcoming shows, and the next one's an artful shot of him onstage, hands curled around a microphone. In a group photo with him and his bandmates, his arm is looped around the female drummer's waist. I feel suddenly sick with panic. Is *she* the reason he didn't make a move? Based on his brazen flirting, I had assumed he was single; if he's not, and if I'm fated to fall for a cheater, I'd like to register a formal complaint with whichever force in the universe is responsible for this disaster.

I navigate to the drummer's page, and scroll until I can exhale in relief. There's a picture of her in a dimly lit bar, embracing a woman with doe-eyed adoration. "Happy Valentine's Day, my angel," the caption reads. Theo and the drummer are just bandmates. Friends.

I return to Theo's page. The white message button is tempting. My head is too muddled from my roller coaster of a day to write anything coherent to him right now, but I like knowing I can reach out to him anytime. I haven't missed my window of opportunity—not yet.

I exit the restroom and return to our table.

"Meet anyone interesting?" Gloria asks.

"I did," I say, surprised by how confident I sound. "This morning."

five

We pack a lot into our Portland weekend—a drive to Cape Elizabeth to see the lighthouse, a celebratory round of cocktails at Blyth & Burrows, an afternoon of shopping for little white dresses on Congress Street, the pedicures I promised Gloria, and, fine, somewhere between seven and twelve visits to Theo's Instagram—before I head home on Sunday night. My family is staying an extra day, but I have back-to-back events for work on Monday.

Unlike my last experience in an airport, I'm fully relaxed this time around. The Portland airport is tiny, so I show up a half hour before the gate closes and breeze through security in all of five minutes. A flight attendant checks my boarding pass and waves me into the line forming on the gangway. I scroll through my phone, narrowing down all the photos I took this weekend into the best options for Instagram. I'm inching forward in line, scrutinizing ten nearly identical, swoon-worthy shots of Max proposing to Rae, when I hear a deep voice that sounds very much aimed in my direction.

"So, we meet again, huh?"

I know that voice. I spin around to see Theo in line. His headphones rest around his neck and his mouth crinkles into an amused grin.

"What are you doing here?" I ask.

"It's wild, I have this thing for hanging around airports," he says, deadpan.

"You're flying home. Duh. Right," I say, recovering. The line shuffles toward the plane. "How long were you standing there behind me?"

I'm bowled over by the sheer luck that I happened to be staring at my own photos and not his Instagram. *That* would have been embarrassing.

"Only long enough to make sure it was you," he swears.

The passengers behind him are giving us curious looks, but I don't care. I cross the threshold into the plane and file down the narrow aisle.

"How was your dad's birthday?"

He shrugs. "It was all right. I don't see my family much, but it's good to come together for occasions like this, I guess. My mom made this insanely rich chocolate cake that I wish I could take home with me. And your sister—she's engaged now?"

"Yep." I show him a photo of the proposal on my phone.

"Precious."

I double-check the seat number on my boarding pass. "Are you 11B again?" I guess.

"You're still 11A?" he asks, laughing.

"Of course."

Under any other circumstances, I'd chalk it up to coincidence. It's not outrageous to bump into the same passengers on the same airline's flights between two cities a few days apart. But it's more than that—it's fate. It's proof my love story is unfolding right before my eyes. It's further evidence that Gloria, as always, is right. Theo has to be my soulmate. Not the men at the bar on Friday night. Not any one of the hundreds or thousands of strangers I must have crossed paths with at JFK or in Maine. Theo. That knowledge injects me with a burst of confidence.

"You know, you forgot something on the plane last time," I say.

Worry puckers his forehead. He pats his pockets. "Did I?"

A flirtatious smile curls across my face. "My number."

I don't know where I got the chutzpah to be so bold. This is a move out of Rae's old playbook; I've never had the guts to speak like this in my life. Theo's jaw drops a fraction of an inch before he catches himself. He clears his throat.

"Believe me, I was kicking myself all weekend," he admits.

Is it my imagination, or do his cheeks look pink?

"Were you?" I ask, relishing the moment. My confidence surges.

He rubs his hand over his face. "I got nervous," he says shyly.

I look him square in his ocean-blue eyes, taking in his high cheekbones, straight nose, and full lips. He fiddles with his hair, mussing it even further into a casually sexy mop.

"Nervous," I repeat skeptically, like he and I both know he must be kidding. "*Sure.*"

He talks quickly, like he's been struck by an idea. "But if you'd let me, I'd like to make it up to you in two ways."

I raise an eyebrow. "I'm listening."

"First, I'd like to ask you for your number now. And second, when the beverage cart comes around, I'd like to buy you a drink."

~~~

Fifteen minutes later, after a conversation that could win an Olympic gold medal in Flirting at 30,000 Feet, my number is stored safely in his phone and we're clinking plastic cups: gin and tonic for me, whiskey for him.

"Thank you for the drink," I tell him.

"Thank you for making the first move," he says. He pauses, like he isn't sure he wants to say what's on his mind, but continues. "I didn't ask you out the other day because I didn't know if you were single. I was try-
~~~

ing to work out a smooth way to ask, but then the flight was over, and I figured, you know, I'd missed my chance."

"I'm single," I confirm with a coy grin.

For the first time in six months, this feels like a boon.

"And you? Do you date groupies?" I ask, mostly joking.

"We're definitely not famous enough to have actual groupies."

"Yet."

"That's the spirit! Thank you. Actually, though, I've been single for a while."

"Oh?"

An ideal twist of fate to ensure he'd be available when we were destined to meet? I know that even if two people are meant for each other, there's no guarantee that getting together will be easy. Mom's brother, my uncle Dave, is proof of that. When he met Aunt Holly, she was traveling cross-country as a trapeze artist in the circus, and so he chased after her through Providence and Columbus and Reno. She turned down his first two proposals before she proposed to him, and even then, they bicker more often than not. That's how they are—fiery. And in love.

"When did the last album come out?" he mutters to himself, then pauses to think. "I guess it's been two years."

"It's all breakup songs?" I guess.

"There's, uh, a few." He snaps his fingers. "The breakup was two years ago, the album was one."

"So, you write songs about the women you date," I say, piecing it together—the theme of his newest album, the inspiration behind his old song "Shameless." "That's why the lyrics are too personal to talk about."

"Women, among other subjects," he admits.

I file this bit of knowledge away for when I finally get the chance to hear the album. There had been too much going on over the weekend for me to fully dive into his band's music.

"You know, this is far more information than I typically like to reveal on a date."

"Oh, so this is a date?" I crow. I run my fingers down the armrests and pretend to admire the mesh seat-back pocket. "Interesting location. Very romantic."

I'm not necessarily a wallflower around new people, but I rarely feel this instantly comfortable being 100 percent myself on dates. I can banter like this with a very select handful of people: Rae, Shireen, plus Jonah when we were still together. Max made the short list eventually, but it took the better part of a decade. So, for me to feel at ease around Theo already is some kind of magic.

He rolls his eyes. "You know what I mean."

"No, you're right, this is kind of like a date."

"Where do you like to go on dates?" Theo clears his throat. "You know, when you're not confined to a plane. Just, uh, hypothetically. If someone needed to know these sorts of things about you."

I laugh loudly enough that the woman in the seat across the aisle turns to gawk at us. I dig Theo's style.

"I like bars that can make a decent cocktail."

He nods deeply. "Noted."

"Or any excuse to put on a swanky outfit."

I watch his reaction closely. I always feel deflated when I show up to a date in a sharply tailored dress or a thoughtfully arranged mix of jewelry, only to meet a guy who threw on a hoodie. But—of course—I shouldn't have worried.

"Glamour. Got it."

"Or something like the gallery openings in Chelsea, or a walk through a museum, or a concert, or a burlesque show," I finish.

"Saucy," he says, lifting an eyebrow.

"I like the costumes. I'm a stylist, remember?"

He chuckles. "Right, because everyone goes to burlesque shows for the *costumes*."

"They're amazing performances," I insist, delivering a light punch to his arm.

It's the first time we've touched. I get a nervous thrill.

Twenty minutes later, after telling Theo all about my favorite annual burlesque show, the Hanukkah-themed Menorah Horah performed by drag queens, the plane touches down. Theo repeats the same polite gesture of retrieving my carry-on suitcase from the overhead compartment. We talk while filing out of the plane and walking into the airport—and this time, he doesn't scoot away with a wave. Instead, we make it past the restrooms, beyond Starbucks and Jamba Juice, and all the way through the terminal to the taxi stand.

The person manning the cab kiosk asks where I'm going. As he marks up a receipt, I realize Theo and I live close enough that we could reasonably split a cab. But inviting him to do that would be officially considered coming on too strong. Just because I feel an eerie pull toward him doesn't mean he feels the same way about me. At least, not yet.

A cab driver walks toward me to pick up my luggage. I turn toward Theo, not quite sure how to part ways. I could get sucked into staring at those warm blue eyes all night if I don't make my exit soon.

"Well, I guess I'll be seeing you," I say.

He steps forward and kisses my cheek. His hand brushes my waist. "Get home safe."

Long after he pulls away, after he closes the cab door, after the car starts, and the airport retreats in the distance behind me, I feel the warmth of his kiss lingering on my skin.

six

The next day, work is nonstop. I file invoices for two photoshoots I did last week, negotiate a contract with a fashion editor on a tight budget, dart around the city returning garments I had on loan, and fiddle with a moodboard for one of my favorite clients, the twenty-two-year-old socialite Sadie Sakamoto. She goes through cocktail dresses faster than most people go through underwear. I'm relieved when the day is over and it's time to head to SoHo for a press preview. I finagled a plus-one so Shireen can join me. She'll want to grill me on every second of my interactions with Theo.

Press previews are a useful way for me to discover new designers and forge strong relationships with the publicists. They're rarely just about the clothes. I've been to the launch of a new accessories brand at a bar serving custom cocktails based on your birth chart; viewed a womenswear collection inspired by the supernatural at a secret, abandoned underground pool beneath a Midtown hotel (it's rumored to be haunted by very chic ghosts); tried out a new activewear line during a complimentary ballet lesson taught by members of the Rockettes; and celebrated the launch of an over-the-knee boot collection that doubled as a private Ariana Grande concert.

Tonight, I'm going to the press preview for Annabelle Crosby, a buzzy, woman-owned workwear brand that specializes in suiting. It won a grant from the prestigious Council of Fashion Designers of America last year. And naturally, the press preview will also double as a fireside chat by a renowned career coach—clad in one of Annabelle's latest ensembles, of course—who will deliver a presentation featuring tips for nailing job interviews.

My pulse speeds up when I enter the subway. It's rush hour. The train platform is packed. Ever since my breakup six months ago, I've developed a painful habit of scanning every face in crowds like these, nervously searching for Jonah's. My gaze darts from person to person, searching for round glasses and cozy sweaters.

My heart lurches when I spot a lanky figure with dark hair leaning against a column. His back is toward me. I feel a disproportionate wave of panic, more like I'm in the path of an oncoming train than an oncoming man. What could I possibly say, *Forgive me for leaving? I had to take a risk? I think it's paying off, though, because I might have just met the man I'm supposed to be with—even if part of me still wishes that man could be you?* No.

The guy turns to check the status of the next train, and that's when I see it can't possibly be Jonah. This man is bearded with a sharp nose and deep-set eyes. My breath returns in a gush, but it takes longer for my nerves to simmer down. I don't like living like this, in fear of seeing someone I once loved. I hope the paranoia subsides as I gain more distance from the breakup. But somehow, I worry it won't.

When I emerge from the subway, I weave around a soft pretzel cart and a group of teen girls trying very hard not to look like tourists, and turn down a cobblestone side street. Annabelle Crosby's showroom is in one of those classic cast-iron Soho buildings I'd give up my firstborn to live in, the kind with ornate façades, high ceilings, and wide windows framed by Corinthian columns. Shireen is already there waiting for me, dashing off something on her phone. She looks annoyingly chic in a tailored black pencil skirt and a sleeveless cream blouse tied in a bow. On someone less poised than Shireen, the outfit might look slightly stuffy, but she looks completely herself.

"Hiiiii!" she trills, giving me a hug. "I'm so glad to see you. I need to hear everything."

"We'll discuss everything."

"There's going to be wine and cheese at this thing, right?"

This is not her first press preview rodeo. In our early twenties, she was always my plus-one. We'd stack two or three events like these back-to-back and pick through enough passed apps and complimentary flutes of rosé to feel full and pleasantly buzzed. It was our way of living large on our meager salaries.

"I would almost bet my life on it."

We take a rickety freight elevator up to the third floor, where I see DeeDee, the publicist who invited us, standing with a clipboard at the entrance to Annabelle Crosby's showroom. She's tall and lanky, with natural hair in an Afro, clad in an aquamarine short suit from the spring/summer line and gold sandals that lace up her ankles. She greets us warmly and checks our name off her list. Her assistant hands us each a signature cocktail on our way in.

A raised, L-shaped platform stands on one side of the airy, spacious loft, where models showcase sleek jackets and high-waisted flared pants in punchy tones of forest green, Barney purple, and burgundy. The models are all close to six feet—not even counting their dizzyingly high heels—but they range in size and shape, from thin to voluptuous.

As Shireen and I wind our way through the showroom, oohing and aahing at the slickly tailored suits on display, I tell her all about Rae and Max's engagement and meeting Theo.

"Stop it," she says, wide-eyed when I tell her about bumping into him the second time. "That did not happen."

I grin. It really does sound like a fairy tale, doesn't it?

She prods me to show her pictures of him, and when I do, her eyebrows—dark, thick, dramatically arched, not touched by anyone but the one threader she trusts in all of New York City—shoot up.

"You didn't tell me he's practically a male model!" she says.

The actual model standing above us gives us an amused look.

"He's very handsome," I admit.

Shireen tilts my phone toward the model on the platform.

"The dude's hot," she agrees.

"Okay, okay." I grab my phone. "What's the latest at the French Embassy?"

She almost exclusively dates Parisian transplants. I bestowed the nickname on her love life shortly after she broke up with the second consecutive Henri (or was it after Jean-Luc?), and it stuck.

"I broke it off with Raphaël last week. I gave him a fair shot for three dates, but I wasn't feeling the chemistry. And then—oh my god, I need to tell you about this guy Louis."

She pronounces it the French way, *lou-EE*.

"Our first—and last—date was on Saturday. He's the biggest name-dropper on the planet. He told me the CEO of Target owns two puppies descended from his dad's dog? And that he's still really close friends with his ex-girlfriend, Felicity, a prima ballerina? And that he hired a publicist for his startup who is, I quote, 'one of the top females in China.'"

"I'm sorry, *what*? Top . . . what?"

"I don't know!" She throws up her hands. "And that wasn't even the end of it! He bragged that his grandfather was the first doctor to be imprisoned in Auschwitz."

I wrinkle my nose. "That's morbid."

She sighs heavily. "So, obviously, the next day, I sent him a text that was like, 'It was so nice to meet you, I didn't feel a romantic connection, blah blah blah.'"

"Standard."

"Right—except he shot back five patronizing texts insisting he wasn't attracted to me anyway."

"Better to find out he's a lunatic now rather than later."

"True." She drains her cocktail. "Anyway, I have another date with this new guy, Romain, next week."

We're interrupted by "hiiii"s and air kisses from people I know: Ayana, the fashion editor I bonded with at the Rockettes class; Talia, the former *Bachelor* contestant–turned–fashion influencer who's nicer than any other reality star alive; Frank, who does not work in fashion (or seem to work at all), and yet somehow makes an appearance at more industry parties than any of us.

DeeDee moves through the room, encouraging everyone to take their seats for the conversation portion of the evening. As the career coach talks, Shireen takes detailed notes; she's been gunning for a promotion for months. I try to focus, too. There's plenty I could learn about setting rates with new clients. But instead, I find myself replaying my conversations with Theo in my head, wondering when he'll text me. I'm antsy for him to reach out, but part of me wants to savor the anticipation. The chapter of my life as a single girl is coming to a close, and I might as well appreciate the last few days of it.

After the press preview, I'll ask Shireen if she wants to keep the night going. We could dip into Bloomingdale's next door to try on outrageous gowns, or grab a real dinner at Charlie Bird, or even go out dancing at Beauty Bar on Fourteenth Street. Entering a new relationship certainly won't mark the end of wild nights out with Shireen, but I know from experience that the prospect of crawling into bed next to the man I love has a funny way of making me want to turn in early.

Tonight, we're both single. A whole city's worth of possibilities await.

seven

Shireen and I did it all. In true New York fashion, I came home late, got up early, dabbed concealer over my dark circles, downed a huge coffee, worked a jam-packed day, and went straight back out for another night. I have dinner plans with Rae and Max at Shalom Japan, the trendy fusion spot run by a Jewish husband and Japanese wife chef team in our neighborhood. One of Max's friends will be joining us. I missed a call from Gloria earlier today, and as I walk to the restaurant, I call her back.

We talk on the phone at least twice a week. She once complained that I only call her while running from one place to the other, but when I asked if she rather I sit around at home with no plans, she changed her tune. "You're right, go be young and interesting and busy," she had said. As I listen to the line ring, I hope she picks up; I want to tell her about seeing Theo again on my flight home.

"Hi, dollface." She greets me in a voice cracked with age. "I couldn't leave a message—your voicemail box is still full."

That's because I've saved every one of her recordings. I'm afraid that one day, I won't get to hear her calling me dollface and *bubbeleh*. She won't recommend the best brand of nylons (I don't wear them) or invite me to join her for a manicure. Her voicemails are keepsakes.

"I'll have to fix that," I promise, a white lie. "How are you doing?"

"Well, I'm still here, aren't I?"

I don't know what to say to that. She's as healthy as someone her age can be, but still, I worry.

I've been calling everyone to tell them Raezie's news," she adds.

"I'm going to dinner with her now."

"Good," she says firmly. "My two girls."

"I'm calling, actually, because I wanted to give you a funny update."

"Oh, yeah?"

I can hear her waiting breathlessly.

"Remember the guy I met on the plane?"

"The musician!"

"Guess who happened to be on the same flight back to New York?"

Through the phone, I can hear the faint sound of her palm slapping her knee. She marvels, "Isn't that a hoot! So? What did you do?"

"I gave him my number, and we're going to go out soon."

I've thought about this moment before—how delightful it would be to share news about my fated match with Gloria, to provide closure for her long-ago prediction. Considering her age, there was no guarantee she'd be around for this. I'm grateful she is. So many long-awaited moments fall flat, but this one is completely satisfying. I can't stop myself smiling as I turn the corner onto South Fourth Street.

"Did you kiss him?" I can practically hear her grin.

"Gloria! No. We were on a plane."

"Flying used to be very sexy."

"It's definitely not anymore."

"Well, let me know when I can meet this fella. I have to make sure he's good enough for my granddaughter."

I laugh. "Give me some time to get to know him. I want to make sure he's the right guy."

"Okay. I'll let you get to dinner—go enjoy and give your sister a kiss for me."

"I love you. Bye."

"Love you, *bubbeleh*."

Inside the restaurant, soft summer evening light spills in through the tall windows, reflecting the sky streaked with hazy washes of purple and pink. A chalkboard by the bar announces specials, including a matzo ball ramen soup and chirashi bowl with lox. Rae and Max sit together on the same side of the table, holding hands in her lap. Since my breakup, seeing their affection has hurt; it's a bittersweet reminder of how comfortable I used to be with Jonah.

They're across from a man I vaguely recognize, but I can't recall his name. I slide into the empty seat beside him against an exposed brick wall.

"Edie, this is Bennett," Max says. "We grew up together in Illinois. He moved to the city a couple of weeks ago."

I remember hearing about him now. Max's childhood best friend.

Bennett offers me a handshake. He looks a little square for this neighborhood, dressed in a pale gray suit with a starched white button-down underneath. He wears tortoiseshell glasses that frame warm, dark eyes and pop against his tan skin. His thick head of dark hair is combed back neatly, though one lock springs forward. I don't even need to see his shoes to guess that they're shined.

"Bennett Garcia. Nice to meet you."

"Hi," I say, thrown by the formal greeting.

Max is the kind of guy who calls T-shirts without words on them "dressy." I didn't know exactly what to expect from his oldest friend, but this wasn't it. I pick up a hint of amber cologne.

"I'm glad you two are finally meeting!" Rae says. "We're so excited Bennett moved here."

"What brought you to New York?" I ask.

"I've always wanted to live here, and a job made it happen." He leans his elbows on the table, talking fast, like his new city energizes him. "I was working in politics in Chicago, and I moved here to manage the campaign of my friend from college. She's running for Congress. I'm her second campaign manager, actually—she fired the last one, who was a mess, but she still managed to win the primary last week, anyway. If she wins the general election in November, she'll be the youngest person to serve in the House."

"If you don't cut him off now, he'll spend the rest of dinner convincing you to canvass for him," Max warns.

"No, no, no," Bennett says, shooing him away. His eyes crinkle when he smiles at me. "It's cool, just remember to tell everyone to vote for Kiara Walker for New York's ninth congressional district."

Ordinarily, I'd think he was cute. But it doesn't matter. I know he's not the one for me.

"How do you like New York so far?"

He beams. "I'm so happy to be here. It's everything I love about Chicago, only bigger and weirder and I don't think my eyelashes will freeze shut come winter."

"The timing of your move couldn't be better," Rae tells him.

"When a promising candidate asks you to run their campaign, you don't tell them, 'Later'—you move."

"No, I know that, I mean—" She darts a look at her fiancé.

Max shrugs and smiles. "Go for it."

Her face lights up with an infectious grin. "We wanted to ask you both something very important." She ducks down to reach for something under the table. "We love you both very much and wanted to ask if you would be our maid of honor and best man!"

"Yes!" I squeal. "Obviously."

Bennett presses his palm to his chest. "Of course, I'm honored."

"Proposing!" Rae shouts. "What a thrill. I could do this all day."

"Please don't," Max says mildly.

She chuckles and kisses his temple. Then she reveals what she's holding under the table: two white paper bags overflowing with sparkly confetti.

"We got you gifts, assuming you'd say yes," she explains.

"I said yes years ago," I recall.

One weekend when I visited her in college, Rae had a ridiculous amount of jungle juice and forced me and half the girls in her sorority to promise we'd be in her bridal party someday. She was so drunk and yet still so scary.

Rae bites her lip. "Oops. We were thinking, like, a pretty low-key wedding party . . . as in, you two, plus three others each."

"Delta Nu will be crushed," I say solemnly.

She swats me. "For the last time! You know that's not what it's called!"

I duck just in time to avoid her palm, the wrath I get for invoking the name of Elle Woods's sorority in *Legally Blonde.* Joining Pi Phi made sense for Rae since the Clifton social scene revolved around Greek life. But for me at FIT? Not a chance. The only rushing I did was to the front of the line at sample sales.

Bennett and I open the bags to reveal handwritten cards and gifts swathed in layers of white tissue paper. He pulls a gold ribbon off a small, narrow black box and lifts the lid. When he sees what's nestled inside, his jaw drops.

"It's the—" Max begins.

"Cross Townsend pen," Bennett finishes, sounding awestruck. "This is way too extravagant. You can't be serious."

"This makes up for all those years of only buying you shots on your birthday," Max counters.

Bennett gently pries a heavy-looking, lacquered black pen plated with gold from the box and holds it out in his palm, admiring its weight.

"This is what Obama used to sign legislation," he explains. "Bush and Clinton, too."

"And the last one," Max adds quietly.

Bennett makes a face and waves him off. "Yeah, but Obama used twenty-two of these to sign the Affordable Care Act—one or two for each letter of his name," he explains. "And they all became priceless pieces of history."

"So will this one," Max insists. "When you sign your landmark bill."

Bennett makes that sentimental face men make when they're trying not to cry. "I love you, man. This is awesome, thank you so much."

"Your bill?" I ask.

Bennett tucks the pen carefully back into its case. "Long story, I'll tell you later. It's a downer."

I have a hunch about what he might be referring to. When Max was in high school, there was a shooting at their school. I wonder if he's interested in gun control legislation, but this isn't the time to ask.

"What did you get?" he asks.

My bag feels suspiciously light. I peel back the layers of tissue paper until my fingers close around a small velvet drawstring bag. It's not like Rae to get me jewelry. She knows I'd have too much fun shopping for myself to even try picking anything out. Curiously, I tip the contents into my palm, and out slides a gold wedding band on a chain. It's thick, too big for my ring finger, and scratched from years of wear. I recognize it instantly.

"Grandpa Ray's ring?" I ask, fighting back sudden tears.

He died a year before we were born, but he lives on in Gloria's stories about the slick-haired man who swept her off her feet, in faded photos of Mom in his arms, and in the physical items he left behind, like the silver cocktail shaker he used to mix drinks, and this ring, kept safe for many years in Gloria's jewelry box. I stumbled upon it in high school, and Gloria said one of us could wear it if we promised to keep it safe. Although we both coveted it for its significance (decades of marriage! What a good omen), Rae insisted she had dibs on it because he was her namesake. We fought over it, but I had to concede. She's worn it on this chain around her neck ever since.

"I wore it while falling in love with Max," Rae says, reaching for my hand. "It's a good luck charm. And now it's your turn to wear it."

"But it's yours," I protest.

"It can be yours for now," she says firmly, like she's already thought through how to push back on me. "It's your turn to fall in love. You can give it back to me if Max ever decides he gets sick of me."

I laugh and sniff to keep from crying, knowing that won't ever happen. "All right—but I'm holding you to that."

I clasp it on. All this love it carries.

The waiter comes by, and we order a bunch of plates to share. Over sake-infused challah and Wagyu pastrami sandwiches, we get down to business.

"I'm not going to go full bridezilla on you, so don't worry—you two won't be up until three in the morning making centerpieces or helping me choose between identical swatches of chiffon," Rae says.

"But I'd *like* to choose between identical shades of chiffon," I say. "I'm good at that. I get paid for that!"

"We can't afford you," Max says.

"You're a designer?" Bennett asks.

"Stylist."

"Max and I talked about it and we really only have one teeny, tiny, eensy-weensy request of you," Rae says.

"This sounds like a big request," Bennett mutters to me.

"We thought it'd be fun to do a joint bachelor-bachelorette party," Max explains.

"One amazing weekend of partying on a fabulous beach!" Rae says, getting loud with excitement.

"And lots of down time," Max adds pointedly, as if they've had this debate already. "To chill. Quietly. And relax."

Rae rolls her eyes. "Right, lots of relaxing. And penis straws."

"Relaxing and penis straws," Max says seriously. "That's our final compromise."

Bennett accidentally snorts some of his sake. The couple seated at the table next to us, who have been talking about a drag queen named Dixie Wrecked since we sat down, don't even blink.

"Where are you thinking?" Bennett asks.

"We were talking about Miami," Max says.

"And you two could maybe plan it?" she asks, looking hopeful.

Mopping his face with his napkin, Bennett leans in close to me and stage-whispers, "Relaxing and penis straws—what do you think?"

"Extremely tacky, but she's my sister."

"You're in?"

"In."

"We'll do it," he announces.

"Amazing, thank you so much," Rae says. "Oh, and it has to be sooner rather than later. This is a secret for the next few weeks, so don't tell anyone else . . . but Olivia is pregnant."

Olivia, her best friend from Clifton, a dermatology resident who got married last year.

"Really! Oh my god, wow. That's so exciting."

Rae's eyes gleam. "Isn't it crazy?"

If I know my sister—and I do—she's picturing Olivia on the night of her twenty-first birthday, when she smashed Clifton's record for the fastest time in the Jell-O Shot Olympics, women's division. And soon, she'll be a mom.

"So, even though Max and I aren't talking about having the actual wedding until sometime next year, I'd rather do this trip maybe this fall or winter so she's not super pregnant or like, legitimately giving birth on a beach somewhere."

"Noted," Bennett says, eyes going wide with alarm.

"Hey, speaking of exciting news—did you hear from the plane guy?" Rae says brightly, leaning forward over her meal.

"Not yet," I say, as if this exact question has not kept my eyes glued to my phone for days.

She makes a face. "He'll text you. I'm sure of it. Pull up his Instagram again? Max hasn't seen it yet."

I do as I'm told. Theo's Instagram handle auto-fills in my search history. Regardless of the prophecy, I'd want to go out with him again. Something about our connection felt easy, reminding me of the quick spark I felt the first time I met Jonah. How could I not pursue that?

Max thumbs through the photos, then passes the phone to Bennett, who raises a skeptical eyebrow.

"This is the guy you like?" He bites his lip like he's trying to suppress a laugh. "He knows The Strokes aren't accepting applications for new members, right?"

I snatch my phone away, annoyed. "Suits aren't everyone's cup of tea," I reply.

"I'm just saying you can do better than this guy," Bennett says, holding his hands up.

I roll my eyes. "Thank you for your feedback."

"Oof, I'm sorry, that came out wrong," he backtracks.

"I'm sure it did," I say tightly.

"I don't know him—maybe he's great," he says.

"We'll find out," I mutter, exchanging glances with Rae.

He winces, clearly realizing he's in the wrong. "Sorry, let me get back into your good graces."

I laugh. "Shoot."

"Hear me out. Kiara—my friend, um, my boss—is pretty stressed about what to wear for a few upcoming campaign events."

"Ooh . . ." My mind flashes to the suits I saw last night. How amazing would they look on the campaign trail?

"How much do you charge for styling?"

"I'll give you my friends-and-family rate. Three hundred dollars per event."

The truth is that my rates typically start at $350 for up-and-coming clients, escalating up to $750 for more successful ones. But I like the idea of working alongside a political campaign—that's appealing enough to give Bennett a friends-and-family discount and then some.

"I think we can swing that," he says.

He fishes a business card out of his wallet and carefully uses his beloved new pen to jot down the dates of Kiara's upcoming events. He looks giddy at the smooth strokes.

"Max, seriously, I can't thank you enough." He admires his handiwork, then slips me the card.

"Enough business, we have a wedding to plan," Rae says. There's a mischievous look in her eye I know all too well. She flags down a waiter. "I think we're going to need another round of sake shots."

Max groans, burying his face in his hands and pushing his dark curls off his forehead. "Again? We did this last night!"

"You signed up for a lifetime of this, bro," I say, testing out how the nickname feels for the very first time. "Welcome to the family."

eight

Two days later, I'm on a folding chair in Kiara Walker's field office, a glass storefront on Franklin Avenue in Crown Heights. Bennett suggested I meet Kiara here. It's bustling with energetic post-grad organizers shoving "Vote for Walker" pamphlets into tote bags, interns crowded around open pizza boxes dotted with grease, and volunteers repeating the same message into their respective phones: *Hi, I'm calling on behalf of Kiara Walker, a congressional candidate in your district, and I'd like to talk to you about making a donation today* . . .

Bennett emerges from behind an office door, and two people jump up to talk to him. In the time it takes for him to stride across the room—eyes glued to his phone, fingers typing quickly—he's answered both questions and shooed them away.

"Hi, she'll be with you in a minute," he says, seemingly unfazed by the chaos.

"No rush."

When I researched Kiara last night, I understood exactly why Bennett felt she was worth uprooting his life and moving halfway across the country. A Crown Heights native, she worked for Clinton's 2016 campaign and at a D.C. nonprofit that helps women run for office, supporting herself with waitressing shifts and freelance writing about politics in between. When her mom contracted COVID and spent ten days in the hospital on a ventilator, Kiara wrote a viral op-ed about America's oppressive health-care system, leading to a face-off with a conservative talking head on FOX that racked up millions of views. In liberal circles, she's a progressive icon; in conservative ones, she's a spitfire nightmare.

The ninth congressional district contains both Crown Heights, a Caribbean neighborhood that's quickly gentrifying, and Park Slope, a mostly white yuppie one. It had historically gone blue. But in the last election, the rapidly growing Hasidic population, which votes nearly unanimously conservative, pushed Republican Glen Vernon into office. Kiara's primary win against Liz Janetti, a more experienced Democratic candidate, had been a surprise victory. But defeating Vernon in the general in November might still be an uphill battle.

"Do you want pizza?" Bennett asks. "Or can I get you to knock on doors or make phone calls while you're here?"

"Stop bothering her," Kiara says, gently admonishing him as she breezes in through the front door.

He throws his arms out wide. His indignant smile could light up Times Square. "I'm only trying to help! I'm dedicated!"

"Don't I know it." She purses her lips. "I'm Kiara Walker. You must be Edie Meyer?"

"It's great to meet you."

She appraises my outfit, a ruffled navy dress toned down by a beat-up vintage denim jacket. I paired it with punchy red clogs and matching lip.

"See, this is why you do what you do, and I do what I do." She gestures to her own drab gray slacks.

Kiara brings me into her office and shuts the door, blocking out the noise of the rest of the field office. I sit across from her desk.

"So, how does this work?" she asks.

"I know you have a million more important things to do today, so I'll make this quick. I'd love to get a sense of what you need—what your days look like, what events you have coming up, what kinds of pieces you feel most comfortable in while working."

"Well! Where to begin. Up until the primary last week, I spent most of my time out—getting signatures, knocking doors, high-traffic canvassing, meeting voters at community events like festivals and fairs and food drives, going to fundraisers, debates . . . And then, of course, hiring up the team, filming ads, doing interviews . . ."

"So, basically, your days are crazy long, you're running around all the time, and you need to be comfortable."

"But professional. I don't go too crazy with work clothes. Black, gray, or navy pants, a button-down or blouse, and a blazer if I need one."

The wheels in my head are turning. "I wish I could see your closet."

"Oh, is that what you typically do?"

I nod.

"Bennett didn't tell me that." She looks annoyed. "I live a few blocks from here. You up for a field trip?"

"I don't want to inconvenience you—you must be so busy."

"We're paying you to work for us, aren't we?"

"Yes."

She laughs. "Then we might as well get our money's worth. Let's go."

On the walk over, she tells me about the early days of her campaign. In order to get on the ballot for the primary, a candidate theoretically needs 1,250 signatures—except, in practice, you need at least four or five times that number to be safe. She would practice what organizers called the five-finger test, pressing five fingers on buzzers outside apartment buildings, claiming she had delivery for a neighbor, and getting inside to chat up residents so she could ask for their signatures.

"Especially after 2016, there was this big push to get women running for office at all levels. Sounds great, right?"

"Yeah," I say warily, sensing this story doesn't have a happy ending.

"Except you need a minimum of two hundred thousand dollars to run a viable campaign. It's an open secret that most people get it from their rich family and friends."

"That's insane."

"I was lucky—I had a pretty significant following on social media before I chose to run, and I could fundraise all that money and more online. But this system is so broken, it's absurd."

I follow her up enough flights of stairs that I lose track, until we turn down a hallway and she unlocks the door to her apartment.

"Sorry about my roommates," she says, as I step over a pile of sandals by the door that apparently don't belong to her. "I used to have my own place, but then I moved in with my mom to take care of her. I stayed for a while after she got better, but optics-wise, it didn't look good to be living with her anymore. Imagine the *New York Post*'s dumb headline—'Entitled Millennial Runs for Office from Her Mom's Living Room,' or whatever. This place is kind of cheap and I'm basically never here."

She leads me to her bedroom. There's a sunny yellow bedspread underneath a colorful wall of Obama '12, Clinton '16, and Biden '20 pennants. Bookshelves prop up economics textbooks and the collected works of bell hooks and Roxane Gay. A photo of her and her mom is framed on the nightstand.

"Everything's in the closet or the dresser—feel free to look around."

I riffle through the wire hangers in her closet, taking in the worn-in Banana Republic and J.Crew business casual pieces. A few H&M and Express tags are mixed in, too. If I had to guess, Kiara bought her work wardrobe straight after college and hasn't updated it since.

"Please don't take this the wrong way, but your closet makes me think you dress the part of a politician a little too well."

She smirks. "Are you calling me boring?"

"No! But your wardrobe might be. A tiny bit."

"I know it is," she admits.

"What did you like about these pieces when you bought them?"

"Most of this stuff is old," she explains. "I looked at what other interns or junior organizers were wearing and bought the same things. I wanted to fit in."

"And now?"

"I'm going to stand out regardless." She shrugs. "Not that many twenty-something Black women run for Congress."

She glances at her closet and sighs. "Everything is a calculation, including what to wear. It didn't used to be this bad, you know, before." Before she went viral, it's implied. Before people paid attention to her every move. She continues, "There's so much to take into consideration. What voters will like, what voters won't like. What's considered too expensive for me to wear, or too cheap. What the press will pick apart versus what they'll love. And that goes double for people like me—one of the only Black women to have ever run in this district, super grassroots, a former waitress. You know Anthony Weiner won seven consecutive terms in this district? He was probably sexting the whole time."

She rolls her eyes at the thought of the disgraced congressman and continues. "There's no rulebook for what to wear when you run for Congress before your thirtieth birthday. So, I've been playing it safe. I guess I want to look polished—no, better, *powerful*. But not like I care too much about what I'm wearing. No offense."

"None taken."

The word *powerful* echoes in my head. That could mean so many different things to so many people: well-tailored suits, or tough combat boots, or luxe leather accessories.

"If you could dress like anyone at work, who would it be?"

She thinks about this for a moment. "Is it bad that the first person who comes to mind is Olivia Pope from *Scandal*?"

"No, I love that!" I say, getting excited. "There's so much we can work with here. Feminine, strong suiting. Interesting pieces with clean lines. There's this designer I love, Annabelle Crosby. Her clothes would be amazing on you."

I sit next to her on the bed and start showing her photos from Annabelle's line. I'm careful to ease her into the idea, starting with the neutral ones, and hiding the green and purple ones for a more adventurous day, maybe after she gets elected.

"Ooh." She nods approvingly. "Very Olivia."

But then, a flicker of worry crosses her face.

"And you don't think these are too . . . I don't know . . . flashy?"

"I really don't," I tell her honestly. "These are like the suits in your closet, only tailored a little bit sharper. It's like, 'Hi, I'm professional, but I'm also young, and cool, and have a personality.'"

"Hmmm," she says, like she's deciding whether to believe me.

"There's nothing more professional than a killer suit. And these happen to be really fabulous. You'd be supporting a local Black-owned business."

Plus, Annabelle is a rising star, too. I flick to the next picture on my phone.

"What about this navy suit?" I ask. "Great tailoring in a classic color."

She considers this. "Sure, that could work . . . for a stick," she says skeptically, eyeing the six-foot, size-zero model.

I flip to another photo, showing her one of the plus-sized models wearing the same suit. The tags on clothing in Kiara's closet suggest that she wears sizes 12 to 14, meaning she falls on the border between straight sizes and plus sizes.

"Oh!" She sounds pleasantly surprised. "That could work. How much?"

"Well, if we work together, I can borrow samples for you on a regular basis. You'd pay me for my time, but the clothes would be free—unless there's anything you loved so much you wanted to buy straight out. Normally, though, this would be about six hundred dollars off the rack."

"Wow. I do like it, though."

"Then I'll put together a rack of samples for you to try on, and from there, we can figure out what to borrow for specific events."

She grins. "Bring it on."

This already sounds like an all-around win: Kiara gets to look and feel fiercely powerful in a suit from a buzzy brand, Annabelle Crosby will probably be thrilled by the association with her, and I get the satisfaction of a job well done.

"Can I see what you have for shoes?"

She nods and gestures to the shoe rack at the bottom of the closet. There are two neatly organized rows: the lower one is filled with sensible flats and modest pumps in neutral colors, while the upper one includes pink bejeweled stilettos and a badass pair of leopard print ankle boots—her off-duty shoes, I guess.

I spot something out of place: a pair of men's loafers. I pick up one shiny, tasseled shoe.

"These are yours?"

She gives me a coy smile. "Do my feet look that big to you?"

Getting dressed is an intimate business; this wouldn't be the first time a client revealed something about their personal life. I don't want to pry.

She gives me a silent once-over, like she's sizing me up. "How much did Bennett tell you?"

"I'm not sure what you mean."

She gives the loafers a pointed glance.

It clicks into place.

"*Oh!* I didn't realize you two were together." It's not my place to ask for gossip, but I'm intrigued.

"We're not," she rushes to say. "Well, that's not true. We are. But it's so new. We've been friends forever, since freshman year of college. Right after he took the job and moved to New York, we were out talking strategy over a pitcher of margaritas, and one thing led to another, and . . ." She trails off, suddenly shy, and looks away, fiddling with her earring. "We're keeping things quiet for now, at least until the election is over. We don't want this going public before we figure out if we could really make things work for the long haul."

"I won't say a word." I slip the loafers back into place.

"Thank you," she says, exhaling. After a moment, she laughs softly. "And good for him, not telling you—I should really give him more credit for keeping his mouth shut."

"He's really proud of you, you know that? He was raving about you."

She gives me a tiny, satisfied smile.

"So, next steps," I say. "I'll pull some pieces for you this week, and then you'll try everything on, and we can go from there. Sound good?"

"Absolutely."

We say goodbye. I've barely made it to the sidewalk when my phone lights up with a text from an unfamiliar number with a Maine area code.

> Hey there, it's Theo. I'd like to take you out for a decent cocktail at a place where you can put on a swanky outfit. Any chance you're free this week?

nine

I'm fiddling with the tiny ankle strap buckle on my Victoria Beckham heels when my doorbell rings. It's Sunday night. Date night with Theo. My first real first date in nearly three years. And he's five minutes early. He asked if he could pick me up at my front door, which is sort of a ridiculous concept in New York—neither of us own a car, and we're only going to Sweetwater, a restaurant a few blocks away—but I'm not complaining. I do a lurching scramble into the living room with one shoe dangling uselessly from my foot.

"I'll be right down!" I say through the intercom.

"Can I come up for a second? I have something for you," he says.

I'm caught off guard. I didn't expect him to come upstairs. I glance at the pile of shopping bags on the couch and the magazines spilling across the coffee table. There isn't enough time to straighten up.

"Yep!" I buzz him up.

I live on the second floor of a walk-up, so I have all of twenty seconds before he's at my front door. I crouch down to finish buckling my shoe, then grab one of the tubes of red lipstick lying on my mantel—they must reproduce and multiply when I'm not looking—and swipe it on quickly in the mirror. I snatch a napkin from the counter and blot aggressively until

I hear a knock at the door. I whirl around, feeling the frantic motion of every single individual butterfly in my stomach.

First dates used to have different stakes. I sought adventure and entertainment, or at least someone to fill up the lonely space on the other side of my bed. (Falling for Jonah was a bittersweet accident.) I knew none of those outings would pan out into anything real, so I figured I might as well have fun while I could. I don't know how fate will change that, exactly. Will tonight go smoothly because that's what the universe has in store for me? Or only because the overwhelming pressure will push me to be my best?

It's time to find out. I open the door to find Theo in a chambray button-down with the sleeves rolled up, clutching a bouquet bursting with pink and red peonies that makes me feel momentarily speechless.

"Hi," he says, eyes going wide at the sight of my dress, with its puff sleeves and mini hem. "You look beautiful."

Words sputter to life in some dusty corner of my dumbstruck brain. "Thank you."

He brushes a kiss against my cheek as he crosses the threshold. "I like your place," he says, taking in the leopard print armchair underneath the gallery wall of iconic '50s *Vogue* covers I meticulously assembled from Gloria's collection. He'd never know it, but the two fashion photography books stacked on the coffee table were gifts from Jonah. I couldn't bear to get rid of them.

"Thanks," I repeat, still trying to find my bearings. "You're quite the gentleman, you know, picking me up here with flowers."

He grins. "Just trying to make a good impression."

"I can tell."

I take the bouquet from him. As I find a vase and fill it with water, he wanders over to the wheeled rack of clothes I keep against one wall.

"You tried on all of these for tonight?"

"No, those are all for work!" I explain, laughing. "I called those in for clients."

"So, there's no way I'd see you in this?" he asks, examining a skimpy lime-green halter top dripping in fringe.

"Not a chance." Sadie Sakamoto requested a sexy after-party look to change into after the Greenpeace gala next week.

He bites his lip. "Bummer," he says in a voice sexy enough to make me briefly consider if we really want to leave my apartment.

I haven't had a man in my home since I was dating Jonah, and that felt entirely different—we were comfortable. I don't know how to comport myself with this alluring stranger. I arrange the fragrant flowers and step back to admire how pretty they look on my kitchen counter.

"They're gorgeous, thank you so much. Shall we?"

He holds open the door. "After you."

We head downstairs. It's a magnificent summer night: the sky has softened from an afternoon blue to a moody dusk and the heat has broken over concrete sidewalks. Side by side with Theo, I itch to hold his hand, knowing it's too soon. We turn the corner onto Bedford Avenue, where people spill out of bars and streetlights twinkle gold. An odd sense of déjà vu settles over me as we approach the restaurant. I've walked this same route on plenty of date nights before. Jonah and I used to eat here all the time.

Behind Sweetwater's weathered blue and gold façade is a dimly lit restaurant that looks like the love child of a swanky French bistro and a pre-war Brooklyn brownstone. Diners nestle into deep red leather booths beneath the intricately embellished tin ceiling. There's a long wooden bar softened and scuffed by age, stormy oil paintings, and charming crown moldings. Specials like French onion soup and grilled octopus are spelled out by hand on chalkboards.

"Theo, reservation for two," he tells the host.

She leads us to a pair of bar stools. I drink it all in: the flowers, the reservation, the way his chambray shirt makes his eyes look an even brighter shade of blue. This is a man I could get used to.

After we order, he tells me, "This is where we—me and the band—came to celebrate booking our first big show. We spent more than we earned, but it was worth it." His eyes crinkle into a smile at the memory. "We felt like we had made it."

"I want to hear more about the band. Who's in it?" I ask, as if I had not read the entire "About Us" section of the band's site three days prior.

"So, I sing and play rhythm guitar. I knew Mika, our drummer, from school. We performed together at Oberlin. She wound up living in this random apartment from Craigslist with this guy Ethan, who's now our lead guitarist. And then I knew Giancarlo, on keyboard, from a billion years ago at summer camp, and we stole Callum, our bassist, from another band playing around here because he's insanely talented and I love him."

He squeezes a lemon wedge over an oyster and tips it into his mouth.

"I still can't believe I was lucky enough to convince them all to play the songs I wrote. Callum hooked us up for our first gig, and when it turned out we didn't completely suck onstage together, we were able to get more."

"Is it scary, performing in front of people?"

"It's my favorite thing in the world. You can't half-ass anything up there when people are watching. I feel more like myself onstage than anywhere else."

"You're lucky that you can make a career that way."

"Well, sort of. It's not a full-time gig yet. But we're actually in talks with a record company out in LA, and I'm hoping they'll sign us. If they do, it could change everything."

"Holy shit, that's big."

Power couple big. I get a flash of an image of us working happily side by side, him plucking out notes on a guitar and testing out lyrics, me on the floor surrounded by a mess of clothes.

"Like, our music would be on the radio and we'd be touring across the country and we'd move to LA— that kind of big." His eyes glow and his voice shimmers with enthusiasm.

If this were any other first date, I wouldn't jump to conclusions. But because our lives are fated to intertwine, my head spins with questions: When would we have time to see each other? Would he want me to join him? There's no way I could work like that, skipping from city to city every night. And LA? No way. I can't imagine ever leaving New York.

"But they aren't convinced we've found our hit single yet," he says, snapping my focus back to the conversation.

"And you wouldn't mind moving to California?" I do my best to keep my voice casual.

He makes a face that says, *Are you kidding?* "Well, the best music producers are all out in LA, so that would make the most sense for us. And touring would be the absolute *dream*. I'd love to go out on the road and perform every night. But enough about me. How did you get into fashion?" I swallow all my follow-up questions about his plans. An interrogation wouldn't be cute right now.

"My favorite thing growing up was playing dress-up in my grandma's closet, and working in fashion makes me feel like I'm still doing that. She's the most glamorous, fabulous person on the planet, and I do my best to follow in her footsteps. I worked my way up as an intern and assistant before launching my own styling business."

I don't mention I opted to pursue styling over, say, working in-house at a fashion magazine or in fashion PR partly because I wanted a career that would allow me to set my own schedule. That'll come in handy when I'm a mom. But that's too much to drop into conversation on a first date.

"You know, you always light up when you talk about your family."

"Ha, do I? We're tight. Especially me and my sister. We're twins. I've quite literally never known life without her."

"She's older?"

"By a minute. She's so damn impatient, she had to rush out first."

I've used that line a thousand times before. All siblings are compared to a degree, but it's different with twins. We settled into our respective grooves early on, defined as much by our contrasts as we are by our similarities. The roles were seemingly assigned at birth: she's the tomboy, I'm the diva; she's the academic one, I'm the artistic one.

"What's your family like?"

He fiddles with his fork and drops his gaze like he'd rather not have this conversation. "Ehhh . . ."

I didn't mean to pry. I make a show of eating an oyster to take the spotlight off him for a moment.

He clears his throat. "My parents are good people, don't get me wrong. But we're not alike. They're both professors—my mom's in astrophysics, my dad's in archaeology—and that's their world. Research, academics, all that. I had a hard time focusing in school as a kid. Later, I was diagnosed with ADHD, but at the time, I felt like I sucked at the one thing my parents built their lives around."

"That must have been hard."

He ruffles up his hair; I'm noticing it's his nervous tic. "Between boarding school and summer camp, I didn't spend much time at home. I think they wish I did something a little more high-brow than music."

"I'm sorry they're not more supportive. Any siblings?"

"An older brother, but he moved to Hong Kong a few years back to work in finance there, so I almost never see him."

"Huh." I can't imagine a life that doesn't involve family poking into every part of it.

"But the band feels like a family," he adds. His voice turns ten degrees warmer. "We do a massive Friendsgiving together every year, and we all have matching tattoos."

He extends his inked-up forearm and shows me a tattoo of a sound wave, The Supersonics' logo, near the crook of his elbow. I run my finger over it.

"We got them on a trip to Hollywood," he says, telling me the story of their adventure.

But it's hard to focus on what he's saying—I can't help but notice how enthusiastically he describes visiting a city three thousand miles away from New York. I've been there on vacation, and while I liked window-shopping on Abbot Kinney and the proximity of the beach, it didn't feel like home.

We order a second round of drinks as an excuse to linger even after we've finished eating. He asks me more about styling, and I entertain him with absurd work gossip. He almost chokes on his drink when I tell the story about the pop star with such unwieldy long nails, she needed my help putting on her own underwear. He tells me about his now-defunct favorite band, a couple who performed as an indie rock duo before their nasty breakup; these days, they perform separately as solo artists who write dagger-sharp lyrics about nightmarish exes. I cop to having a very embarrassing fashion blog back in college, and he levels with me by playing a downright mortifying video clip of the time he auditioned for *American Idol* in high school, back when that show was cool. (Simon Cowell eviscerated him.) We agree Coachella is overrated and disagree about the best midnight snack—Crif Dogs' hot dogs are definitely not better than a classic slice of cheese pizza at Joe's, but he's cute enough that I'll let it slide.

I find myself swiveling on the bar stool to face him, as if pulled by a gravitational force, and his fingertips dance lightly over my knees. He's close enough that he could easily lean in and kiss me. I wish he would.

"Are we going for round three?" the bartender asks, butting in.

I hadn't even noticed our glasses were empty.

"What are you thinking?" Theo asks me.

I don't want the night to end, but I'm not sure if it's greedy to eat up another hour of his time.

"What do you want to do?"

"How about the check?" he asks the bartender.

I hope the disappointment isn't visible on my face. Theo removes his hand from my knee to reach for his wallet. I scramble for mine, too, but he beats me to it. Maybe he's only paying to be polite.

"Want to take a walk down to the waterfront?" he suggests.

I feel flushed with relief. He doesn't want the night to end, either.

"Yeah, definitely."

After Theo signs the check, we emerge onto the street as the last rays of sun slip into dusk. He slips his hand effortlessly into mine and we take off toward Domino Park, which spans the waterfront along the East River. The walk is just a few blocks, but it's ample time to appreciate watching Theo amble through the familiar sights of my neighborhood. It's not a stretch to envision us strolling hand in hand to the park, or up Bedford on sunny weekends, or across the "hall" to Rae and Max's place.

The best part about the waterfront isn't the breezy air or the gentle slosh of the river. It's the majestic view of Lower Manhattan's skyline, spanning from the gleaming peak of One World Trade through the low-slung brick buildings of the East Village to the neon top of the Empire State Building. Theo leans his elbows on the railing. We drink in the sight of the city lit up by countless glowing windows and spires.

"What a beautiful night," he says.

It's not just the view.

"It's perfect," I agree.

He nudges my elbow with his. I turn to look at him. We're so close, I can see the glittering skyline reflected in his pupils. The nerves I felt before our date melted away two hours ago, and in their place, I feel a grounding sense of peace.

Theo kisses me softly. It's nothing like the chaste peck on the cheek he gave me at the airport. This time, his full lips are on mine, his hand cups the curve of my jaw, and I could melt right into the East River. He pulls a half inch away, nuzzling my skin. I've been waiting for this moment ever since I met him on the plane last weekend, or maybe it's more accurate to say since I was sixteen and learned without a doubt that my soulmate was somewhere out there.

I straighten up, craving more of him, and he responds like he can read my mind. He kisses me again, open-mouthed this time. One hand slips over my hip to bring our bodies closer and another hand snakes into my hair. He smells like leather and tastes like citrus cut through with brine. I press against the cool metal railing and arch toward him, sliding my arms over his shoulders.

There's an infinite number of ways this moment could have played out differently, if Theo didn't ask me about my magazine, if Max didn't tell me to get on a plane to Portland, if I hadn't chosen a life in New York, if I hadn't believed Gloria at all. There are countless other universes out there in which strange versions of me might be kissing other people, or kissing nobody at all. I could be alone or already in love with an engineer in Philadelphia or married to a teacher in Toronto, except I'm not. I could be with Jonah, but I'm not. Fate brought me here, to the waterfront in a city I've made my home, wrapped in the embrace of a musician with a soulful baritone and an adventurous spirit. This is how it should be.

"I've wanted to do that all night," he admits quietly.

"Me too." I rub a red mark off his lower lip. "I'm sorry you have lipstick all over you."

"I don't mind."

His fingers graze the small of my back, sending a tingle up my spine. I kiss him again, completely undoing my cleanup work.

I know I'm going to fall for him. I don't have a choice, but that's not the result of the prophecy. I don't think anyone has a choice. You like someone, you love someone, and that's it—logic switches off. You want who you want.

"Can I walk you home?" he asks.

"Only if you're a gentleman and say goodnight on my front stoop."

I'm not merely saying that for his benefit—I want to stretch out the process of discovering each other like taffy. This isn't the kind of romance that fizzles out in favor of a greater love down the road. This is *it*. I want to savor the experience.

"I wouldn't dream of doing anything else."

"Yes, you would," I say, smirking.

He laughs. "You know me too well already."

I smudge the lipstick off his face one last time and intertwine our fingers. "Let's go."

We set off in the direction of my apartment, but as we exit the park and turn north up Kent Avenue, our steady steps turn into a slow, meandering stroll. Even so, we make it to my building before I'm ready to say goodnight.

"When can I see you again?" he asks.

"Will the next date be as fabulous as this one?"

"Of course."

I give him a coy smile. "Then I'll be available next weekend."

He glances at my stoop behind me. "Can I give you one last kiss?"

"That would be an excellent idea."

I get upstairs eventually. It takes a while. But I don't mind at all.

ten

When my alarm blares on Monday morning, it takes me a few bleary moments to remember that what happened with Theo last night on the pier wasn't a dream. I press my face into my pillow, letting images pop into my mind like fireworks: the heat of his body sitting so close at Sweetwater, our fingers interlaced on the walk to Domino Park, his lips flush against mine, blocking out the entire dazzling length of Manhattan's skyline. In a city of eight million people, he made me feel like I was the only one worth looking at. I roll out of bed and check the kitchen, where the vase on the counter still overflows with vibrant blooms—proof it all really happened.

I whip through my morning routine in a giddy haze. I catch myself actually humming in the shower, and I can't help but put on a piece I almost never wear—a saccharine-pink shirtwaist dress like I'm Rachel McAdams in the goddamn *Notebook*. This doesn't feel like the early days of falling for Jonah, when every dangerous burst of excitement came tempered with the knowledge our relationship had an expiration date. No, this time, I feel like I'm floating.

My goal for today is to put together a rack of options for Kiara to try on, and I'm going to start by visiting Annabelle Crosby's showroom to pick up as many suits as I can carry.

On the subway ride to Annabelle Crosby's showroom, I try to text Theo.

Hey there. Last night was really—

Delete, delete. I try again.

Thank you so much for treating me to a wonderful night. I had—

No. I lose my nerve to text him first and delete everything. Instead, I text Rae.

Come over tonight? I want to tell you everything about my date with Theo. Spoiler alert: I could happily make out with him for the rest of eternity.

I know she's currently in the middle of a shift, so she'll get back to me later. Next, I tackle my email inbox: I answer an inquiry about my availability and rates from the fashion editor at an indie mag and schedule a styling session with Eliza Roth, a local jewelry designer in need of a glam look for her vow-renewal ceremony.

At the showroom, DeeDee, the publicist, is waiting for me.

"Hi! Come on in." She waves me toward the racks of clothing by the window. "I pulled some pieces I thought you might like."

I had emailed her ahead of time to explain what I needed: no-nonsense suiting in sizes 12 and 14.

"Oh, look at these!" I say, delighted.

I run my hand over a row of sleeves done in black, charcoal, navy, and white.

"You like?"

"These will be fantastic. Can I borrow one of each?"

"You sure can."

She gets to work covering the suits in garment bags to protect them for transportation. Meanwhile, I examine the blouses and shells on hangers and select a few samples in pearl pink, olive green, and copper.

"Thank you so much for thinking of us for Kiara. Is she a new client of yours? I didn't realize you worked with politicians."

I can guess what she's thinking: How many other rising political hotshots can she dress in Annabelle Crosby?

"Not typically, but her campaign manager is a friend of my family's."

DeeDee zips up the last garment bag and smiles. "Well, isn't that lucky for us."

I have a few more stops to make in SoHo for Kiara. At Zara, I find sleek top-handle bags in imitation leather that look chic without costing the kind of fortune that would inevitably piss off right-wing morning show talking heads. At Duane Reade, I pick up gel inserts to make her pumps more comfortable for long days on the campaign trail. Laden with bags, I take a cab back to Brooklyn. On the ride, I dash off an email to a publicist who reps an indie jewelry line about potentially borrowing some pendants and earrings.

Back at my apartment, I steam the Annabelle Crosby samples to get rid of the wrinkles that set in while I ran around town. I snap a picture of the rack of clothing and send it to Kiara.

All set for you! I write.

Bennett made me promise to keep him in the loop about my work for the campaign, so I text him next.

Styling Kiara is going really well. I attach a photo of the lime-green halter top that caught Theo's eye last night.

His response bubbles up immediately. Please tell me you're joking.

Before I can respond, he sends another text. No, you know what? I'm assuming you're joking, or else, I'll have to kill you.

I shoot him a winking emoji and silently appreciate the image of him tearing his hair out in terror. Next, I check my messages for any texts I might have missed from Rae, but she must still be at work. There are no messages from Theo—which is fair enough. He invited me out. He paid for the date. The least I can do is send the first text today.

I draft a message and hit send before I can lose my nerve: Hey! Last night was really great. Can I ask you out again, or would that be pushing my luck?

That wasn't so scary, was it? The paralyzing nerves I felt about texting him all morning melt away. I realize for the umpteenth time how silly it is to worry about playing the game right with Theo—whatever move I make *will* be the right one. It has to be.

I sink onto the couch to wait for his response. I wonder where he is, what he's up to. Teaching music? Plucking notes on a guitar, experimenting with a new song?

My phone lights up. There it is.

Permission granted.

I can practically see the flirtatious way his lips are curling up into a grin right now.

Are you free next weekend? I ask, remembering the slew of events I RSVPed to for this week.

Anyway, if absence makes the heart grow fonder, I don't mind making him wait several days for another date.

Let's do Saturday. Should I make a reservation somewhere you can wear a proper ball gown?

I eye the flowers sitting across the room.

You treated me last time. Let me arrange this one.

Very chivalrous.

My mind whirs with ideas.

I'll keep you posted on our plans.

I see his response bubbling up, but then it disappears. A moment later, the bubbles are back. And a moment after that, my screen lights up with another message.

I'm excited to see you again.

Me too.

My buzzer blares. I lean toward the window and see Rae on my stoop, still dressed in scrubs, ready for gossip. Smiling, I get up to buzz her in. Her footsteps clatter up the stairs.

eleven

I wanted to treat Theo to something special, so I made Saturday night reservations at The Llama Inn, an upscale Peruvian restaurant wedged into a skinny triangular block under the Brooklyn-Queens Expressway. It's all teal brick on the outside, magical inside, with cool olive-green furniture, angular lampshades made from interesting textiles, and plants dangling over floor-to-ceiling windows. As I perch on the bar stool, I do my best to discreetly adjust the strappy black lace teddy hidden under my clothes. It's an outrageous thing to wriggle into unless you plan on taking it off within the next few hours, which is exactly the point.

Theo appears in the doorway, wearing a soft white T-shirt and a denim jacket that makes his eyes look even more piercingly blue. He spots me at the bar and joins me.

"Hey, good to see you," he says.

"You too."

He looks around the restaurant. "No llamas here," he observes.

"It's not a *zoo*."

"I see that now."

"You thought I'd take you to a zoo on a date?"

"Oh, shit, this is a date?" he asks, giving me a blank stare.

My jaw drops as he leans in to deliver the most casual of kisses on my cheek, as if I hadn't been daydreaming about our last kiss all damn week.

"I'm kidding, I'm kidding, of course this is a date," he says playfully.

His hand lingers on my hip and his thumb skims soothingly over the fabric of my dress. I wonder if he can feel what's underneath.

"You thrive on giving me shit," I say, recovering.

"Oh, absolutely."

A waiter appears in front of us with two menus. "Can I bring you to your table?"

Theo ushers me forward. "After you."

We sit and order a tasty spread: grilled carrots; ceviche soaked with lime, plantain, and habanero; pork with charred onions; and two Llama Del Rey cocktails made from sangria and pisco.

"So, why is that?"

"Why what?"

"Why is everything a joke to you?"

I don't mean it aggressively. I genuinely want to know.

"Does it bother you?" He leans forward onto his elbows and stares down at the blond wood table between us.

"No," I admit. "I like that you keep me on my toes."

Theo, as a concept, is predictable: Of course I fell for the man I met on Friday, June 24. But Theo, the *person*, is anything but. He keeps me on edge in the best way possible. I never know what he'll say next.

He rolls the bottom ridge of his glass against the place mat like he's rolling a thought around his head.

"It started as a defense mechanism, I guess. Back in school as a kid, I wasn't at the top of my class, but I could be the class clown."

"And clearly it stuck," I say, amused.

"Entertaining people makes me feel good," he says, not fully meeting my eyes. "It's the one thing I can do well. Or try to do well."

I get the sense he's serious—for once—and don't want to ruin the moment. "You don't have to try around me," I say gently.

He exhales. "I like that I don't have to. It's weird, isn't it? This feels easy."

His gaze connects with mine now; he clears his throat and stumbles quickly over his words.

"I mean, not that I'm not trying to look decent in front of you and show you a great time, because I am—but I mean, I feel like I can be myself around you, and you won't think I'm a loser."

I almost spit out my drink. "You're *not* a loser."

He presses his lips into a tight line. "I'm not an astrophysicist, either."

Like his mom. I realize, maybe for the first time, how his family's expectations shaped his life. That's something I can understand.

It's too soon to tell him about my family's strict adherence to Gloria's prophecies and how that's molded my own experiences, so I find myself telling him more about my own mom. She never explicitly told me and Rae to follow in her footsteps and become an accountant, like she is, but she didn't hide the fact that choosing a career crunching numbers meant we would always be comfortable. Still, she was supportive when I chose to take a risk and enter a creative field. I used to worry that my professional choices would make me look vapid in comparison to Mom or Rae, but hearing them affirm how hard I work mostly keeps the insecurities at bay.

I tell Theo about how I got into this industry, starting with my first internship in the fashion closet at *Seventeen*. I was in awe of the way fashion editors and stylists could transform a pile of garments into a cohesive look that transported the viewer into another world. That's where I met Florence Choi, the stylist who worked on our prom spread. She was unflappably cool and I loved her off-kilter glam aesthetic. She became my biggest career idol. I interned with her for the rest of college, became her full-time assistant after graduation, and worked for her for three years before she said I was ready to strike out on my own.

"Sorry, you must think this is so boring."

The ceviche is long gone.

"Not at all." He reaches under the table to rest his hand on my knee. "I want to hear it all. This is your origin story."

"Well, no, that's a different beast that involves a turkey baster." I start to explain.

His eyebrows shoot up. "Sorry, what?"

In kindergarten, I had misunderstood the full story and drew a family portrait complete with a flock of turkeys. I got the details ironed out eventually. Mom and Pops, and later Allen and Rocco, did a great job teaching me and Rae that families come together in plenty of different ways.

"Oh my god, no. I mean, like . . . this is how you became who you are. Ambitious, hardworking, cool as hell."

"Stop," I say, embarrassed. His praise feels like sunshine: warm and blinding.

"You're not very good at taking compliments."

"Yes, I am."

At work? Always. From Gloria? I was raised on them. But Theo's make me feel flustered. It's overwhelming to watch him fall for me.

"See, you do it like this," he says, grabbing his cocktail glass like it's a microphone. He drops an octave into a ridiculously deep Elvis impression, swoops toward me over the table, and coos, "Thank you, thank you very much."

I roll my eyes at him, my hunk of a spotlight-loving date. He beams.

Beneath the bravado, I'm starting to see the real him: not always confident in himself, though he can build himself up with the energy that radiates off a crowd—even if it's a happy crowd of one.

But here's where I could find myself in trouble. Falling for him. The real Theo. This is the danger with Gloria's prophecy. To Theo, I'm just another woman. He could be seeing any number of other people for all I know. In his mind, this could be the last chance he's offering me to see if potential blooms before he sends one last well-meaning text: It was great getting to know you, but . . . If that's the case, he might not come around for years. Decades. I would have to claw my way back to him somehow, and who knows how long that would take? How difficult it would be? The prospect makes my chest feel tight. I shake my head as if that can clear out those anxious thoughts.

Theo tells me about his plans for tomorrow, including a 6 p.m. recording session with The Supersonics at a studio.

"I'm just glad it's not too early. Last time, Mika booked a 9 a.m. slot and it was terrible."

"Not a morning person?" Unbidden, an image comes to mind: soft morning sunlight illuminating his dark tattoos against my bright white sheets.

"Definitely a night owl." He casually spears a sliver of pork off my plate and pops it in his mouth. I like that he's comfortable enough to do that.

It's just the encouragement I need to say what's been on my mind all night.

"Would you want to come back to my place for a drink after dinner?"

I don't care that it's a transparent line. It's all I can manage with my heart thudding in my chest.

His eyes sparkle. He stretches back in his chair so a sliver of abdomen, dusted with a trail of golden hair, peeks out from the hem of his shirt. His lips curl into a smile.

"I'd love to."

Twenty minutes later, we're at my place. "I hope you like a mean martini, because that's the only thing on the menu here."

I had picked up the check after dinner, despite his protests—I'd invited him, it was only fair—and we ambled through the neighborhood hand in hand. Once we made it inside, I did my best to set the mood: I put a thrifted jazz record on an old-fashioned turntable and lit a candle on the table next to his flowers. The scent of fig, amber, and sandalwood flows throughout the apartment. The half of my living room I typically use for work is often cluttered, but this morning, I fastidiously organized the hanging rack of clothes, rows of shoes, and trays of jewelry so that they wouldn't spill out into the rest of my apartment. I spent an extra five minutes making my bed look crisp and neat in case he happens to see it. Now that he's here, I'm glad I put in the effort.

I rummage around the kitchen, pulling out bottles of gin and vermouth and a glass jar of olives soaked in brine. The cocktail shaker is on a high shelf I can't reach without a step stool; Theo reaches for it instead. I could get used to that.

While I measure out the ingredients, Theo flips through the stack of take-out menus on my counter. He waves the paper brochure from Sage with my favorite Thai noodle dishes starred.

"So, this is the secret to your legendary home cooking."

"It's usually best for me to leave cooking to the professionals. But drinks I can do."

To prove my point, I fit the cap on the shaker, rattle it hard, and strain out two perfect martinis. He takes one and tastes it slowly, licking a dot of liquid off his lower lip. He raises an eyebrow.

"Yes, you can."

We clink glasses. I move to put the bottles away and rinse the cocktail shaker out in the sink.

"Hey," he says tenderly, coming up behind me to wrap his hands around my waist.

He presses a kiss into my hair, which makes it nearly impossible to focus on the task in front of me. I feel him gathering my hair into a low ponytail and twisting it over my shoulder.

"Did I mention you're an excellent bartender?" he adds in a low voice between kisses.

"Mmm, you did."

His full, soft lips brush the top of my ear. "And a very thoughtful host."

Every second he's talking is another second he's not kissing me.

"Shut up," I tease.

"Gladly."

Now, he uses his mouth to plant a distracting row of kisses down the exposed nape of my neck. I savor the way his lips make my skin buzz with anticipation, then flick off the tap and turn to kiss him. He draws closer to me, so I lean against the sink, arching up to meet his lips. I could happily spend hours like this, with his mouth probing mine and my hands exploring the edge of his jaw, the expanse of his chest, the belt loops around his hips.

He follows me to the couch and unlaces his shoes. I curl my bare feet up under me, soaking in the jazz floating through the room, freezing this moment for a snapshot I can return to when I'm eighty and wrinkled and looking back on a lifetime of love. He kisses with enthusiasm, like he's been looking forward to this moment all day, too. His movements are sweet and sexy—slow enough to tease me with anticipation for what's coming next, and smooth enough that I know I'll be replaying the mental footage on sleepless nights for a long time to come.

We find ourselves horizontal, legs tangled, his clothed and mine bare. My dress is hiked up to my thighs. His fingers brush the strap and it falls down. I pull away slightly, enough to see his long, golden eyelashes and the euphoric expression on his face. It gives me a rush.

"The zipper's down the back," I say softly.

His eyes flutter open. "Yeah?"

I sit up and hold my hair to the side so he can slide it down.

"Whoa," he murmurs.

I've worn lingerie for Jonah, and for a handful of other men I've gotten to know over the course of several hookups, but I've never been brave enough to wear it on the first night with someone new. More than anyone, though, I know that fashion is a powerful tool of armor. It can be used to set a scene, evoke an image, and broadcast your intentions. Tonight, I wanted to feel sexy. Glamorous. Unforgettable. I turn to see Theo looking awestruck, and I know I've made the right choice.

I stand, wriggle my arms out of my dress, and push it down my hips to the floor. I turn toward the bedroom, but he stops me.

"Look at you." His voice is low and gritty with desire. "I need a moment to admire you."

Theo takes in the full effect of the black bodysuit—the plunging neckline, the straps that crisscross my ribs, the sheer lace that dips between my hips—then pulls me by the hand toward the bedroom.

We nearly make it there, pausing in the doorframe. His fingers slip under the band of lace beneath my sternum. Between kisses, I tug off his T-shirt. His hands roam my body, but I keep him in one place long enough to undo his belt buckle and push his chinos to his knees. He kicks them off. His black boxer briefs are tantalizingly tight. I'm torn between an insatiable lust that drives me to keep going, and a vague recognition that I should slow down so this moment can stretch on forever. My body overrides my brain, and my fingers and tongue and hips move instinctively on their own.

I pull him into the bedroom and flick off the lights, letting us feel our way to each other in the darkness.

twelve

When Theo and I are both blissfully exhausted, we lie in bed with my head on his chest and his fingers splayed out over my ass. It must be late; usually, the windows of the apartment across the street from mine glow golden yellow into the night, but they're dark now. The album is over, but the record player keeps spinning in silence.

"I wanna know everything about you," Theo says.

"Everything?" I echo. "That's a lot."

"Like . . ." He taps his fingers thoughtfully against my skin. "Like, your first memory."

I pause for a moment, thinking. "It was at this beach we used to go to as kids," I remember. "Rae and I must have been three or four, and she pushed me into the sandcastle we were building. I got a whole mouthful of sand, so I pushed her back, and then we were both crying."

"You two must have been terrors."

"Double the trouble," I say, rolling my eyes.

"Tell me about your first concert."

"Avril Lavigne. I was eleven."

"'Sk8er Boi' is still kind of a jam."

"Oh, it definitely holds up."

"Tell me about your first time."

"Like, first time having sex?" I clarify.

He hesitates. "Yeah. Is that a bad question?"

"Ergh, no thank you," I demur. "Nothing special to report."

I have no interest in recounting the tale of losing my virginity to the junior varsity tennis captain in the backseat of his dad's Toyota Corolla parked behind the supermarket.

"Fine, then, first impression of me."

I laugh because there's no way I could possibly tell him that I instantly guessed he would become the love of my life.

"Um," I say, stalling.

"Yeah?" He props himself up on his elbow, very clearly intrigued by whatever I'm about to say.

"Well . . ." I begin, even though no coherent thoughts are forming, like, at all.

"Oh, *interesting*." There's a playful, animated surge to his tone. "You're speechless! Trying to come up with a nice way to say I was bothering you, keeping you from reading on the plane? And haven't let you alone since?"

He buries his face in the crook of my neck and kisses a trail along my collarbone, down my chest. He slides in bed beside me, resting his chin on my stomach and gazing up at me with those ocean-blue eyes.

His question catches me off guard. I can give him an easy, normal answer, or I can explain the truth—that I was looking for someone that day. I hadn't yet decided when or how to tell him about Gloria's prophecy. I always assumed that telling my match about it would be a delicately orchestrated conversation involving a speech I workshopped with Rae and rehearsed over several weeks or months. Now, though, my mind is blank. I could blame it on the way his body wiped my brain into a molten haze, or maybe on tonight's cocktails. I want to treat this conversation with care, because I only get one shot to explain this to Theo the right way. But I have to have faith—I *do* have faith—that no matter what I say, all will be right in the end.

"My first impression of you was perfect," I say honestly, easing us into the subject.

"Perfect?" He laughs. "That's a pretty high bar."

"It is. But you cleared it."

He beams back at me, and I feel a wave of confidence. I trace a constellation of freckles on his forearm as the right words begin to form on my tongue.

"Theo, do you believe in fate?"

I can feel my heartbeat thumping in my ears.

"Fate? Not really. I mean, no. I didn't grow up with any sort of . . . religion, beliefs, spirituality, whatever you want to call it."

This is one of the many reasons I never dared to dream of telling Jonah; he wasn't primed to believe in fate. But if Rae can convince Max, a literal research scientist, that Gloria's powers are real, then Theo can get on board.

"I'm not talking about what your parents taught you," I say, forging on. "I'm asking about you personally—what *you* believe."

He squints. "I don't know how exactly to put it into words, but sometimes I wonder if there's some sort of . . . force? In the universe. As in, whatever kind of energy you put into the world, it comes back to you somehow."

"Okay, okay, yeah!" I say, encouraged by this development. "So, I believe in some sort of force in the universe, too. Actually, my whole family does. It all starts with my grandma Gloria."

I take a deep breath and start from the beginning, explaining her first eerie vision of a date three months ahead in 1958, followed by meeting Grandpa Raymond on exactly that day.

"This is his wedding ring." I show him the gold band on the chain around my neck.

I tell Theo that she predicted when each one of her siblings would meet the loves of their life, too, and then her cousins, her own kids, and her grandkids, stumbling a little over the details I know by heart.

"Grandkids?" he says, jerking his head back.

"The day we met, that was supposed to be . . ." I lose my momentum, my confidence. I swallow and try again. "That's my day. The one my grandma predicted for me."

Theo has rolled back by my side. His head is propped up in his hand, and his lanky torso disappears under the covers. I can practically see his wheels turning.

"So, you're saying . . . it's you and me?" he asks.

I nod, afraid to say anything more. Dazed, he ruffles up his hair.

"That's . . . wow. That's a lot."

"I know." Silence stretches out between us, and I rush to add, "And I don't mean to put any pressure on you, or make things weird between us, or make you think I'm crazy."

He sucks in a sharp breath. "So, this is like love at first sight?"

"No," I say quickly. "I'm not in love with you *yet*. We just met, okay? I'm just saying, you know . . . in time, it could happen."

"But someday?"

I hedge. "Maybe."

He kisses me softly at first, then more intensely, pinning me to the bed, rolling his hips against mine. At first, I only intend to indulge him for a second or two, but he's unfortunately very sexy, and I get sidetracked. The kiss gets heated before I remember we're in the middle of a life-changing conversation, and so I cut it short and force myself to focus.

"I don't want this to change anything between us," I tell him, forcing myself to speak bluntly so there are no misunderstandings. "I like you, and I want to keep going out with you, and only you, and we'll see where this goes."

"I like you, and only you, too," he says, grinning. Then his smile falters. "But does the prophecy mean . . . marriage? I don't know if that's for me."

My stomach drops. I try to play it cool. "It's always been described to me as the love of your life. But if you found a forever love that was guaranteed to work out, why not get married?"

In the darkness, it's hard to see anything more than a glint of moonlight reflected in his eyes. I wish I could study his expression more clearly.

"I don't know if I believe in that happily-ever-after, till-death-do-us part kind of thing. I mean, relationships are tough. I've never been good at them. And marriage is a lot of pressure. Isn't it better to be with someone long-term because you both choose to commit? Rather than staying together because a piece of paper says you should?"

I have a hard time understanding his point of view. Whenever I've thought about my future, I've always assumed marriage would be a part of it. Even though I grew up knowing that Mom regretted her first marriage and that Pops and Rocco never felt the need to tie the knot after New York legalized gay marriage, *I* wanted to get married. There's something incredibly romantic to me about standing up in front of your family and friends and vowing to cherish another person for as long as you both live. The commitment of marriage symbolizes the kind of everlasting love the prophecy promises. Giving up on that would sting.

"I don't think of it like that," I manage finally. "More like, isn't it nice to have someone you love and trust who will always be on your team? Isn't life better when you have someone to share it with?" I hope I sound sturdier than I feel.

"Sure." He waves his hand abstractly. "But who says you need the government involved to prove you love someone?"

"Of course you can love someone without getting married—like my dads. They're not married but they're in it for the long haul." I feel like I'm sliding backward. Am I losing this argument? *Is* this an argument? "But I think it's a nice show of commitment."

He shrugs. "For some people."

We're so close, I can feel the heat radiating from his chest. I pull the covers tighter around my body, shielding my nakedness.

"I must be freaking you out," I say.

He traces the underside of my chin with his finger, gently lifting it so we're eye to eye again. The gesture is so tender, I can't imagine why anyone wouldn't want to embrace a lifetime of this.

"I can't promise that I'll be here forever, but I'm here for now," he says uneasily. "I'll give this a try."

"Okay," I eke out.

My cheeks burn with shame.

"I'd like to keep seeing you, but I also understand if this conversation changes things for you—if it makes you think I'm maybe not the right guy."

"Oh, no," I say quickly. "Trust me, you are."

Anyway, now there's no way for me to retrace my steps from June 24 and figure out which other men I crossed paths with. I've already put all my metaphorical eggs in Theo's basket. Eventually, we'll figure out the future together. There's no need to hammer out every detail right now.

Theo shifts the subject, maybe in an attempt to ease us out of dangerous territory. He tells me about a psychic reading he got on the Coney Island boardwalk last summer; she apparently predicted he'd meet an "enchanting lady" very soon. "So, that must be how we crossed paths," he jokes. It hits too uncomfortably close to Gloria's prophecy for me to really laugh. We talk about the last vacation he took, when he crashed on a friend's couch in LA for a week while soaking up the music scene there. I offer up my own travel wish list, destinations I want to visit while I'm young, before kids make vacations tougher: Hawaii, Portugal, Morocco. My head lands on his chest again, and between the warmth of his arm wrapped around me and the weight of the covers, it gets harder and harder to string words together.

"I bet your eyes are closed," I mumble.

"My eyes are closed."

My eyelids feel so heavy. Sleep would be nice.

"My eyes are closed, too."

"Night, babe."

I shift closer to him, relaxing into the rise and fall of his chest. I could get used to falling asleep like this. I'd like to do this night after night for a long time to come.

thirteen

In the morning, I roll bleary-eyed across the bed and find the other half empty. For a moment, I worry that my conversation with Theo has driven him away permanently, but his clothes from last night are still scattered across my floor. I wrap a silk bathrobe around myself and peek into the kitchen.

Theo, bless him, is sitting at my kitchen table in his underwear, sipping from a mug.

"Morning, sunshine. I took the liberty of making us coffee."

He cranes his neck toward me, and I kiss him, morning breath be damned.

I pour myself a mug and join him at the table. His hair sticks up in eleven different directions and my robe sags open in a way that probably looks sloppy, not sexy. Over coffee, he tells me stories about the ridiculous antics he got up to in boarding school, and later in college, and even throughout his twenties with his bandmates, his best friends. I can't remember the last time I laughed this much or this loudly so early on a Sunday morning. We're both hungry and my fridge is bare, so we opt to get dressed and head out for brunch.

Williamsburg might be the brunch capital of the Eastern Seaboard, so we spend a half hour meandering from restaurant to restaurant, putting our names down with frazzled hostesses. Realizing it could take anywhere between forty-five minutes and two hours to get a table, we ditch the brunch plan altogether and pick up bagels to go from Bagelsmith on Bedford: smears of lox spread for me, jalapeño-cheddar cream cheese for him. We unwrap them while lounging in the grass at McCarren Park. Theo plays DJ, wafting a playlist of indie rock music through the warm air. He rolls up his chinos to his knees and takes off his shirt so we can sunbathe properly. I force myself to pretend I'm not staring at his abs.

When I finally bother checking my phone, I'm surprised to see that two easy, lazy, sun-drenched hours have slipped by. We're in firm afternoon territory now. But neither one of us make a move to part.

"You know what I love to do on weekend afternoons?" I say.

"What?" Theo asks.

He's playing with a blade of grass, using it to tickle the inside of my knee.

"I like to go sit at The Bitter End and listen to the open mic. Entertaining, cheap, delightful."

"Is that an invitation?"

"Only if you aren't sick of me yet."

I don't want to give him the impression that I'm trying to ensnare him into settling down with a girl he's known for two weeks. I really do want to spend more time with him today, but not at the expense of making him feel prematurely trapped in a relationship he's not ready for.

"Let's go," he says, flicking the piece of grass at me.

New York City's oldest rock club is on a vibrant and buzzing stretch of Bleecker Street in Greenwich Village. College kids spill out of the sports bar on the corner, tables of friends share appetizers at the Indian restaurant across the street, and tanned sunbathers carry beach towels toward nearby Washington Square Park. Under the bar's blue awning, the wood-paneled front is papered over with weathered magazine clippings about past shows and torn flyers promising upcoming ones. Icons performed here: Etta James, Billy Joel, Bob Dylan, Joni Mitchell, Patti Smith. These days, the open mics attract a laundry list of aspiring musicians and comics. They rarely live up to the institution's hallowed history in terms of talent, but they make up for it with character. I fell in love with this place when I was in college. The bouncer always made a show of checking IDs, and didn't seem to care that we all had fakes.

Inside the dimly lit club, we order a round of no-frills beers and settle in at one of the tables. The varnished wood is slightly sticky with the residue of spills from decades of not-exactly-sober patrons. The open mic is already underway. Onstage, a painfully earnest middle-aged man is warbling his way through John Mayer's "Your Body Is a Wonderland." Behind him, a brick wall displays a black flag with the club's name.

Theo slips his hand into mine. The performer croons, "I love the shape you take when crawling toward the pillowcase," and goes wide-eyed with confidence at the success of pulling off such a line. He slides into the chorus with a surge of energy and breaks out jazz hands.

"Mmm, yes," Theo muses quietly. "He's really getting me in the mood here."

"Shut up, this place is great."

"No, it is, it's fantastic." He gestures toward the guy onstage. "I love this man. He's a gem."

"Have you performed here?"

"Of course. Doesn't every wannabe musician in New York get their start here?"

"I think you count as more than just a wannabe at this point."

The guy onstage attempts a falsetto for the song's final chorus. The emcee, a surly man holding a clipboard, loudly claps him offstage a few moments early.

"Thank you, thank you," the emcee grumbles.

He announces the next act and the act on deck.

I nudge Theo. "You should put your name down."

He smirks. "Oh, I see. That's the real reason you brought me here."

"Excuse me for bringing you to an iconic music venue for an afternoon of entertainment."

"You want me to?"

"If you want?"

He considers it, then scoots his chair back and goes to talk to the emcee. I see the guy scribble down something on his clipboard.

"I'm sixth in line," Theo says when he returns.

"Are you going to sing one of the new songs you're working on?"

He shakes his head. "Nah, those aren't really ready yet. I'll do something our band already performs."

"I can't wait."

He squeezes my thigh.

We listen to a teenager plucking away at a Fleetwood Mac cover, a gruff comic working through an excruciatingly raunchy set of jokes about his attraction to his ex-wife's sister, a singer who can most generously be described as "very loud," a comedian who has a bone to pick with her tap-dancing upstairs neighbor, and an enthusiastic performer who remembers most of the lyrics to the Spice Girls' "Wannabe."

When it's Theo's turn, he hops up on the stage with ease and borrows another entertainer's guitar. As he adjusts the mic, he says, "I'm doing my best to impress a girl here, so please feel free to be a generous audience."

That gets a laugh and a hearty round of applause out of the room. He flashes a wicked grin my way.

"I'm Theo Larsen, I'm in a band called The Supersonics, and this is our most recent single, 'Over the Top,'" he announces.

He proceeds to dive into a fast-paced, jangling melody. If this is the stripped-down version, I can only imagine what the song would sound like with a full band. His baritone is rich and warm, and he slides his hands up and down the guitar with confidence. It's like all the swagger and charm I'm learning to love about him offstage gets turned up a notch onstage. The effect is mesmerizing and I can't look away. I bop along to the beat.

The lyrics tell the story of a lovesick guy totally smitten with a woman who won't look twice at him, and the increasingly endearing attempts he makes to win her affection. The song is infectious, but I can't help but think it rings false—I can't imagine anyone turning Theo down. I shimmy and groove in my chair. I'm not the only one—he's roused the crowd to clap, dance, and sing.

A pair of college girls sitting in the front row stare at him with open desire. Their longing makes me feel self-conscious. Is this what Theo wants? To go on the road with his band, make it big, jump from woman to woman without ever being tied down? It's clear to me now that he thrives off the energy of a crowd. He's good up there; he deserves to be up on stages across the country. I don't know how to reconcile that with the settled-down, paired-off life I see for myself. I know they have to fit somehow, but it makes me nervous that I can't figure out how we'll work.

He strums the final notes of the song with gusto, then relaxes and swoops a hand through his hair. He catches my eye and beams.

"Thank you, everyone, you're a beautiful audience," he says.

He patters down the three short steps from the stage to the floor, nodding at the emcee who—for once—doesn't look irritated to be here.

"Nice job, man," the emcee says.

Then he refers back to his clipboard and sighs heavily before announcing the next act.

Theo slips back into his seat in one smooth motion, squeezing my knee and taking a sip of his beer.

"How'd I do?"

His rock star bluster is gone, replaced by a hopeful gleam in his eye.

"You're a hell of a performer." I lean in to give him a peck on the lips.

He does that dopey Elvis impression, the one he mentioned last night. "Thank you, thank you very much."

He tucks a stray lock of my hair behind my ear and looks at me with such tenderness, I'm toast. Today has been one delight after the next; I adore the way our relationship is unspooling. It's far too early to fall in love with him, but I *like* him—a lot—and for now, that's more than enough. As I lean in to kiss him again, a thought stirs from the back of my mind, where I tried to stuff it down last night: I hope we can find a way to be happy together, even if I see marriage in my future and he doesn't. But there's no point in worrying about that just yet. For now, I only want to savor the start of this love story. It's the last and most important one I'll ever have.

fourteen

On Wednesday morning, I pack up everything I need to bring to Kiara's apartment. She needs to look flawless tonight for a fundraising dinner where she'll meet with high-profile donors. As I dart from my living room work space to my closet to my purse, crossing each item off my checklist as I go, my brain wanders off toward the bedroom, where Theo made my limbs feel like jelly as recently as this morning. I've been listening to The Supersonics' most recent album ever since he left. After a few replays, I've decided that "Over the Top" is even better with the full band than it was at The Bitter End; Theo's lyrics soar over an infectious beat and a thumping bass line. It's the kind of song you want to turn up on the radio. But I also like "Stay," a less flashy song toward the end of the album. Theo sings the tender lyrics hesitantly, like he's afraid of what they mean: "Saturday night, you love me / Sunday morning, you turn me away / I hate that you don't want me to stay."

I understand now why Theo declined to get into the specifics of his songwriting on the plane. A random listener wouldn't think twice about lyrics this personal. But if you know Theo, as I'm getting to, it's easy to recognize him in these songs. It's almost too much, like listening to his diary. "Stay" makes me wonder if—despite his feelings about long-term relationships—he secretly craves the security and comfort a commitment would bring.

We haven't revisited our conversation from Saturday night. I don't plan on bringing up the M-word—*marriage*—again until Theo and I get to know each other better. Instead, I've channeled all my anxiety into conversations with Rae and Shireen. They both tell me not to let Theo's comments freak me out, but that's far easier said than done.

Once I've gathered an Annabelle Crosby suit and blouse in two sizes—so Kiara has options—plenty of accessories, and my mini travel steamer, I call an Uber to go to her apartment. When I knock on her door twenty minutes later, Bennett opens it.

"Oh, hi!" I say.

I can't tell if he's here for official campaign business or a personal visit. If he were here as Kiara's boyfriend or fling, or friend, or whatever he is—it's early enough that he could still be in pajamas. But he's not. He's dressed in jeans and a faded Obama '08 T-shirt. The slogan *"Sí, se puede!"* clings to his chest.

"Come on in." He leads me through the apartment.

It's a whirlwind: one roommate flips eggs in a pan in the kitchen, while a second lounges in front of the TV in the living room with her head in a woman's lap. In her room, Kiara paces as she reads notes off her phone, mumbling to herself about an initiative for police reform. She lights up when she sees me with the garment bag.

"Hi, thanks for bringing this over! Should I try everything on now?"

"Works for me."

I hang one suit in her closet and give her the other. I've learned over time that it's better if clients try on the larger size first and request a smaller size if necessary, rather than starting off with pieces that might be too tight.

"Um," she says, darting a glance at Bennett. "I'm going to change . . . here?"

Bennett makes a show of turning around.

"I don't mind." I laugh. "I'll give you some privacy."

I've seen plenty of clients and models naked; I wouldn't blink twice if Kiara undressed in front of me. But I respect that not everyone is as instantly comfortable with nudity.

"Yeah, actually, same," Bennett says.

I step out into the hall and he joins me, closing the door behind him.

"She told me, you know," I say.

He cocks his head. "Told you what, specifically?"

"That you're dating. Or together. Or not together. Whatever you're calling it."

"Oh, so you know." He leans against the wall and gives me a shy grin, rubbing his jaw. "Yeah, it's new. We're figuring it out."

"Does Max know?"

He nods. "Of course. And so do they," he adds, indicating the roommates down the hall. "And I think Kiara's mentioned it to a few close friends. But everyone's sworn to secrecy. The way the press hounds her, it's not a good idea to let this get out before the election. She works way too hard to let the headlines be about her personal life, you know?"

"Makes sense."

Kiara opens the door, looking uncertain. "What do you think?"

She brushes past us toward the bathroom to see herself in the mirror.

I analyze the fit. "The pants are great. I want you to try the jacket in the other size. This one looks a little roomy on you."

I swap the jacket she's wearing for the size 12, and it fits like a dream. Her face lights up in the mirror. She tugs appreciatively on the sleeves and swivels to see the back of the suit.

"I look *good*," she says.

"It's fabulous on you," I say.

"You look amazing," Bennett says, looking her slowly up and down.

Kiara shoots him a silent look, a tight-lipped smile that sits somewhere between *stop, you're embarrassing me* and *don't stop, I love it.*

She fiddles with the buttons on the jacket. "Open? Closed?"

"I'd button the top one if you're standing and leave it open when you sit," I suggest.

"Got it."

She changes back into her regular clothes and looks at the accessories I brought for her while I steam the pieces she'll wear tonight. The purse gets an approving nod, and she looks appreciatively at the array of jewelry.

"Ooh, I love these," she says, examining a pair of chunky gold earrings. "You're amazing."

I can't help but smile at her compliment. "I'm glad Bennett connected us."

"He is good for some things, isn't he?" she says breezily.

He frowns. "Hey, hey. I'm useful."

"As a campaign manager? Absolutely. Saving me *the leftovers* like you promised? Not at all!" Kiara says pointedly, like she's resurrecting an old fight.

"It was so delicious, I'm so sorry," he says mournfully. "I couldn't help myself."

"Yeah, I've heard it was very good. You keep telling me."

Their eyes glitter with an entire unspoken conversation—his apology for eating her share of the food, her stony refusal, his playful pleading, and finally, Kiara's good-natured eye roll. She forgives him. I watch their exchange, feeling a little self-conscious. I had thought that Theo and I were moving along so smoothly, but we're not anywhere near this level of intimate communication yet.

"I'll never eat a midnight snack out of your fridge again," Bennett promises.

"Try it and you won't have access to my fridge anymore," Kiara warns.

They argue like they've been together longer than a month—their history as friends is very apparent.

"Edie, do you have time to join me on a very important errand?" he asks.

"I'm free until two."

This afternoon, I'm meeting an aspiring stylist for coffee, then pulling some pieces for that indie magazine's upcoming photoshoot. My old boss Florence was so helpful to me when I was still in school that I try to connect with people looking to break into the fashion industry at least once or twice a month. It's my way of paying it forward. Then tonight, I'll be at a launch party to celebrate a denim brand's new collection. The publicist promised a seamstress would be on the premises customizing complimentary pairs with personalized embroidery.

"Good. I'm heading out to get some apology food for Kiara, and maybe along the way, we can start hammering out details for Max and Rae's wedding party trip."

I laugh. "Sure, why not."

Kiara narrows her eyes at us. "I'm counting on you, Edie. Watch him. Make sure he doesn't eat one bite."

~

Bennett takes me to Chavela's, which he claims serves the world's best enchiladas outside of Mexico or his dad's own kitchen. As we walk over to the restaurant, he scrolls through the calendar on his phone, cross-referencing a list of Kiara's campaign events with the weekends Rae and Max suggested for the trip.

He walks fast and talks faster, like his mind is already hopscotching ahead to map out every detail all at once. Even in jeans and an old T-shirt, he's laser-focused; he doesn't need a suit to carry himself like a professional.

"On Rae's side, it's me, Shireen, Max's sister, Alana, and Olivia, Rae's best friend from college," I recall. "And on Max's side, it's you . . . and who else? Noah?" I guess the name of one of Max's best friends from growing up.

"Yep, Noah. And Max's cousin Zach and coworker Trevor. I'll get everybody's number and start the group text," he offers.

"Let me take care of that. I already have most of the party's numbers. I can start scouting out locations, too."

He sighs. "Does that leave me with official penis straw research? It's not the *strangest* thing I've ever managed, but . . ."

I laugh. "That sounds like a story."

He exhales heavily. "I'll be dead if this ever gets out."

"Your secrets are safe with me."

"I can trust you?" he asks.

"Pinky-promise," I say, extending my little finger.

He interlocks his with mine and gives it a good shake before diving into a tale from his intern days, when he was responsible for sending Mother's Day bouquets to both a senator's wife and a woman who was very much *not* his wife. It was absolutely crucial that each bouquet went to the correct person, as the senator's wife was terribly allergic to daisies, but his mistress loved them. There was a rumor around the office that three years prior, another intern had mixed up the orders. He never worked on the Hill again.

"I just wanted to learn about how to whip up support for a bill!" Bennett says. "I had no idea I was in for a crash course in Adultery 101."

"You know what? Let me get the penis straws. I've got this," I insist. "You've clearly done enough."

He grins, holding open the door to the restaurant. "Thank you."

Inside, elegant chandeliers dangle from an old-fashioned tin ceiling in a vibrant shade of purple. The walls are tomato red and inlaid with brightly painted tiles. The bar is lined with bottles of tequila. Bennett catches a waiter's eye.

"Hey, man! Back again?" the server asks.

Bennett replies in Spanish. I can't quite catch his meaning, but the waiter laughs.

"You can take your usual table," he says.

"You're a regular already?" I ask. "You just moved here."

"This food is legit. I'd eat here forever."

After we sit and order (enchiladas for us, plus takeout for Kiara), I text Max for Zach and Trevor's numbers. Bennett and I already have the rest of the wedding party's contact information.

Max shoots back the numbers along with a *thank you* for organizing the weekend, and I draft a note to the crew.

> Hello, hello! Welcome to the official group chat for Rae and Max's wedding party! Rae and Max asked me and Bennett to plan a joint bachelor/ette trip, and we've narrowed it down to the following dates. Any conflicts with these?

I write out the options and slide my phone across the table to Bennett. "How does this look?"

He glances up from his own phone and peeks at my screen. "Excellent," he says, approximately three-quarters of a second later.

"Do you always move at ten million miles a minute?"

He gestures helplessly to his phone. "I'm very busy right now."

"Campaign stuff?"

He nods and flicks his gaze back to his phone. "Approving the language for our next fundraising email and coordinating some volunteer efforts."

"Simultaneously?" I ask incredulously. "While I wrote this one extremely basic text message?"

He flips his phone around to flash a black-and-white grid at me. "I'm also doing my damnedest to beat my mom doing the *New York Times* crossword. We compete against each other to see who can get the fastest time."

I feel slight relief knowing Bennett isn't the most terrifyingly productive human being on the planet. It makes me feel an ounce better about my own work ethic. I hit send on the text.

"This one's in your wheelhouse—'Dominican couturier,' nine letters," he says.

I think for a moment. "De la Renta. Oscar de la Renta."

"Thank you very much," he says, fist-bumping me.

He taps answers into his crossword app, and I watch as the group text fills up with responses. Alana and Trevor note they have conflicts with one date, but it's shaping up to look like there's one weekend that works for everybody.

When the food comes, we put our phones away and converse like humans with actual social skills.

"You said you're working on a bill, right? Or want to someday?" I ask, recalling what he had mentioned the night we met.

"I'd like to eventually, yeah. The reason I got interested in politics in the first place is because back when I was seventeen, there was a shooting at my school. Four kids died, including my brother, Gabe. He had just turned fifteen."

So, I was right at dinner with Max and Rae two weeks ago. He had told her about this early in their relationship; the shooter was a former classmate, a dropout who had been radicalized by hateful manifestos he had read online. Max had said that he knew one of the victims well, but I didn't realize that was his best friend's little brother. It's devastating that Max had to live through such trauma, but I feel even worse for Bennett. I can't imagine losing a sibling in such a violent way.

"That's awful. Just horrible. Living through that, losing him—I am so sorry."

Bennett swallows. "I was on a field trip that day," he says grimly. "I wasn't even there. I started a petition in our town to provide better security for the school, racked up thousands of signatures, and managed to convince the town government to take real steps to keep students safer."

This has to be a deeply painful story, but he doesn't flinch. It's clear he's had practice telling it. I can only assume he feels some sort of brutal survivor's guilt for being away from the school the day it happened.

He continues, "Not that it was much of a challenge—what was the town going to do, turn down a grieving kid? Snub a whole school full of traumatized students? No. That sparked my interest in politics. I realized that I liked organizing efforts to make a difference. So, that internship? The Adultery 101 internship? I wound up there because that senator was working on a gun-control bill. I was hoping to learn from him and to see it pass. It didn't, of course."

"That sucks." As I say it, I hear how much of an understatement it sounds like—but what else is there to say?

"It does," he concedes. "But it also means there's room for me to draft and pass an even better one someday."

While we eat, he tells me about the research he's been doing over the past few years, digging deep into public safety measures and mass shooting statistics from across the country. He's connected with organizations like Everytown for Gun Safety and Americans for Responsible Solutions, and intentionally stayed in touch with the members of Congress who had supported the original bill, buttering them up so he can curry their favor when the time is right. If Kiara gets elected, *she* could sponsor a bill. He's not vain about who gets the credit for it, so long as it passes.

"This might sound cheesy, but I can't wait to see you in office someday," I tell him after we've finished eating, as we wait for Kiara's take-out order to be brought to our table.

He sighs softly, like he's been waiting forever for that day to come. "Me too."

"Tell Kiara I wish her the very best luck tonight, not that she needs it," I say.

"Every little bit of luck counts these days. Vernon is a tough competitor."

"Do you think she can make it up?"

He hesitates. "If anyone could do it, it would be her."

fifteen

As July slips into August, Theo and I become regular fixtures in each other's lives. I forgot how quickly this happened with Jonah—how suddenly, almost overnight, routines develop. Habits form. Inside jokes pop up. I sleep at his apartment in Bushwick sometimes, but we stay at mine more often than not. He clears out a chunk of closet space for me at his place, anyway. In the mornings, he makes coffee, and he's established himself as the official DJ; our every move plays to a soundtrack of indie rock songs, like we're in a movie.

Once, when I was on set for a magazine photoshoot and went a few hours longer than usual without responding to Theo's texts, he followed up with, Bloop. Thinking about you. We send it back and forth all the time now as shorthand—*bloop* to mean "good morning," *bloop* to mean "it's been forty-eight hours and I miss you like crazy," *bloop* to mean "I saw a hot dog stand on the street, and it made me think of you because you told me once they're your favorite midnight snack, and it's too mushy to say that out loud, so I'm just gonna go with *bloop*."

After leaving Jonah, I worried that any other relationship would be a pale imitation of the one I had with him. I couldn't imagine sharing diner omelets and making silly poses for the camera on long, meandering walks up and down the city with another man. I should have realized that there would be new routines—not because I've changed or suppressed some essential part of me, but because my chemistry with Theo is undeniably different than mine and Jonah's. It has to be. My connection with each man feels distinct and special in its own way.

It goes unspoken that Theo and I spend at least part of every weekend together now—in addition to some weeknight sleepovers in between—but today, Sunday afternoon, I'm pulling myself away to play mah-jongg with Gloria, Mom, and Rae. Gloria learned the Chinese tile game, beloved by Jewish women in the U.S. for nearly a century, from her mother, and passed the tradition down to us; if Rae and I have daughters, we'll pass it down to them someday. She's played with the same group of ladies for decades, rotating players in and out of the league as they've moved to Boca or given up the game due to dwindling eyesight or, all too often, died. She doesn't get to play with her friends much these days, so we serve as her opponents instead.

Her Upper East Side apartment has barely changed since she bought it in 1958. There's an orange mid-century modern couch and a pink brocade chair in the sunken living room. Dozens of framed photos and little crystal tchotchkes line the mantel. I cover the dining room table with a pad so the mah-jongg tiles don't scratch the wood. Rae shuffles and stacks the glossy white tiles into four neat rows lined up against colorful plastic racks. Mom sets out a spread from Gloria's kitchen: chopped liver from Zabar's on Ritz crackers, egg salad on challah, a bowl of diced cantaloupe, four slices of homemade jelly roll.

"Don't forget, there's a box of rugelach on the counter," Gloria says.

I retrieve the pastries, biting into a raspberry one. Gloria doesn't understand why I thrive on Italian and Indian takeout when, according to her, all you really need is a little egg salad, a little tuna salad, maybe some blintzes for breakfast. What she doesn't realize is that if I ate her favorite Jewish deli staples regularly, that food wouldn't taste quite so sweet. I can't see rugelach out at a bakery without thinking of her every time.

"You know, my mother wouldn't buy me a mah-jongg set until I was married?" Gloria says over the *click-clack* of Rae dealing out four hands.

We've heard this before, but none of us mind listening again.

"And I worked! I could afford to buy my own set. But I didn't, because my mother didn't want me to have one until I was married. Imagine that."

We're playing using Gloria's original set from 1958—which was, indeed, a wedding present. She made a point of buying Mom, Rae, and me our own sets on principle when we were teenagers.

My hand is a jumbled mess, as it always is at the start of a game. I organize my thirteen tiles into suits (craks, bams, dots) and categories (flowers, winds, dragons). The goal is to trade, draw, and discard tiles until your hand matches one of the predetermined ones listed on your mah-jongg card, which changes annually. Gloria buys new cards for each of us every year. *You wouldn't want to be caught without one*, she says.

I study this year's card and strategize to pick one or two hands I have the best chance of winning. In order to focus, I have to quiet the steady stream of thoughts of Theo that otherwise float through my mind. I like to play mah-jongg because it's another way to feel connected to the Jewish women who came before me. I'm not particularly religious; I don't keep Shabbat or keep kosher, and I'll admit I don't know much about the Torah. But here, I know the complex litany of rules. I know the one bam tile looks different from the rest of the suit, like a funny little bird instead of a stick of bamboo, and that the soap tile actually functions as a white dragon. To me, that's enough to feel Jewish, full stop.

We pass tiles around the table seven times, per usual, and then the game picks up speed.

"Eight dot," Rae says, throwing out the first tile.

"Two bam," Gloria says.

"Flower," Mom says.

"Seven crak," I say.

"I want it." Rae stretches out a triumphant hand.

She rests my discarded tile on top of her rack alongside two identical ones from her own hand. The game continues. Mom makes dramatic, purposeful eye contact with each of us and lays down a joker. Rae and I groan. There are only eight jokers in play and they're coveted because they make winning exponentially easier. Once one has been discarded, it can't be picked up and used by another player. Mom's signature move is to discard them gleefully, rubbing it in our faces that she's so good, she doesn't need them to win.

"You know who else used to do that?" Gloria muses. "Doris. A real piece of work."

"Sorry," Mom says flatly, spearing a cube of cantaloupe.

"Remind me, how are we related to Doris?" Rae asks.

"She was married to my first cousin Roger," Gloria explains.

"The one who hated Barbra Streisand," Mom prompts.

"Oh, him!" Rae says.

Roger was a man of many strong opinions, including a fervent dislike of one of the most gifted singers of all time. In an ironic twist of fate, the Streisand family happens to own the cemetery plots next to his in Queens; when Barbra dies, she'll spend eternity haunting his grave.

Gloria predicted he'd meet the love of his life one day in 1966. He gleefully came up with a plan to wait outside the Barbizon School of Modeling and Acting on Fifth Avenue and ask out the prettiest girl he saw. He spotted this bombshell coming out the front door, all legs and eyelashes, and invited her to lunch on the spot. She said yes; he thought he hit the jackpot. He took her to lunch at a diner around the corner, sat down at a booth, and sure enough, fell in love with the waitress taking their order. She wouldn't ever be accepted to modeling school, but Roger didn't care. He was smitten.

"Doris could talk your ear off," Gloria recalls. "She never shut up—ever. She always insisted on hosting every holiday and serving the most watered-down matzo ball soup you've ever tasted."

"Oh, give it a rest," my mom says. "She's been gone, what, twenty, thirty years? Enough about the soup."

"It was terrible soup."

Once, in a fit of feeling sentimental about my heritage, I asked Gloria for her famous matzo ball soup recipe. She recited it over the phone, and I made it in the one pot I owned, the one I usually kept on the floor to catch drips from my leaky A/C. She told me I could add a little parsnip for flavor, but I got confused at the grocery store and grabbed what I thought was parsley instead. Rae had to point out that it was kale. I sympathize with Doris.

"Were Roger and Doris your first predicted match?" Rae asks.

"Third, right?" Mom corrects. "You first, then Morris?"

Gloria nods and tosses out a tile. She predicted her brother would meet his other half on a winter day in 1961. The date came and went without any word from Morris, and he married a preschool teacher named Nancy in 1964. But Nancy walked out a year into their marriage after she caught Morris writing love letters to Beverly, the college girlfriend he had kept a secret from the family because she wasn't Jewish. As Gloria predicted, they had met in the dining hall on campus on December 12, 1961, and have been inseparable ever since.

"But did you know I did some matchmaking before that?" Gloria asks.

"I didn't, no," I say, amused.

"Just a few couples, nothing much. When I worked as a secretary, some of the other gals around the office had crushes on the ad men, but were too shy to say anything. I'd fix them up."

"That's adorable," I say.

"Speaking of romance," Mom interrupts, "how are things with Theo?"

I feel myself light up. "Great. I'm really happy. I know it's early, but I'm having an amazing time getting to know him."

"So, you'll be the next to get engaged," Gloria says absentmindedly, running a lacquered pink nail down the list of hands on her card.

"Well, he doesn't necessarily believe in marriage," I say lightly, rearranging my tiles on my rack.

"Oy." Mom rolls her eyes. "He's one of those."

She and Gloria share a skeptical look. Their resemblance is even more pronounced when they each arch an eyebrow.

"Have you told him?" Mom asks.

"About what?" I play dumb, not wanting to deal with this subject.

"Come on, you know."

"I did."

"That's soon, isn't it?"

They exchange another look.

"It felt like the right moment," I insist. "He wasn't scared off or anything." I wish my voice didn't sound quite so defensive.

Rae doesn't seem fussed. "He's not going to freak out. I mean, it might take him eleven years before he's ready to propose, but . . ."

In truth, it was Rae's reticence that caused the wait. For a long time, she thought about marriage the way most toddlers think about vegetables: allegedly good for you, but not so tasty. A few years back, Gloria gave Rae the recipe for *Glamour*'s Engagement Chicken—a roast chicken stuffed with lemon, topped with herbs, and apparently imbued with magical powers, because it's inspired dozens of proposals. She simply returned the slip of paper with a polite, "No, thank you, not now."

"Or maybe you just live happily ever after, no marriage certificate required," my sister suggests. "Take it from me, weddings are *expensive.*"

Mom snorts. "Edie's getting married. She's always wanted to get married. Remember her with the veil?"

When we were ten, Rae and I were both flower girls at Mom and Allen's wedding. Mom was nearly late walking down the aisle because I got my hands on her veil and wouldn't take it off.

"I have a passion for accessorizing," I say defensively.

"When can we meet this fella?" Gloria asks.

I recoil. "Oh, isn't it kind of soon?"

Rae leans forward on her elbows, making very eager eye contact. "No."

I resist the childlike urge to stick my tongue out at her. But it's too late—Mom and Gloria are already backing her up.

"*I'd* like to meet him," Mom says.

"Why don't you bring him for Rosh Hashanah, hmm?" Gloria asks.

"Next month," Rae says. "September."

I glance down at the table, now a sea of tiles, to stall. We've only been dating for two months, and I don't want to put too much pressure on us too soon.

Gloria drops an eight bam. That's the last tile I need in order to win.

"I've got mah-jongg," I announce.

I scoop up Gloria's eight bam and add it to my rack along with the rest of my hand.

"Ugh, I was so close!" Rae yelps.

Gloria only gives me a warning. "Don't think your win gets you off the hook from this conversation."

sixteen

Two weeks before Theo turns thirty, we're drinking iced coffees in Domino Park, taking in the breeze rolling in off the East River, when he casually says, "So, my band is playing a show at Baby's All Right on my birthday. Want to come? Hang out with us after?"

I've been hoping for an invitation like this. "Of course!"

The significance of meeting his friends isn't lost on me. He keeps disappearing to band practice, friends' parties, and drinks with the guys. I never push for an invitation. I want him to open up his life to me at his own pace.

"Great. They're excited to meet you."

"I can't wait to meet them, either. What else do you want to do for your birthday?"

"Nothing serious." He looks unbothered.

"No big celebration?"

"I'll go all-out on a huge party when the band gets the record deal," he says.

At *that*, he sighs, looking out across the river at the towers and spires that pack the length of Manhattan. I know he wants to make it big more than anything. The Supersonics' meeting with the record label keeps getting pushed back. I've stopped asking for details—it seems to stress him out. He says the meeting will happen when it happens.

Theo's birthday arrives during a heat wave at the tail end of August, when even the ice cream truck's jingling siren droops with exhaustion. I had proposed we celebrate with an excursion to Rockaway Beach or Coney Island, but it's too hot to brave the subway. Instead, we bake under the sun in McCarren Park until the fear of heat stroke forces us to retreat into the cool darkness of my apartment. I have a personalized gift and handwritten card waiting for him there.

I had spent a painstaking amount of time figuring out what to write. What can you possibly say to a person who composes love songs for a living? He skims the card, tosses it aside, and opens the box with the present. I had found a designer on Etsy who makes custom guitar straps and had one made with The Supersonics' logo, the same squiggly sound wave Theo and his bandmates have as tattoos. Considering we met so recently, I didn't have the nerve to splash all out on something more extravagant. He goes to switch out the old strap on his guitar.

"I can't wait to show it off tonight onstage," he says, kissing me.

He heads over to the concert venue early to help set up The Supersonics' gear, finish the sound check, and listen to the opening act. I'm slightly relieved by this arrangement; if I had plenty of time to hang around the venue while the band got ready, I'd probably try too hard to make anxious small talk and distract them from their work, or I'd cling to Theo out of nerves. This way, I'll have Rae and Max by my side, plus a drink from the bar to settle me down. I changed my outfit three times, finally settling on my favorite cutoff Levi's and a silk camisole—my attempt to strike the right balance between cool and effortlessly sexy.

When we arrive at Baby's All Right that night, the air-conditioning is cranked up to full blast, but it's still not enough. The crowd of people in shorts and loose tees glistens with sweat. Max goes to retrieve drinks from the bar. "I'll drink anything as long as it's cold," Rae says, holding her hair up from the back of her neck and fanning her face.

We're somewhere in the middle of the crowd, but once Max returns with our ice-cold beers, Rae pushes through the audience, muttering, "'Scuse me, 'scuse me.

"You deserve to be front row," she says.

"You're acting like a bigger groupie than she is," Max says.

The Supersonics come out onstage, waving as the audience cheers. Theo manages to look rock-star cool in a black leather jacket for all of eight seconds before he whips it off and tosses the jacket toward the back of the stage.

"Whew! Anybody else burning up in here?" he asks.

He sweeps his gaze over the audience and holds eye contact with me long enough that I feel as if there's a spotlight on the front row.

Rae squeezes my arm. "Oh my god, *look at him*."

"Seriously, thank you all for coming out tonight," he continues, sliding his new guitar strap over his head. "I know you'd probably much rather be sitting at home in front of your A/Cs."

He chats easily with the audience as Callum plugs a cable into his bass and Giancarlo settles onto the piano bench. There's no trace of self-consciousness in his casual posture. *I've* been stressed all day, just imagining carrying on a conversation with his four bandmates; I can't fathom how he can be so confidently himself onstage in front of a hundred people who paid to be here tonight.

He introduces each member of the band: Giancarlo on piano, with a tangle of dark curls pushed off his forehead with a rolled-up red bandana; Mika on drums, who waves to the crowd with both arms covered in colorful tattoo sleeves; Ethan on lead guitar, who gives a stoic nod; and

Callum on bass, who salutes the audience with an excitable "Oi, oi!" in a loose British accent.

"And I'm Theo. I sing and play rhythm guitar. Thank you in advance for putting up with me tonight." The audience laughs. "We're The Supersonics, let's have a beautiful night!"

He counts off and the band jumps into "Over the Top." Callum strikes up the thumping bass line and Theo nods deeply to the beat. His fingers curl around the mic as he leans in to deliver the opening lyrics. I've listened to this song often enough that I can sing along. Max teases me for knowing all the words. I call him out for not being cool enough to know any of them. Rae shushes us and takes me by the hand to twirl me as the chorus booms around us.

I dance tentatively at first, feeling self-conscious of Theo's bandmates feet away. It's silly, but I want to make the right first impression on them. But as they play, I realize the stage lights are bright enough that they probably can't see into the crowd. Anyway, if I'm destined to have Theo in my life, his friends are a package deal. I'm sure they'll become friends of mine, too. And isn't feeling compelled to dance to their music the ultimate compliment, anyway?

My limbs loosen. I spin Rae around, and she nudges Max to do more than stand with his feet planted firmly on the floor. I groove to the beat, working my hands into the air and swinging my hips from side to side. When I make eye contact with Theo, he stumbles over a word. His gaze flashes playfully to mine; when Ethan takes over for a guitar solo, Theo bites his lip, watching me dance. Maybe the stage lights aren't too bright after all.

They bounce from song to song. Halfway into the set, Mika hops up from behind the drum set and leaps to the mic.

"You know, it's this dude's birthday? Will you sing for him?" she asks the crowd.

Theo laughs, smothering his face with his hands, as she scuttles back to the drum set and counts off as the audience roars a sloppy rendition of "Happy Birthday." I join in, blowing a kiss for him at the end.

When the song ends, Theo grabs the mic. "That is very sweet, thank you very much. You've all made this an unforgettable day. Next up, we're going to play a new song called 'Soaring.' It's something I wrote recently after meeting someone special."

"Whoop-*whoop!*" someone in the audience interjects.

Theo blushes, ever so slightly flustered. "It's actually our first time playing it live, so . . ." He locks his eyes with mine like the next part is just for me.

In the smoothest, sexiest voice I've ever heard, he says, "I hope you enjoy it."

Rae squeals and elbows me hard. "Holy shit."

"Did you know this was coming?" Max asks.

"Not even remotely."

I used to think that going weak in the knees was something only swooning heroines in romance novels did. I didn't think it was real. But here, gazing up at the stage, I feel heat rising to my cheeks as my legs turn woozy beneath me. I watch intently and listen closely, determined to memorize every second of Theo's performance.

"Thirty thousand feet up / I met this glamour girl / Now I'm living in a whole new world."

He caresses the mic softly, wrapping his hand around it the way he clutches my hip in bed, or my hand when we cross the street. He's dropped the confident bluster, displaying real tenderness instead of bravado for the first time tonight. On either side of me, I can see people in the audience swaying to the beat, oblivious to what's going on. They seem to like the song anyway—it really is good, apparently. That's not my bias talking.

"And now I'm soaring, soaring / High-flying with my Brooklyn babe / Feels so right, it has to be fate."

The bass booms. Cymbals shimmer. The melody crashes into the chorus. As I watch Theo croon the earnest lyrics he wrote for me, I realize he's falling for me. Not just because of the prophecy—but because he's chosen to.

Theo pulls me backstage after the show. I bring along Rae and Max, so everyone meets in a flurry: I kiss Theo to thank him for the song, Mika hugs me, Ethan shakes my hand; Rae introduces herself to Theo; Max congratulates Giancarlo and Callum on the show. There are too many people crammed into the narrow green room, and somebody suggests we relocate to Midway, a dive bar nearby. Callum roars in approval. The crew spills out onto the street, and we walk there in clusters of twos and threes.

I slip my hand into Theo's. "I can't believe you wrote a song for me," I say, equal parts overwhelmed and proud.

"I wanted to surprise you." He looks shyer than I've ever seen him.

"Isn't it everyone else's day to surprise *you*?"

"This is more fun for me," he promises. "What did you think of it?"

I take a moment to get my words right. "I thought it was incredible. It's the most thoughtful thing anyone's ever done for me."

I force myself not to get caught up in dwelling on whether or not that's true. Now isn't the time to compare Theo's music to the night Jonah threw me a surprise party to celebrate the launch of my own styling business, or the time he spent hours on the phone teaching Gloria how to use FaceTime so she could see Rae during the months her ER was overrun with COVID cases. Those comparisons don't help anyone. When I was with Jonah, it felt impossible to imagine that anyone else could infuse my days with so much love. I was terrified to leave him; I had to operate on blind faith that the risk of losing him would lead to an even greater reward. Tonight, I'm starting to see that come to fruition.

I kiss Theo again and pull him by the hand to catch up to Rae and Max a few paces ahead of us.

"So, we finally meet the guy she won't stop talking about," Rae says, eyes twinkling.

"Oh, *really*?" Theo says, intrigued.

"Shut up," I say softly.

"She only says good things, don't worry," Max says.

"I'd hope so," Theo says.

Mika hangs back on the sidewalk while we catch up. She links her arm through mine.

"Usually, we never meet anyone Theo dates. He never sticks around long enough to get to the 'meet the friends' stage," she confesses.

"Huh!" It's all I can say that encourages her to keep talking without seeming like I'm explicitly digging for information.

She gives me a once-over. "So, that must mean you're pretty special, huh?"

I'm suddenly very curious to learn about the other women in his past. Before I can respond, we're at the bar.

Callum pulls open the front door and ushers everyone in quickly. "Come, now, all that beer inside won't drink itself," he says, snapping his fingers. "The bartender on shift tonight has a generous pour."

Midway—named for its Grand Street location on the dividing line between North and South Williamsburg—feels warm and cave-like thanks to its windowless deep red walls. A string of Christmas lights twinkles above the bar. It's crowded tonight, but somehow The Supersonics secure their regular table toward the back of the bar. Theo tries to buy a round of beers for everybody before his friends steal his wallet. Giancarlo orders the drinks instead, taking extra care to ask what I'd like.

"I have stories about your man, you know," he says. "Has he told you about where we met? That Italian immersion summer program in the Alps run by nuns?"

"No!"

I glance back at Theo, who's being forced into a colorful birthday hat by Callum. If, years ago, you asked me to picture what my soulmate's friends were like, I probably wouldn't have landed on this crew. But I can imagine that nights out with them would never be boring—and maybe it's healthy to have a good dose of fun in my life, especially as Rae and Max start settling down.

Giancarlo, unfazed by the sight, points at me as he walks backward to the bar. "I'll be back in a minute. Trust me, you'll want to hear these."

I slide onto an old, scratched wooden bar stool next to Theo. "I didn't know you spoke Italian."

"*Solo un po'*. I've lost most of it by now."

"And you went to summer camp with nuns?"

"Oh, they *hated* me," he remembers, chuckling at the memory. "I used to stash handles of tequila in the eaves of the bedrooms."

"Leave it to you to find handles of tequila in the Alps," Mika says, snorting.

Rae cocks her head. "You sound fun. I approve."

"Already!" Theo trills, clearly pleased.

"I had to work *much* harder for that one's approval," Max tells Theo, gesturing to me.

Giancarlo comes by with the beers and Theo helps pass them out.

"Well, cheers to meeting you," Theo says.

He and Rae clink glasses emphatically, and then the rest of the group piles on to raise a toast in his honor. Amid the revelry of new friends and old, the nerves I felt all day suddenly feel silly. I can't believe I was worried about meeting these people, who are so openly welcoming and couldn't be less pretentious.

Giancarlo returns to tell me all about their rowdy teen boy escapades. I try to pay close attention to every detail, but it's tempting to eavesdrop as Theo and Rae bond. It sounds like she's alternating between reciting my most mortifying childhood stories and grilling him for details about what I'm like in a relationship. I'd strangle her, but she has him laughing hard. At the end of the table, Ethan and Max are deep in discussion about their mutual favorite politics podcast. Mika and Callum are holding court over the pool table, where it looks like she's in the lead, if his loud cursing is anything to go by.

Rae and Max leave early because she has morning ER shift tomorrow. Giancarlo invites me to play pool with him, but I decline because I'm awful at it.

"We'll teach you next time," Ethan says, feeding quarters into the machine.

Underneath the table, Theo slides his fingers over my thigh, resting his hand just high up above my knee that it's distracting. I dart a glance toward Mika, who's at the bar fetching more drinks.

"Mika said something interesting."

His expression darkens. "Oh, no. What?"

"You don't 'stick around' long enough to bring girls to meet your friends?" I recall, using air quotes. "Her words, not mine."

He cringes, then recovers. "You're meeting the most important ones now."

"It doesn't bother me. I was just curious. And kind of flattered?"

Theo takes my hands in his. "I haven't gotten serious about anyone in a while, but that doesn't mean I don't want to give this a real chance. This is different—it *feels* different," he says seriously.

Mika returns carrying three beers pressed close to her chest. "You guys good?"

Theo rolls his eyes at her. "Yep."

Someone clears their throat behind me. I swivel around to find Callum, who slips his hand into mine and fixes me with a serious gaze.

"Lady Edie. Sir Theo's famous muse. It's been an honor learning an ode to your beauty and grace. I hope you enjoyed the song."

"'Soaring'? Very much. You guys are all amazing."

He somberly places a light peck on the back of my hand, then reverts out of whatever (Elizabethan? Medieval?) persona he had adopted and slides back into his usual Essex accent.

"Theo's been right soppy for months, so don't you dare mug him off," he warns.

"Callum, she's not going to dump him!" Mika exclaims. She turns to me for backup. "You, like, can't, right?"

Her question catches me off guard. "I'm sorry, what?"

"Because of your destiny or whatever." She waves her hands like she's conjuring up magic.

Five feet away, Giancarlo goes still, pausing with the pool cue in his hand. Ethan's eyes flick to mine. They all seem to know what she's talking about. Theo must have told everyone. Panic flits through my chest. His hand is still on my leg, fingers slack on my skin, but he's not looking at me. Instead, he's suddenly fixated on the soggy label peeling off his beer bottle.

"I mean, I have no interest in breaking this off." I force a little bit of a laugh, as if to demonstrate how ridiculous the idea is. I hate being on the spot like this.

"Right, but like, you . . . you, what, think you're destined to marry him?" Mika probes, wide-eyed. "Your grandma makes these predictions and so everyone in your family just marries whoever they meet on the right day? Like a game of musical chairs—you settle down whenever the music stops."

"It's a little bit more complicated than that," I deflect, straining to keep my tone friendly.

Mika sits patiently, like she's waiting for me to explain. I cannot believe this girl. I can't believe *Theo.*

"It's kind of personal, actually. I almost never tell anybody about it—just my best friend, really, up until Theo."

"Meeks, chill," Theo says quietly. He pulls off his birthday hat and ruffles up his hair.

"Sorry! I didn't realize it was such a touchy subject. I mean, it's *fascinating*," she says, talking fast now that she realizes she's offended me. "I'm really into tarot. Have you ever had a reading done? I'd love to do one for you sometime."

"Sure." I offer up a weak smile and let the group's focus slide toward Callum, heckling the pool game. I want to tell Theo why I'm upset, but this isn't the time or place.

Theo slings an arm around my shoulders. "You okay?" he whispers, nuzzling a kiss into my jaw.

When his lips brush against my skin, endorphins burst in my brain like fireworks. I can't help the way my body reacts to him; he's hard to stay mad at. "Yeah, I'm all good."

~

We're halfway back to my place, teetering a little on the sidewalk, when I bring up what's been weighing on my mind.

"Hey, I need to say something. You know what you told Mika about the prophecy? I don't tell anybody that. *Anybody.* You're the second person I've told in my entire life."

It's past midnight and the sky is an expanse of ink, but even in the glow of a streetlight, I can see his face fall.

"I'm sorry, Edie. I'm really sorry."

Even through the haze of his birthday drinks, he apologizes with pleading eyes and a panicked tightness to his speech, like he's bewildered to find himself in trouble and is desperate to get out of it.

"I guess I never explicitly told you not to say anything," I say.

I had assumed it would have been common sense not to spread it around, but maybe I can't fault him for that.

"Who else knows?" I ask.

It would be embarrassing if he told his parents. I don't think Max's family knows at all. Mom's first husband used to make fun of the prophecy to his parents and siblings—something she only discovered after they were already married.

"Nobody but the band," he insists. "And I'll make sure they don't tell anyone else or ever bring it up again."

Theo sounds sincere now, but he didn't stand up for me when Mika's tone turned mocking. He was right there, watching the whole thing go down, and he stayed silent.

"I wish you had defended me more back there," I admit.

He bites his lip. "I hate that I let you down."

If this were a conflict with Jonah, it wouldn't end so neatly or so fast. We'd talk it out more thoroughly. But I can't bring myself to keep admonishing Theo—not on his birthday, and certainly not after he demonstrated how much he cares by belting out a love song he wrote for me in front of a packed concert hall. Not now, seeing how quick he is to apologize and how genuinely sorry he looks. Not when the foundation of our relationship still feels as delicate and fragile as a baby bird.

"It'll all be okay," I say, sweeping the conflict away. "We're good."

One of the upsides to Gloria's prophecy is that I know Theo and I have the gift of time. It could take months or years, but I can trust with full certainty that we'll eventually learn each other inside and out. Maybe I'm learning that he shows affection better with actions instead of words. Or maybe he's seeing just how protective I am over the people I love. Maybe he's proved he's not ready to meet my family at Rosh Hashanah—or maybe this is exactly why he needs to meet them all in person soon, so he can see how important they are to me.

I could tell him all of this, but I don't. I know everything will ultimately be all right in the end. I suppress the pit in my stomach with a kiss.

seventeen

After the incident at Midway, I need to have Shireen vet Theo before I feel comfortable officially inviting him to Rosh Hashanah. I've long admired Shireen for her no-bullshit demeanor; I know she'll be straight with me about her opinion. In some ways, I prefer discussing Theo with her rather than with my sister. Rae so badly wants me to have what she has with Max. When I tell her what happened with Mika and Callum after she left, she agrees he should have stood up for me, but is also quick to point out that I never asked him to keep the prophecy to himself.

"Come on, Edie, anyone would be freaked out or psyched or *something* after hearing their entire romantic future has been predicted by some old lady they've never met. Cut him some slack."

I want to believe her. But ever since that night, when I'm waiting for the subway or in line at Duane Reade or trying to sleep next to Theo, the memory of him falling silent next to me at the bar comes surging back to me. So, I need Shireen's take. I trust her to tell me the truth about whether he's a good person who messed up, or someone who just plain falls short. I'm afraid to find out what that could mean for Gloria's prophecy, but I figure I can cross that bridge when I come to it.

Shireen herself has had a string of bad dating luck lately. She liked

Romain, the guy she started seeing after the Annabelle Crosby press preview, but after a month of romancing her, he suddenly broke it off, saying he just wasn't feeling it anymore. Since then, she's had a one-night stand not worth repeating and two dates with men who seemed fantastic on Hinge, but awful in person. She's temporarily swearing off dating—but she's game to meet Theo over dinner and give me her honest thoughts afterward.

Dinner doesn't happen right away. New York Fashion Week dominates a week in early September. Between pre-dawn call-times backstage before shows, styling clients like Sadie Sakamoto and the up-and-coming actress Lana Davenport for their front-row appearances, and occasionally making it to late-night after-parties myself, I'm too busy and exhausted to even think about Theo. The space helps. The frustration I felt after Midway boils off, leaving me to miss him.

The night after Fashion Week ends, we go to San Marzano, which has been in my regular dinner rotation since college. There's nowhere else in the city you can eat this well—wild boar ragù bursting with flavor spooned over handmade pasta with a deliciously cold pitcher of red sangria—for such a good price. It doesn't hurt that the white subway tile walls, cozy wooden bar, and moody lighting make a gorgeous backdrop for dinner.

Theo takes my invitation to meet Shireen in stride. If he's nervous, he doesn't show it.

"You feel good about this?" I ask when he slides into the seat next to mine at the restaurant. He kisses me.

"Yeah! Shireen sounds awesome. Two triplets down, one to go."

He knows me so well. I don't even remember when I told him about our childhood inside joke—but clearly, he does.

Shireen pushes through the front door, looking chic as ever in cropped black cigarette pants and a thin gray cardigan. She joins us at the table, resting the black leather Chanel bag she bought with last year's bonus on the empty seat next to her. Theo stands and Shireen delivers a double-cheek kiss. He gamely follows along.

"It's so good to meet you," he says.

"I feel like I know you already from Edie's stories," Shireen says. "Plus, full disclosure, she sent me that song you wrote about her, 'Soaring.' I listened to it like, at least five times."

He gives a bashful grin. "I really appreciate that."

"Do you write songs about all the girls you date?" There's a challenging edge to her voice, like she's daring him to give the right answer. *I* don't even know what the right answer would be.

"Whew, you go straight for the kill, don't you?" He shakes his head a little in surprise.

She holds his gaze as I flag down a waiter and beg for a pitcher of sangria to loosen up the interrogation.

He clears his throat and attempts to answer. "I mean, dating, love, sex—" I flinch at his use of the word, recalling one particularly memorable night last week. The image of Theo's fingers curled into mine, knuckles turning white, shoots a shiver down my spine. ". . . heartbreak, it's all inspiring. That's what people care about the most, oftentimes, so that's what I write music about."

"That's not a straight answer, Romeo."

"Remind me, did Edie say you're a lawyer?"

"I work in executive search—recruiting for C-suite roles at big companies." Her favorite part of her job is grilling pompous men who want to be CEOs. She's a natural at it.

"Shireen, let him out of the hot seat, he hasn't even gotten a chance to look at the menu."

"You can't go wrong with the pappardelle," she says with the tone of an apology.

"Noted, thank you." He reaches for my hand under the table.

A minute later, when she and I both rattle off orders without looking at the menu, he asks if this is our regular spot.

"Since forever," I say.

She points at a table across the room. "That's where we were sitting when Edie convinced me to move here after graduation."

"And that's where we sat when Rae and I had our birthday dinner here one year." I indicate the long table by the back wall.

She knocks on our current table. "And this is actually where we sat when we celebrated my last promotion."

"Hallowed ground," he says, looking around the restaurant.

He tells us about the day he and Giancarlo learned to make pasta from scratch while in Italy. Shireen jumps in with a story about making pizza; she likes to cook to clear her head from work. Theo teases me for my lackluster kitchen skills, and Shireen commiserates with him. I don't even mind that they're roasting me—I'm happy they found something to bond over.

We're digging into our pastas when Shireen tosses out the question of the night.

"So, what did you think when Edie told you about Gloria's prophecy?"

Theo darts a glance at me, like he's checking to see if it's all right to discuss what he knows. I smile and tilt my head as if to give him permission.

"I was definitely surprised," he admits.

"Did it change how you felt about her?"

I am breathless with nerves. I take a long sip of sangria just to have something to do other than stare Theo down.

He hesitates. "Yes and no."

Shireen arches a skeptical eyebrow. She can wield her manicured brows like weapons; it's not a good thing to be on the receiving end of one of them.

"Explain."

"It didn't make me like her any more than I already did, which was a lot," he says. He speaks slowly, choosing his words carefully. "But I'm not going to lie, it's pretty clear that we currently have different views about marriage. That's not a dealbreaker for me, but I understand if it is for her."

He turns toward me now. "I'm actually really glad you told me because it gives me a better understanding of how seriously you're taking this. So, I know not to mess this up. Like, I get your point of view, and you've heard mine. Though, of course, I'm open to having my mind changed."

Shireen watches him closely. "Edie can be pretty persuasive."

"Oh, yeah?"

"I'll never forget the time she talked me into wearing a fedora for school picture day in ninth grade. I looked like an aspiring pickup artist."

"It was trendy at the time," I apologize.

Theo laughs. "She hasn't hijacked my wardrobe yet."

"I like the way you dress," I point out.

"And I like the way *you* dress," he echoes.

"What else do you like about her?" Shireen asks. She tosses off the question playfully, but I know she's listening with razor-sharp ears.

Theo tenses up ever so slightly beside me.

"God, Shireen, this isn't a job interview, or the SATs," I groan. I wanted her to vet him, but not this obviously. "You can chill with the questions."

"No, I respect it—you want nothing but the best for your best friend," Theo says, putting on a diplomatic smile. "Well, the first thing I noticed about Edie, of course, is that she's beautiful and stylish. Her fedora days are behind her. And then as I got to know her, well, she's accomplished, creative . . . and she makes a mean martini."

With that, he swirls a long piece of pappardelle around his fork. I hide my face-shattering grin behind another long gulp of sangria.

"Yeah, Edie's all right," she tells him. "You could've done a lot worse."

He smirks. "Trust me. I have."

"Guys, stop it, this is mortifying."

Shireen shrugs. "You invited us."

Later, after we've finished our pastas and Shireen has attempted to disguise grilling Theo on everything from his voting history to his views on feminism as breezy dinner conversation, he excuses himself to use the restroom. When he's beyond earshot, I lean across the table.

"So, what do you really think of him?"

"I like him."

"Really?"

She ticks off reasons on her fingers. "He's confident enough to handle all my questions, he's funny, and he seems pretty smitten with you."

I search her eyes for a flicker of doubt. I know what she looks like when she withholds the truth: I've seen her fib to our seventh-grade classmates that she definitely, totally already got her period for the first time. I've seen her hand over a fake ID to a bouncer without blinking.

"Come on, Shireen. There must be something you're not telling me."

She fidgets with her necklace. "It honestly doesn't matter what I think. All that matters is if you're happy."

"And I'd be happier if I knew your take on him."

She sighs. "Okay, I'm only saying this because you really asked, but if it turns out you fall madly in love with him, we have to pretend this conversation never happened. Got it?"

"Deal." My heart thumps against my chest. Time slows down as I wait for my eagle-eyed friend to fill in what I've been missing.

She presents her theory slowly and gently. "So, we know he tends to flit from girl to girl, and he's rarely that serious about any of them. And from the way he described you—'beautiful,' 'stylish,' 'accomplished'—it's like he's only seeing the surface of you. Like you're his Manic Pixie Dream Girl muse. But you're so much more than that." She pauses and cringes. "You're not mad at me for saying that, are you?"

"What? No. But we've only known each other for a little over two months," I remind her. "It's not like he can learn everything about me overnight."

"He could say you're incredibly thoughtful—you just got him that custom birthday gift, right? Or he could appreciate your ambition, your work ethic, the effort you put in to stay close with your family. You're an amazing friend, a great listener . . . I mean, I hate to bring this up, but remember what you and Jonah were like after two months?"

I groan. "Don't remind me."

He didn't just call me beautiful; he took photos that captured me at my most radiant. He didn't just brag about my accomplishments; he helped me achieve them, introducing me to his friends in the fashion industry. He saw me when the pandemic hit, then dragged on, and I felt like a shell of myself, when the prospect of showering or changing out of my bathrobe felt unfathomable without a reason to leave the apartment. My styling projects had stalled to a halt. And I was still his dream girl then. His appreciation for me wasn't superficial.

"And I wonder if the prophecy plays right into Theo's commitment issues and his whole Manic Pixie Dream Girl thing," Shireen continues. "You're not just another girl, you're not just another muse—you're bringing the supernatural into your relationship. I mean, that's fodder for a whole album right there. Wouldn't that be catnip for a guy like Theo?"

She winces at the weight of her words. I slump back in my chair, overwhelmed. I don't think Theo is calculating enough to date me solely for musical inspiration. Even if the prophecy appeals to his subconscious, he isn't cruel enough to use me like that.

"So, where does that leave me? How do I get him to care enough to see me in full?"

She bites her lip. "If he's really right for you, he'll catch up soon enough on his own."

"I guess it's kind of stupid for me to expect that everything would be seamless right away," I mumble.

"Not stupid. You're optimistic. Romantic. Starry-eyed. That's how you've always been," she reminds me. "You deserve so much love. It's just a matter of whether he's able to give that to you."

I'm still chewing on that idea when the man in question returns to his seat.

Later, after the sangria is gone, the bill is paid, and we've parted ways with Shireen, Theo stands above me on the L train back to Brooklyn. Ever the gentleman, he let me take the sole remaining open seat. We're deep underground, zipping below the East River. He's talking about something Shireen mentioned at dinner, but I'm having trouble focusing on what he's saying. Across from me, a couple sits side by side with their hands interlaced in her lap. She rests her head on his shoulder, and he absentmindedly fiddles with the rip in the knee of her jeans, like she's a continuation of himself. They look intertwined and at peace. I miss that. I want that.

If dinner with Shireen and Theo was intended to give me clarity about my relationship, then in that regard, it was a success. I know now that I want him to meet my family soon. Maybe the more he sees of my life, the more he'll truly see *me*. I can't let Shireen's comments make me shrink away from Theo. If anything, I have to do the opposite.

"Hey, you know Rosh Hashanah's coming up? My family is getting together. You could come. Everyone wants to meet you."

He pauses and gives me a curious look. "Your mom and stepdad?"

"And my grandma, plus Rae and Max, and Pops and Rocco."

"Everyone—wow."

Mika's comments from the bar echo in my head. Maybe asking him to meet my family is asking for too much.

"But if you're not ready, you don't have to—"

But he presses a single finger to my lips, warmth already bubbling up in his voice.

"Edie, I'd love to. When is it?"

eighteen

The new year is a new start, the rabbi tells the congregation on the morning of Rosh Hashanah. It's a time both to celebrate our good deeds of the past year and remember those who came before us. The holiday commemorates the creation of the world, so he tells the story of Adam and Eve, but I zone out halfway through. For me, religion itself doesn't mean very much, but family tradition certainly does. I'm here in temple because we're all here—Rae, Mom, Gloria.

Lack of faith aside, one of the reasons I have such a soft spot for Rosh Hashanah is because dressing up for High Holiday services was my first taste of feeling like a stylist. When Rae and I were little girls, Mom would take us to a children's boutique every September and let us pick out frilly, formal dresses with high necks and taffeta bows, or prim skirts with matching cardigans, and patent leather Mary Janes. If we were particularly well behaved, Gloria would let us borrow a piece of her own costume jewelry to wear with our new outfits. Two decades later, even though it would be more than appropriate to dress in business casual for temple (Mom is in the no-nonsense black slacks she wears to board meetings), I'm still drawn to fussy dresses and family jewels for this occasion. Today, I chose a garnet red dress with pretty bell sleeves. Grandpa Ray's wedding band rests against my chest.

The rabbi transitions into singing a Hebrew prayer I don't remember learning the words to, but sure enough, I know every single one. Then, to conclude the service, he picks up the shofar, a hollowed-out horn, and trumpets out the traditional one hundred blasts, like he does every year on this holiday. He goes red-faced with effort.

I wait with Gloria on the sidewalk outside the temple as Mom and Rae cross the parking lot to pull around the car. The four of us are going to lunch at a nearby deli, just like we always do.

"Big Rosh Hashanah crowd this year," she observes.

I love her Brooklyn-tinged Hebrew with the warped, flat vowels: *Rusha shunnah.*

"And they say the Jews dwindle further every year." She tuts. "You'll keep this up after I'm gone, won't you?"

"Of course," I say, making the same promise I've already made about continuing to play mah-jongg and stocking my kitchen with chopped liver and rugelach from Zabar's.

But I know it won't be the same without Gloria. It breaks my heart that my own children will likely only know her through stories and photos—and neither of those come close to capturing a person's full essence.

My stomach growls for pastrami and half-sour pickles. I slip my phone out of my purse and check it for the first time in hours. Theo's name lights up on my screen. He had asked if he should join me for services, but I told him that he didn't need to sit through two hours of prayers, half in a language neither of us understand. He has last-minute questions about what to wear and what to bring, followed by, Blooooop. I know you're busy, but I wanted to say that I miss you.

This might be my best year yet.

Theo rings the doorbell at Mom's house in Mount Kisco while holding a massive bouquet of daisies. He's hidden nearly all of his tattoos under a gray button-down and has even combed his hair neatly. I'm touched by the effort.

He greets me with a kiss.

"*Shana tovah*," he says proudly. "Did I say that right? Happy new year?"

I laugh. "Yes, you did. Come on in."

Mom sweeps into the foyer, clearly pleased by the bouquet. She opens her arms in a hug. "Theo! Welcome to our house, welcome to our family."

"Oh my god, *Mom*." Mortifying.

"What? He understands, right?" She turns to Theo expectantly, daring him to be unflappable in the face of fate.

He chuckles. "*Shana tovah*, Ms. Meyer."

"None of that, call me Laurie. But keep up the Hebrew and my mother will love you."

She excuses herself to the kitchen to find a vase.

When we're alone, he exhales, going wide-eyed for a moment. "Whew, your mom means business."

"Can you handle this?" I keep my voice light, like I'm joking around, but deep down, his stress worries me.

He swallows. His stage face slips back over his regular one. "Absolutely."

"Just wait until you meet my grandmother."

I take him into the living room, where Allen, Pops, Rocco, and Rae are sitting with glasses of Crown Royal. Theo shakes hands with my dads and gives my sister a hug.

"Good to see you again," she says.

"Can we make you a drink?" Pops asks.

Theo looks at the matching glasses of whiskey. "Sure, thank you so much."

Before he can sit, I pull him into the kitchen to meet Gloria.

"Leaving us already?" Rocco protests.

"He'll be back," I call.

For as long as I can remember, Mom and Gloria have been in charge of our holiday meals. Max has been a more recent addition; once we all realized what an excellent cook he is, Rae and I were banished to the living room while Max has been roped into making side dishes. Mom always promises that he'll be able to make the main course—the brisket—next year, but next year never quite seems to come. She's too proud of her own version to let anyone else touch the dish.

I lead Theo through the kitchen, where every flat surface is covered with platters of food. Mom trims the stems of the bouquet to fit in a glass vase, and Gloria stands at the stove, taste-testing her soup.

"This is Theo," I say, introducing them.

She leans forward so he can stoop to kiss her cheek.

"*Shana tovah.*"

"You like matzo ball soup?" she asks.

There is only one correct answer to this question, and unfortunately, he doesn't give it.

"I actually don't think I've ever had it," he admits.

"Ha! Well, come taste it. Does it need salt?"

She gives him a spoonful straight from the pot shimmering with filmy, golden liquid.

The second he swallows, he heaps praise onto the soup like it's the greatest thing he's ever tasted.

She flips a hand at him. "That's nice, but excuse me for not trusting your palate—yet. Edie, come taste."

I consider a sip of fragrant broth. "A pinch more salt."

"Salt. Good girl." She moves to sprinkle some over the pot.

I fix myself a martini, and Theo and I rejoin the group in the living room. There's a tray on the coffee table with slices of apple and a small bowl of honey. I dip the gleaming red fruit into the amber and hand it to Theo. "We eat this to represent the sweetness of the new year."

He pops it into his mouth, but not before the honey drips a little onto his hand. He grabs a napkin from the table.

"This was once all new to me, too," Rocco says. "You'll catch on soon enough."

I wish his words didn't make me think of Jonah. I never brought him home for holidays, even though he implied he'd like to come, because it felt cruel to weave him into the fabric of my family's life when I knew he wouldn't be a permanent fixture. But he's Jewish, too; he would have understood all of this instantly, intimately, without explanation. He would have fit in seamlessly. *Shana tovah* would roll off his tongue. He'd be able to properly taste-test Gloria's soup and would know the symbolism behind the apples and honey. For the first time, it occurs to me that when I think about my ideal partner, I think about someone who could slip into this dinner and feel instantly at home. I thought that keeping Jonah away from my family's traditions would be easier in the long run. It didn't occur to me back then that I'd feel his presence here nine months after our breakup. I had taken Jonah for granted. I loved him so much. I would have married him. I really would I have—but I couldn't.

I take a deep breath to center myself and try to tune back into the conversation in front of me. My dads lob softball questions at Theo, like whether he follows the Giants, where they can see his band play next, and if he's joining me next weekend in Miami for Rae and Max's bachelor/bachelorette party (he's not an official member of the wedding party, so no, he's not coming). I had wondered if they'd go into full protective dad mode and grill their daughter's new boyfriend, but I guess the prophecy has softened them. What's the point of putting Theo through the ringer when he's destined to be perfect for me?

I hear Mom calling out to me from the kitchen. "Edie, can you set the table?"

Theo gets up to help me, but that's not necessary. "You can stay," I offer.

In the dining room, I unload the stacks of Mom and Allen's wedding china from the credenza. Tonight, we're nine people, but as I put out the dishes—creamy white, decorated with fine periwinkle, ringed with gold—I realize we only have place settings for eight. I scrounge around the credenza for a spare plate and an extra bowl for Theo, but the hand-me-down china from Allen's long-deceased parents is chipped around the edges. The patterns clash. We've never needed an extra place setting; our holiday dinners have always just been the eight of us.

When dinner is ready, I sit next to Gloria like always (*the two single ladies must stick together*, she said every year), with Theo on my other side. Tradition remains tradition, even as life changes all around us.

The meal begins with brief prayers in Hebrew over the candles, wine, and challah. I recite them quickly by memory with the rest of the family while Theo sits quietly. Everyone gets a hefty serving of matzo ball soup for starters, and Mom and Max carry out the rest of the food: Max's noodle kugel and tzimmes, Mom's brisket and salad, more apples and honey, and gefilte fish (only because we've always served it, even though none of us particularly like it). Theo gamely scoops a little bit of everything onto his plate, including the fish.

"Nobody would judge you if you didn't eat that," I say quietly, nodding at the pale, slippery mass on his plate.

Theo gives my hand a grateful squeeze under the table. "That is *awesome* news," he whispers.

I never gave much thought to my match's religion. It truly didn't matter to me. But even so, I didn't expect that walking Theo through tonight step by step would make me feel so hyper-aware of the differences between us. You can't choose the family you're born into, and despite nurture's best attempts to override nature, you can't really choose who your kids become, either. You only get one shot at choosing your family, and that's through love, partnership, or marriage.

Even so, I'm not deterred from falling for Theo. If anything, it makes me want to work harder to teach him about everything that matters to me, so that someday, this will feel like home for him, too. Maybe he's supposed to become a part of this family because he never felt at peace with his own.

I explain what's in each dish, which ones we eat on other holidays, and which are specific to tonight. That turns into a tangent about why Jews eat Chinese food on Christmas; Chinese restaurants are almost never closed on that day, but the tradition dates back to when Jewish and Chinese immigrants lived side by side on the Lower East Side at the turn of the last century. And anyway, Chinese food isn't exactly kosher, but it rarely mixes meat and dairy—that's close enough for plenty of Jews.

"You want New York history?" Gloria chimes in. "I'm an old broad. I *am* New York history."

"You don't look a day over seventy-five," Pops says, serving Rocco an extra slice of kugel.

"This is why I love you," she says.

Once, many years before I was born, Gloria apparently hoped Mom and Pops would get together, prophecy (and his sexuality) be damned. I think she was relieved when she got to keep him in the family. I wouldn't be surprised if she was the one who planted the idea in Mom's head.

"I grew up in Flatbush," Gloria tells Theo. "You know Flatbush?"

A neighborhood south of where we live in Brooklyn.

"Sure."

"It used to take forever to get into the city. There were three different subway systems back then: the IRT, the BMT, and the IND. We used subway tokens back then, not these new MetroCards."

MetroCards haven't been new since my fifth-grade field trip to the Natural History Museum, but I don't correct her.

She and Theo fall into every New Yorker's favorite pastime, alternatively defending and complaining about the subway. I scoot my chair back an inch or two so I can watch them connect. Seeing two of my favorite people get along so smoothly is a ridiculous thrill.

Once Gloria has thoroughly reviewed all of his opinions on the mass transit system, she places her hand on my knee, beckoning me closer.

"I like your fella," she says. "But those tattoos? *Hmmm . . .*"

I didn't realize there would be a performance review at dinner. Theo tugs his sleeves down to cover his wrists.

"But he's smart! Polite! Handsome! And he ate two servings of my soup because he knows what's good for him."

"It was delicious," Theo says.

I'm relieved Gloria adores him. Just because someone is fated to be a match doesn't mean the extended family will approve—look at her infamous cousin Roger and his wife. Doris still gets trash-talked decades later.

"Are you two lovebirds staying over tonight?" Mom asks from the other end of the table, where she, Rae, and Max have been deep in debating the merits of a wedding DJ versus a band.

"Here?" I ask.

"Oh, I . . ." Theo turns to me out of deference.

The word catches me off guard. "Lovebirds." I've been in love before, and that's how I know I'm not quite there with Theo yet. I'm close, for sure. The more I get to know him deep down inside, insecurities and all, the more I enjoy what I see. He's all wild swagger on the outside, tender and sensitive on the inside. I like that we're a power couple brimming with creativity, me in fashion and him in music. But as charming and alluring and fascinating as he is day to day, I still have doubts about our long-term potential. Can our relationship go deep enough? Do we want the same kind of life? I want to wait to use that word with him until

I'm 1,000 percent confident in my feelings. They're still developing. Just because we're fated to fall in love doesn't mean it'll happen overnight. I trust it will happen eventually.

"I think we'll head back to Brooklyn after dinner," I say.

"You know there's always room for you here," Mom says.

"Maybe next time," Theo offers.

Next time. I like that.

There's a sweet and moist honey cake for dessert, and then we help clean the kitchen. Rae, Max, Theo, and I take the train back to the city. I like having him in tow with my family, and it's all too easy to imagine us taking this same route between Westchester and Brooklyn for holidays, birthdays, and weekends to come. I'm sleepy from the martini and the wine and the honey cake, and I curl up in the seat, resting against Theo. Rae naps, too, and Max reads. Theo puts on his headphones, and I can faintly hear the hum of his music. I don't mind it.

But as the train hurtles toward Grand Central, a song starts up with a distinctive opening melody I'd recognize anywhere. Suddenly, I'm wide-awake. It's my song with Jonah. We listened to it over and over that fall he moved from his Morningside Heights apartment into a new place downtown, the one he wanted me to move into with him. I resisted and said no. I told him I wasn't ready yet. I wasn't brave enough to tell him I wouldn't ever be ready.

The sound of the chorus transports me back to the day I helped him move. I remember standing over an open box of toiletries and towels while he came up behind me in the bathroom, studying our reflection in the long mirror that hung over the back of the door. He kissed a trail down the back of my neck and wrapped his hands around my middle. He said, "It's not too late for you to change your mind and move in." His voice was heavy with longing.

The memory is sharp enough that it hurts. I have to concentrate on pushing away the lump in my throat, just like I pushed away Jonah. I interlace my fingers with Theo's, rubbing my thumb over the back of his hand. The sensation of skin against skin grounds me in the present moment again.

When we switch from the train to the subway, I ask Theo, "You'll come home with me, won't you?" even though I think I know the answer.

"Yeah, of course."

I like that there's no question about whether he'll stay the night.

In the bedroom, he unzips my dress and slides it off my body. I crawl under the covers, rolling toward him so my bare chest is flush against his side.

"Tonight was really nice." His voice is soft as he strokes my hair.

"I'm glad you liked it. It made me really happy to see you getting along with my family."

Even as I appreciate how sweet and comfortable this moment is, my mind is still thick with memories, thanks to that song. It's like Jonah's ghost lingers in the air. As I nestle my head onto Theo's chest, the questions that started to nag me at dinner come flooding back. Am I overthinking what love feels like? Am I afraid that fate is pulling me toward a relationship I wouldn't have chosen with my own free will? Did I make a mistake by leaving behind a man I once loved?

I tilt Theo's face toward mine, kissing him deeply. He responds softly at first, then enthusiastically. He rolls on top of me, propping himself up on his elbows. I can feel how hard he is against my hip. In the dark, the brush of his lips against my throat and on the inside of my thigh feel like sparks. His touch clears my worries until all I can comprehend is sheer gratitude for the man right in front of me.

nineteen

Boarded the plane, I text Theo at the crack of dawn on Friday. Streaks of peach and gold sunrise begin to warm up the sky on the first morning of Rae and Max's bachelor/bachelorette weekend.

Oooh, exciting, he shoots back. I know flirting on airplanes is kind of your thing, but . . . try not to hit on whoever's sitting next to you this time, all right?

The aisle is to my left, and across it, there's Rae, napping on Max's shoulder; to my right, Bennett is filling in today's *New York Times* crossword puzzle at impressive speed, biting his lower lip in concentration. While the rest of us—me; Shireen; Rae's best friend, Olivia; Max's cousin Zach; and his coworker Trevor—are groggy and bleary-eyed, most of us clutching large coffees to keep ourselves alive, he's in a starched button-down, as alert as ever. Thanks to his job, he's used to this kind of sleep deprivation.

You have *nothing* to worry about, I text Theo.

I figured, he says. Have a safe flight!

I'm not thrilled to be up at this hour, but the coffee has me too wired to even attempt sleep. I pull a magazine from my bag.

Bennett nudges me. "Jewish ravioli, eight letters."

"Kreplach."

"Spell that?"

"Isn't that cheating, asking for help?"

He purses his lips. "We have house rules."

This is a man who finds time to iron his clothing and apply hair gel before a 6:35 a.m. flight.

"Of course you do."

"No Google, no dictionary, no thesaurus, no texting people for help," he rattles off. "But asking a friendly neighbor? Not off-limits."

"Fine." I give him the spelling.

I watch him fill in a few more words and scroll by a few other clues that stump him, then return to my magazine. The plane rumbles down the runway, and as it takes off, I reach across the aisle to worm my hand into Rae's. Her eyes flutter open enough for her to survey the action outside the plane window and squeeze my grip, like always.

"Here we go!" she says.

"One step closer to your wedding," I point out.

She looks fondly over at Max, who's sleeping with his jaw hanging open. "I can't believe it. And you're sure you're okay that Theo's not coming?"

"It's really fine. Anyway, nobody's bringing partners. Zach's husband is at home, so is Olivia's." Kiara and Bennett are on the DL, but even so, there's no way she could come this close to the election.

"Yeah, but still. You miss him?"

I roll my eyes. "He slept over last night. I kissed him goodbye literally two hours ago. Honestly, it's way too soon for him to join us for a trip like this. He and I haven't even been on vacation together yet."

"One step at a time," Rae says. "That's the right idea."

Bennett clears his throat loudly. I turn to him. "Yes?"

He shakes his head, lips pressed tightly together, eyes aglow with amusement.

"You seem like you have something to say," Rae prods.

He sighs. "Rae, coming from you, this is absurd advice."

She looks around, bewildered. "From me? Why?"

"Didn't you basically kidnap Max and force him to go camping with you, sharing a one-person tent, like, a week into dating? Three days after you met, you told him you wanted to spend your entire life together. And now you're advising Edie to take things slowly."

Bennett doesn't even know about the prophecy, and he still picked up on how infatuated they were right away.

Rae blushes. "Hey, when you know, you know, okay?"

~~~

After landing in Miami, we meet Alana and Noah's flight from Chicago at the airport, then head to the Fontainebleau Hotel. We have a block of five rooms along the same hallway on the ninth floor: Rae and Max are shacking up, I'm rooming with Shireen, Bennett and Noah are together, and then there are the less seamless pairings. Olivia, who's five months pregnant now and looks dead exhausted from the flight alone, is paired up with Alana, who's eyeing the mini fridge. Confident Zach and shy Trevor split the final room. "Don't worry, I barely snore," Zach promises him.

We drop our bags at the hotel and go to Moreno's Cuba for lunch, the first stop on the itinerary Bennett and I crafted with Rae and Max's approval. Today will be go-go-go adventures, per Rae's preference, and tomorrow will be dedicated to lounging by the pool, reading novels as the hotel's cabana boys bring over a steady stream of piña coladas, per Max's wishes. (I love my sister, but Max really needs to teach her that vacations are supposed to be relaxing.)

At lunch, we order a round of mimosas and chow down on plantains, ropa vieja, and flan. Alana regales the table with stories from the first time Rae met Max's family over winter break during their freshman year.
~~~

It was a comedy of errors: he had never invited a girl home before, so he scrambled up to his bedroom early to swap out his rocket ship–print sheets with a more neutral navy blue. Rae found the offending sheets crumpled up under his bed and made fun of him, anyway. Over breakfast, she cheerily complimented his mom on her "super cute shot glasses," only to be told they were egg cups. (It was eight in the morning.) Max's grandpa, slightly senile, hit on her. Dressed in only a towel after her shower, my sister got the layout of the house confused and accidentally walked straight into his parents' room while they watched TV in bed.

"And yet, you all invited me back, anyway," Rae points out, sounding pleased.

Afterward, we meet up with our guide for the bike tour we booked. Trevor, Max's coworker from the lab, is gangly and reserved, so quiet I almost forget he's here with us. But he lights up at the bikes.

"I ride everywhere in New York. Rain, snow, doesn't matter."

"I wouldn't count on snow here," the tour guide says, winking at our group.

Max's high school friend Noah gallantly offers to adjust Alana's bike seat to the correct height.

"Oh, I got it, I spin, like, twice a week," she says.

Noah deflates a little at this. "Right, of course you do." He strains with the effort it takes not to check her out again.

I've heard stories from Max about how Noah used to be this chubby, awkward kid, but his confidence apparently blossomed in college, when he joined AEPi and was introduced to passions like protein powder, flirting with pretty girls, and pretending to know all the lyrics to Drake songs. Now twenty-nine, he's the kind of guy who wears fleece vests to bottomless brunch. He seems smitten with Alana. Whenever she's within earshot, he puffs up his chest and talks loudly about how many pounds he can bench-press.

We bike through Wynwood, an artsy neighborhood with an industrial edge that reminds me of Williamsburg. The trip concludes at Wynwood Walls, an outdoor graffiti museum featuring dozens of colorful murals. The walls are bright, playful, and vibrant, but I don't know if most people are here for the art alone—us included, truthfully.

We take endless iterations of group photos, mostly under the watchful direction of Alana, who has somewhat of a talent for Instagram. (Biscotti, her Scottish terrier, has a solid fifteen thousand followers.) Rae poses with her bridesmaids, Max wraps his arms around his groomsmen, the bride and groom kiss in front of a graffiti wall full of hearts, and so on. Before we leave, Noah works up the courage to ask Alana to take a selfie with him.

"Gotta love puppy love," Rae whispers.

"God, I love watching dudes with crushes," Shireen says. "They're so vulnerable."

Zach sidles up to join us in gawking. "Who wants to make things interesting? I'll bet you fifty bucks he makes a move on her before this weekend's over, and she stops talking to him before the wedding."

Never one to back down from a dare, Rae ups the ante. "A hundred bucks and I'll hold you to it."

"Well, let's hope they make it down the aisle without killing each other," I say.

We can't spend too long in Wynwood, because we have reservations for a cruise around Biscayne Bay. This was high on Rae's list of preferred adventures, since Olivia's bachelorette weekend two years ago also involved renting a yacht (and a male stripper, but Max had to draw the line *somewhere*). Bennett initially balked at the prospect of splurging on a yacht, but Rae explained, "No, no, no, just, like, a very small, chill yacht." So, that's what we found—big enough to accommodate our group of ten, a crew, a bar, a pile of pool noodles and floats, and nothing more.

We all have bathing suits on under our clothes, but I also have the pièce de resistance stashed in my tote bag: ten birthday party hats, the pointy kind with an elastic strap to fit under your chin, customized with a cartoon drawing of Rae and Max, their wedding date, and their hashtag: #MaxsRaeOfSunshine. Rae squeals as I pull them out of my bag.

"I'm only wearing this because I love you," Shireen sighs, positioning the hat at a jaunty angle like a beret.

"If anyone can make this hat look cute, it's you," Rae says.

Olivia holds two hats, pointy tops facing out, over her newly voluptuous breasts. "Do these make my bump look smaller?" she asks, mock seriously.

The captain of the boat reminds us of some key rules—like alerting the crew if a drunk person falls overboard so nobody gets hurt and nobody gets sued—and then we're off. The boat cuts through the sapphire-blue waters of Biscayne Bay, and sunlight dances across the rippling ocean waves. Bennett, who looks less like a future presidential candidate and more like a wildly overgrown six-year-old in his party hat, is handing out fruity rum punches from the bar. Noah hooks up his phone to the boat's speaker system so he can play DJ, expertly lining up one 2000s Top 40 hit after the next. By the time the rum hits our bloodstreams, we're gleefully scream-singing every lyric. Alana makes her way to the bow of the boat to take photos, and after a moment of watching her, Noah follows. I can't hear his opening line over the boat's engine and the dulcet tones of Max and Bennett doing their best Kelly Clarkson impression, but Alana tosses her head back in laughter.

Zach and Olivia are sprawled out on the tanning nets, sunbathing and commiserating about how too many of their friends are moving to the suburbs.

"My husband wants us to move to Long Island or Jersey," Zach says, making a grim face. "I keep telling him I'm not ready to live in a place without drag brunch, dollar slices, mutant subway rats, and the smell of trash."

"Right? My baby doesn't need a nursery *and* a playroom," Olivia says, more like she's trying to convince herself than anyone else.

"City kids are more interesting, anyway." Zach rotates for a better tan.

I can't relate at all to this conversation. I keep moving. Despite what I told Rae earlier, I do miss Theo. Downing rum punches and belting out Pussycat Dolls songs in party hats would be even more fun if he were here.

Bloop, I wish you could be here in the sunshine with me, I text him.

I lean against the railing of the boat and take a selfie that reveals more of my bikini than strictly necessary, and send that along for good measure.

He has band practice this afternoon, so I can't reasonably expect him to respond right away. But still, I feel bummed when my phone doesn't immediately light up with a reply.

Bennett comes up beside me and leans his elbows back on the railing, taking in the party stretched out across the boat. His white linen shirt hangs open, unbuttoned to reveal a smattering of dark chest hair. The usual tension in his posture is gone. I don't even see his phone cradled in his hand. Is Bennett . . . relaxed? What a world. He holds out his rum punch and clinks it to mine.

"We did good." He nods at Rae and Max canoodling on a pool float tethered to the back of the yacht.

I take in my blissed-out sister, our happy little group of vacationers, and the Florida sunshine.

"I see why you're so great at your job—you get shit done."

He pulls off his hat and examines it. "I could say the same about you. These are . . . Chanel? From the fall collection?"

"The cruise collection, obviously."

"Chic."

I hear someone calling my name and I whip around for the source of the noise. Like Bennett, it turns out Shireen is ready to blow off steam, too. She barrels toward us with an armful of pool noodles and presses a purple one into my hand.

"Let's jump in!"

She pushes one at Bennett and then tosses two more overboard to Rae and Max. I pull off my hat and ditch my phone. The screen is still blank, which momentarily disappoints me. But then, my best friend pulls me into the water, toward my sister and my soon-to-be brother-in-law. The shock of ocean water is refreshing. When I bob above the water, I hear Fergie winding up to the chorus of a Black Eyed Peas song. Rae is sprawled out on the pool float. I lunge for her ankle and pull her in with me, sun-drenched and cackling with laughter. Happy.

~~~

We have dinner reservations at Scarpetta, our hotel's upscale Italian restaurant featuring a James Beard Award–winning chef, unobstructed views of the Atlantic, and a mouthwatering ravioli dish starring foie gras. Everyone has their phones out—Alana is showing Noah photos of Biscotti, Shireen is snapping shots of Rae and Max, Bennett is only answering one "super fast, really quick work email, I promise"—but I resist the urge to keep checking mine. Last I looked, Theo hadn't texted. I know it's not a big deal. We spoke this morning. But I miss him.

After dinner, we head next door to LIV, the Fontainebleau's club. According to everything I've researched about Miami bachelor and bachelorette parties, this is where soon-to-be-newlyweds go to drink and dance the end of their single days away. I thought I understood clubbing from my college days, when my roommates and I would hail cabs to go ten blocks from FIT to the Meatpacking District. We teetered in sky-high
~~~

pumps around 1OAK, danced on tables at The Gansevoort, and splashed around in the hot tub at Le Bain, feet away from the vending machines stocked with swimsuits. I haven't done any of that in years. Overpaying for sweaty vodka sodas while dodging strangers attempting to grind on you? No thank you. Dancing to Skrillex in stilettos that cause your feet to go numb at three in the morning? I think not. Give me a serene cocktail bar where you can sit down and actually enjoy yourself any day of the week.

Once we make it through LIV's doors, past the line of girls name-dropping their promoters to bouncers, I'm floored. This club makes Le Bain's hot tub look like a kiddie pool. Soaring columns of flashing neon lights illuminate a crush of bodies. Here, the ceilings are higher, the beats hit harder, and the dresses are brighter and tighter than anywhere else I've seen before. The DJ is spinning an electronic club remix of an old Beyoncé song. Rae pulls the group deep into the throng on the dance floor, shaking her ass and tossing her hair. Shireen and I pump our arms in the air.

Noah's shockingly in his element here, and he confidently surges toward the bar to order a round of shots. Trevor, previously frozen with his feet on the floor, offers to help him carry all the drinks. It's a very nice gesture, but not a selfless one; I'm sure he'd do anything if it got him out of dancing. This clearly isn't his scene.

I don't think this is Bennett's scene, either, but he's a delightfully goofy dancer. He bops his head enthusiastically and wiggles his shoulders in what I think counts as an approximation of a dance move. He hypes up Max, he dips Rae, he spins me around. I'm learning more about him: when he takes the weekend off, he is *off*.

As the music slides into a deep house song, Max wipes a glistening trail of sweat from his forehead. He fans himself, catching his breath. Rae's eyes lock with his as she twirls, shakes, and struts. He pulls her close and she kisses him deeply, snaking her fingers through his hair.

I groove backward across the dance floor, giving them some space and privacy to retreat into their own world. Max pulls back an inch to say something to Rae, and although the DJ drowns out his words, I can read them on his lips: "I love you. I can't wait to marry you."

Clubbing is the last thing Max would call fun. But he's here for Rae, because that's what love is. He'd follow her anywhere. The sight of them together ignites a flare of jealousy I didn't know I had. As thrilled as I am for my sister, I'm also impatient for that kind of love in my own life. I'm so ready for it, so tantalizingly close to it—I found my match, didn't I?—but it's not quite clicking yet.

Will it ever? A tiny shred of doubt worms its way into my head. I think about the way Jonah's memory lingers when I'm supposed to be happy with Theo; Shireen's diagnosis that Theo only sees my surface; Mom's worry I revealed the prophecy too soon; Theo's desire to take The Supersonics to the next level, leaving me and my New York roots behind. With him in LA or on the road, my vision of us building a life together—a family together—in Brooklyn feels hazier than the neon fog rolling out from the smoke machine overhead.

I push through the crowd, off the edge of the dance floor, and wind my way through the club until I reach the hallway to the bathroom. The air is cooler out here, away from the sweaty masses, and I can focus on the click of my heels against the floor instead of my tangled thoughts.

My phone buzzes against my hip inside my crossbody bag.

Heyyy, Theo writes. Sorry I've been MIA—was with the band. Having a good night?

twenty

We spend the next morning sprawled out on lounge chairs by the pool. Even though my body feels like the dirty, crumpled receipt you find stuffed in the bottom of your purse, my mood is lighter today than it was last night. Maybe copious amounts of alcohol don't do you any favors when you're hyper-conscious about your new relationship. Theo and I texted back and forth a little last night and this morning, and it became clear that I had no real reason to worry. Like I had known all along, he was at band practice with The Supersonics, and then they wound up getting dinner and going out to a bar.

Bennett sets his strawberry banana smoothie on the side table between our two lounge chairs and eases back into a reclining position, groaning with effort. My thighs and calves ache from our night of dancing, and I can only imagine his feel twice as awful, considering his acrobatic moves.

"How are you holding up?" I ask.

"Just trying not to die."

A dictionary-sized tome about the history of democratic socialism rests facedown next to him, but he makes no move to pick it up.

I pull the glittery package of plastic penis straws from my tote bag. "Pink, orange, or purple?"

"I don't suppose 'none' is an acceptable answer?"

"This is my one job," I remind him.

He plucks an orange one from the bunch and dunks it into his smoothie.

"There you go! Festive," I say encouragingly.

He slurps down a sip. "Don't you dare tell anyone I'm enjoying myself on vacation so close to Election Day."

I take the last bite of my bagel, which I ordered in a calculated attempt to soak up last night's alcohol. "Your secret's safe with me."

He stretches out under the sun like a cat, lazily taking in the lap swimmers, sunbathers, and members of our party recuperating under pool umbrellas.

"How's Kiara doing? I haven't been in touch with her since I dressed her for that *New York* magazine photoshoot."

"She's great. Busy, obviously. But doing her thing. I think she has a real chance of making it."

"That's amazing. I really hope she wins."

"Of course." But there's something different about his tone—he isn't lighting up the way he usually does when he talks about her.

"Are you two still seeing each other?"

He crosses his arms over his chest.

"Yeah. Quietly, but yeah, we are."

I don't want to pry, but he looks more deflated than a *Real Housewives* star's lips in between filler appointments.

"I see."

He squints down at his smoothie.

"I get that she doesn't want anything to distract from the election right now. And as her campaign manager, I think that's fantastic. But as her . . ." He trails off, like he's grasping for the right word. I've never seen him speechless before.

"Boyfriend?" I supply.

He narrows his eyes. "She wouldn't use that word."

"Man friend," I suggest.

He gives a short laugh. "Classy. As her *man friend*, deep down, I have to admit the situation doesn't feel . . ."

Again, a look for help.

"Great?"

"No, not great." He sighs. "I understand she doesn't have a ton of time right now, but the time we *do* spend together outside work, she mostly wants to talk about the campaign. Or zone out with TV. I planned this romantic dinner for her at my place—steak, wine, candles, flowers, the works—and it turned into a strategy meeting. She doesn't seem particularly . . . invested."

I start to respond, but the rest of his thoughts tumble out quickly.

"I know it's stupidly arrogant to think I deserve even a sliver of her energy six weeks out from the election, but part of me wonders if she'd bother keeping me around at all if I weren't managing her campaign."

"I'm sorry. That sounds frustrating."

He nods, flags down a waiter, and orders a piña colada. I join him in day-drinking to ease his mood.

"It's not dumb to want your girlfriend—sorry, *lady friend*, whatever she is—to actually put energy into your relationship," I remind him. "You deserve that, you know."

He shrugs.

"Have you talked to her about this?"

His eyes go wide. "Six weeks before Election Day? Not a chance."

"Why not?"

"There's enough pressure on her as it is."

Pressure. It occurs to me that I'm the last person to advise Bennett on this. I don't feel fully confident about Theo. Not that I would ever admit that out loud. I don't want him—or anyone—to have reason to doubt my relationship. It *will* work out. Eventually.

When the waiter drops off our piña coladas, I dunk a penis straw into the cocktail and take an eager slurp of the sweet rum.

"Maybe things will settle down after the election? She'll be less stressed, and hopefully she'll have more time for you. And if things don't get better, then you can talk to her honestly about how you're feeling."

He nods thoughtfully, then clinks his glass to mine. "I'll drink to that."

I offer up the most morose "cheers" that's ever been uttered poolside on a glorious day in Miami. But then the conversation takes a dreaded turn.

"What about you and Theo? The way Rae talks about him, he sounds like Prince Charming. Should I pencil in your wedding for next week, or are you thinking more like next month?" he teases.

I roll my eyes dramatically. "We're taking things one day at a time, all right?"

"Just so you know, if it comes to this, I make a great ring bearer." He straightens up, suddenly enthusiastic. "I did it twice—preschool *and* kindergarten. I can get you references, too. Should I put you in touch with my uncle Rodrigo?"

My phone rings from inside my bag. "I appreciate your interest in the position," I tell him, fishing through my things. "I'll review your application and get back to you."

Mom's name lights up on my screen. She's probably calling to hear how the weekend is going.

"Hey!" I say brightly.

I hear a jagged inhale. "Hi."

I sit up straight on the lounge chair, scanning the pool deck for my sister. Something is clearly wrong.

"Mom? Is everything okay?"

"I didn't want to call and ruin your big weekend," she says, sniffling.

My mind instantly flashes to the worst place possible. "What's wrong?"

"It's Gloria. She had a heart attack."

twenty-one

Rae and I grip each other's hands when the plane takes off from the runway in Miami. We managed to switch to an earlier flight home. Mom relayed Gloria's medical details to Rae, who asked terse follow-up questions and then swallowed silently. I don't press her for information; I understand she has nothing good to tell me. I'm afraid to ask Rae about Gloria's chances anyway. If I do, I'm certain the lump in my throat will spill out into tears. I can't let myself break down yet.

Instead, I ask the flight attendant for a martini in Gloria's honor.

"Sorry, we don't have vermouth on board. I can get you a gin and tonic? Vodka tonic?"

Somehow, that feels like a bad omen.

We make it to JFK, and off the plane, and through the airport, and to the taxi line, and into a cab, and across Queens, and over the Manhattan Bridge, and finally pull up outside Lenox Hill Hospital on the Upper East Side. There are so many steps. Every one is excruciating.

An antiseptic smell greets us in the lobby. The flurry of people and the maze of hallways make me freeze up, overwhelmed. But Rae doesn't wilt in this environment—this is her domain. I follow as she strides toward the elevator. Half of me wants to rush up to Gloria's room. The other half of me wants to slow down time so I never have to face what's up there.

It is not a shock that a ninety-year-old woman is sick. It's probably more surprising that, up until today, she still mailed handwritten letters to the mayor about her ideas for improving the city, and she still had nuanced opinions about the handiwork of every manicurist in her neighborhood, and she could still make it to her favorite balcony seat at the New York City Ballet without any help. Unlike my friends' grandmothers, who were revered for their kindness or their baked goods or their sheer adoration of their grandkids, Gloria's magic has always been her vibrancy. The prospect of seeing her as a shell of herself is terrifying. I worry the odds are stacked against her.

Upstairs, Rae finds the right door. Mom pulls us in for a hug, one daughter under each arm, and holds us close. Her eyes are puffy from crying.

"I'm so sorry to cut your weekend short, but . . ." She sounds ragged.

"Mom, don't be ridiculous," Rae says.

"We're just glad we could make it—" I'm about to finish that sentence with *in time*, but then I realize I haven't heard any updates on her condition in hours.

"How is she doing?" Rae asks.

"She's weak. She still has chest pain. And she hit her head when she fell."

We hug Allen, who's somber and quiet, and make our way to the bed.

Gloria is swimming in a white hospital gown; it sags around her neck, revealing bony collarbones under translucent, paper-thin skin. She looks shrunken in the narrow bed. The butter-yellow afghan from her bedroom is pulled up to her chest; Mom must have brought it. But otherwise, she's stripped of all her familiar markings: no trademark oversized glasses, no signature pearls. She smells like a sterile hospital instead of French perfume. Tubes wind from her nose and her arm into a clunky device by her bedside that beeps along with her heartbeat. A speckle of dried spit clings to the side of her mouth. A mottled bruise splashes across her temple.

Her eyes flutter open but don't quite focus. She reaches for us, and the gesture makes me nervous. I'm not good in hospitals. I nudge Rae forward. She takes our grandmother's hand and sits on the edge of her bed.

"Hi, Gloria," she says warmly.

I see why Rae is so good at her job: She's confident in a crisis; she can easily pretend that everything's fine. If the circumstances weren't so agonizing, it would be impressive.

"My Raezie's here," Gloria croaks out. "And my Edie. My girls."

"Your girls." Rae tucks the afghan up under Gloria's arms.

My sister pulls me forward. My chest is tight with fear. I bend down and plant a kiss on her cheek.

"I'm so glad to see you." I'm fighting back tears. I don't want to scare her. "How are you feeling?"

She grimaces. "Not so good."

"Is there anything we can do to make you more comfortable?" Rae asks.

If Gloria were better, she'd crack a joke here. She'd ask us to fetch her a martini, or send in the most strapping doctor we can find. But instead, she weakly pats the bed on her other side.

"Edie, come sit."

I walk around the side of her bed and sit opposite Rae. Gloria slips her hand into mine, so she's holding on to us both.

"Talk to me."

It's all we can do. Rae makes a valiant effort to lighten the mood by regaling Gloria with stories from our weekend in Miami. Max wanted to fly home with us, but we had only been able to switch two tickets to the earlier flight. The rest of the plane was sold out. He hugged Rae long and tight before she left and promised to join her as soon as possible. It went unspoken that she only hoped he'd make it in time.

I had texted Theo earlier with the news. Part of me wanted to call, but I knew if I had to say it out loud, it would sound too real. I wasn't ready to break down yet; if I did, I couldn't guarantee putting myself back together. He offered to meet me at the hospital, but I didn't want to overwhelm Gloria with too many visitors.

Completely understand that, but if you need me, I can be there, he had written back.

Later, on the plane, I had second-guessed my decision to turn him down. If Theo's my future, shouldn't he be here, too? Isn't that what couples do—operate in tandem, especially during moments like these? If I really loved Theo, I'd want him to be there.

A nurse clad in scrubs enters the room. "How are you feeling, Mrs. Meyer?"

Gloria holds up our hands. Her own shake from the effort. "I've got everything I need."

The nurse smiles. "Aren't you lucky? I'm going to need to get in there for a minute."

Rae and I step back so she can adjust Gloria's IV.

When she's finished, Gloria's eyes look heavier than ever.

"Are you tired, Ma?" Mom asks.

She nods.

"We'll let you get some rest," Rae says.

Gloria nods again. I squeeze her hand one more time.

"I love you," I say.

"I love you, *bubbeleh*," she says softly.

Her words make the lump in my throat well up again. As her eyes drift closed, I try to soak in the sound of her voice so I'll always remember it.

twenty-two

The only way I make it through the funeral is by cataloguing every detail Gloria would have despised. The rabbi says, "Gladys, known as Gloria to her loved ones, was fortunate enough to live a long and fruitful life." *Loved ones? How schmaltzy,* she would quip. *Do we have to go with Gladys? Nobody mentioned Norma Jean at Marilyn's funeral. And no need to emphasize "long"—it's not polite to talk about a woman's age.* The cantor wears a shapeless dress with an even more shapeless haircut. *Fashion is expensive, but taste is free, dollface.* The service is held at Temple Emanu-El on the Upper East Side, but the burial will take place later today at a far-flung cemetery in Queens. *Here I was thinking I left the outer boroughs behind decades ago.*

The only time I fail to channel Gloria's running commentary is when Mom delivers the eulogy from the bimah. There's nothing to say. It's flawless.

"My mother was a remarkably gifted woman." She fingers the strand of pearls she clasped on this morning for strength—Gloria's signature. "I know many of you here are thinking, sure, her gift was intuition."

At this, she looks out at the crowd and smiles warmly, taking in the sea of matches Gloria predicted. There's Allen, of course, and me and Theo, Rae and Max, Pops and Rocco, Uncle Dave and Aunt Holly, and so many more. I'm surprised Mom dares reference Gloria's superpower in public—there are people here who aren't family—but she only offers a coy smile. She doesn't elaborate.

"But that's not where her strengths ended. She saw limitless potential in everyone, and when she told you to fix your hair and stop slouching, she wasn't critical just for the sake of being a pain in the ass. She saw that you could be a better version of yourself, and she believed you could get there. That's how she expressed her love."

"Well, then she was the most loving woman on Earth!" Uncle Dave interjects.

That gets a laugh from the crowd. It's like heavy gray clouds had been hanging over the room, only for a stream of sunlight to find its way through a crack.

"She was," Mom says, looking up from the notes she had prepared. Her eyes water as she goes off-script. "And we loved her—everyone loved her. I know that's what you're supposed to say at funerals. But how could you not?"

It's impossible to sum up ninety years of life in a few minutes' speech, but Mom tells a few stories that get at Gloria's essence. She talks about her glamorous ad agency days; her refusal to simply get married at twenty or move to Florida at seventy just because that's what everyone else was doing; her love of ballet and mah-jongg and strong martinis. Her thirty-three years of loving marriage with Grandpa Ray, cut all too short. And now, they can be together again. I sit in the first row of pews, sandwiched between Rae and Theo, legs crossed tightly as I pick off my nail polish. Little red flakes surround my feet like confetti. It's all I can do to keep from bawling.

Theo, noticing this, reaches for my hand. "Hey, c'mere, it'll be all right," he whispers.

He scoots closer to me. The warmth radiating from his body is comforting, but it doesn't take away the sting of grief. The more Mom talks about Gloria, the more I realize how extraordinarily lucky I was to have her in my life for so long. Out of everyone in my family, she and I had something special. It's impossible to tell if I loved her so much because we were naturally similar, or if years of seeking her approval shaped me in her image. Either way, I'm grateful to have been her granddaughter.

After the service ends, I make my way slowly through the pews, up the aisle, toward the door to the lobby. Distant relatives greet me with sympathetic touches on the arm, and I repeat *thank you for coming* so many times, the phrase starts to sound like jumbled words from another language. Theo follows me, his hand slipped into mine. I'm glad he's here to support me, but I also wonder if today would be easier without him. I don't have the energy to make hospitable introductions to second cousins and old family friends, or to explain what it means to sit shiva. We're not yet close enough that he can take one look at me and understand intuitively how I feel and what I need. That kind of intimacy takes time.

I spot Shireen, who makes me tear up on sight. I'm not surprised she's here, but I'm overwhelmed with gratitude all the same.

"You came," I say, voice breaking, as Shireen folds me into a long, tight hug.

"Of course. I loved her. I'm so sorry she's gone."

"Me too," I say somberly.

"Can I fix your makeup? Nobody here is judging you, but I know you don't like when it smudges under your eyes."

I give the world's most pitiful laugh. "Please, fix me."

She pulls a makeup wipe from her purse and erases my running mascara.

"It said waterproof on the tube," I explain.

"It lied."

"Thank you." I pause. "Not just for this, not just for coming, but for making me feel a tiny bit better today."

She hugs me again. "Don't cry this time," she threatens lightly.

I'm so glad she's here.

Maya, Uncle Dave and Aunt Holly's sixteen-year-old daughter, waves me over. Theo follows. She's taller and ganglier than she was the last time I saw her, and her braces are off now. Her eyes are puffy from crying, and I pull her in for a hug.

"It's good to see you," she sniffles.

"I wish it were under better circumstances."

"Is this your match?"

I nod and introduce them. Maya greets Theo shyly; if I'm not mistaken, she looks like she might be developing a little bit of a crush.

"Did Gloria get a chance to predict your date?" I ask quietly.

The prophecy dies with Gloria. As far as I can tell, nobody else in our family inherited her gift. We're the last generation to benefit from it—how strange and sad after three generations shaped by its power.

"I told her not to."

Even Theo raises his eyebrows. "What?" we ask in unison.

"I don't want to know. I'd rather trust my own instincts. Let my relationships develop naturally."

I disagree, but I don't want to convince poor Maya she made the wrong choice, especially not when it's too late to do anything about it. For as much faith as I have in Gloria's prediction, I know it comes with challenges. Before Rae met Max, she felt like the prophecy whittled down all of her life's many potential paths into just one: settling down young. Still, I would never voluntarily choose *not* to know. Knowledge is power, and Gloria's gift is too special to pass up. What would I do, gussy myself up for Hinge dates with men who think liking tacos or quoting *The Office* counts as a personality?

"I mean, no offense," Maya adds. "I just think it takes the mystery and the fun out of life."

In an alternate universe, had I forbidden Gloria from telling me my date, would I still be with Jonah? Would Theo still be here by my side today? Would I have broken things off early on once I realized he and I don't see eye to eye on marriage? I can't let myself explore those questions because I'm not sure I'll like the answers. That would require considering if I truly want to be with Theo for who he is and the way he makes me feel, or if I'm only convincing myself we're right for each other because I want to live up to Gloria's wishes for me. And *that* is not a stick of dynamite I'm willing to touch.

I turn to Theo. "We should get going."

We finally make it through the lobby and out toward the street, where a car is waiting to take various family members to the cemetery. Before we climb in, I lock my arms around Theo's neck and bury my face into his chest, breathing in his leathery scent.

"I'm really grateful you're here today. Thank you so much."

He slides his fingers through my hair, pressing me close to him. "Where else would I be?"

~~~

An hour later, we gather around Gloria's grave. She's being buried next to Grandpa Ray, of course. His name is inscribed on half the tombstone, and the other half is empty—waiting for her. It's the first crisp day of fall, and as the rabbi leads us through the mourner's kaddish, I nestle closer to Theo for warmth. I don't know the words so well, but my older relatives do: *Yitgadal v'yitgadash sh'mei rabah, b'alma di v'ra chirutei* . . . I suppose
~~~

you learn it with age, time, practice. Loss. Theo pulls off his black suit jacket and offers it to me; I shake my head, but he insists. He's right. I'm cold. I nod, grateful as he drapes it around me.

The grave is a gash in the otherwise smooth expanse of green grass. The simple pine casket is lowered down slowly, carefully, as the rabbi explains what will happen next: we'll each take a turn shoveling some dirt into the grave. Mom, standing closest to the rabbi, would be the first one up, but she chokes back a sob and reaches for Allen's hand instead.

"I need a minute," she ekes out.

Uncle Dave steps up, rubs a reassuring hand over Mom's upper back, and takes the shovel. His mouth is a thin, hard line as he drives the tool backward into a pile of dirt—the traditional first move, to signify his reluctance to bury his mom—and tips the contents into the grave. The sound of soil hitting wood makes me wince. It's a sickening reminder she's gone for good.

Mom works up the composure to go next. She says, "I love you, Ma," as she takes her turn. Allen and Aunt Holly follow her, then Rae, who hastily wipes away a tear and leaves a smudge of dirt behind, and then Max. Once he's done, he dabs Rae's cheek clean with such tenderness and wraps her in a hug. I'm up next.

The shovel is heavier than I expected. What would Gloria quip? *Muscle tone, dollface. Use it or lose it.* I think about everything she's given me: pearls to match her own, the trip to Paris for my sixteenth birthday, a new mah-jongg card every year, the vintage *Vogue* covers framed on my living room wall, her secret ingredient for a killer martini. My sense of humor, my confidence, my sense of style. My faith in fate. In return, all I can give her now is this moment.

I grapple with the wooden handle and dig the other end deep into the dirt. It sprinkles over the toes of my black pumps. I inhale the scent of earth, step forward, and tip the shovel over the edge of the grave. There's already a small pile splattered across the top of the casket.

I hand Theo the shovel. He hesitates, glancing uncomfortably at the line of my relatives behind us.

"I don't want to impose. It's not my place," he says, passing the shovel to Maya.

I'm crestfallen. We'd already been over this in the car earlier. You don't have to be family, or even Jewish, to participate in the burial. If he truly felt like one of us, he wouldn't think twice. But either he doesn't feel like one of us yet, or he doesn't want to be. We move away from the grave to make room for others. He shoves his hands into his pockets. I couldn't hold his hand even if I wanted to.

When the procession ends, there's still a mountain of dirt left. The cemetery workers will do the rest later, once we're gone.

"I almost don't want to leave," Rae says morosely. "Once we do, this will be over, and then it's like . . ."

"She's really gone," I finish.

"Exactly."

I'm too sad to keep the conversation going, and apparently, Rae feels the same way. Max and Theo are stoic beside us, each offering their own sort of stereotypically male comfort: Max strokes soft circles on my sister's back and I still have Theo's jacket draped over me. It's not that I'm not grateful—but I wish that one of them would be able to say the right thing. Offer a reprieve from the awful sadness that's blanketed this entire week.

After a few moments of stony silence, Bennett joins our circle. He looks sharp in the black suit he wears to the most formal campaign events. He hugs Rae, then me, Shireen, and Max. The steady rise and fall of his chest remind me to take a deep breath. It's a simple gesture, but a surprisingly comforting one. He's experienced more grief than anyone our age should have to bear. I'm shocked he made the trek all the way out here, but I'm also touched he considers us close enough to come.

"I'm so sorry I'm late," he says. "I never got the chance to meet her, but if she had anything to do with how wonderful you two are, then she must have been pretty incredible."

"She was," Max confirms.

Bennett nudges his shoulder playfully. "And somehow she approved of you?"

It's not a particularly funny joke. But it's enough for me and Rae to exchange small smiles. Today, that's more than enough.

twenty-three

We mourn the traditional way, by wearing black and sitting shiva for a week while loved ones stop by to pay their respects over bagels and platters of whitefish and lox. Gloria used to complain that all her friends had either moved to Boca or died, but that clearly wasn't true. Her apartment was filled with ballet enthusiasts she met at Lincoln Center, the twelve-year-old girl in the apartment upstairs who liked to come by and sample her rugelach, her hairdresser. It's customary to drape the mirrors in dark cloth, as vanity is considered inappropriate at a time when you should be grieving. We pin black tablecloths over the mirrors in the front hall and the guest bathroom, but leave the one in the master bathroom as is. After each bagel, I duck into the bathroom to touch up my red lipstick. I know it's how Gloria would have wanted her memory to be honored.

On the seventh and final day of sitting shiva, we are worn out. When the last of the food has been picked over, it's just me, Mom, and Rae left in Gloria's living room.

"You know what we should do to cap this off?" my sister asks.

She's lying across the couch with her feet propped up on the armrest, letting her toes breathe after stuffing them into a pair of pumps.

"Never eat bagels again?" Mom suggests.

I groan.

"A round of martinis. Not here, but somewhere really decadent. A final toast to Gloria."

"I could go for a stiff drink," Mom says.

"I mean, if you *really* have to twist my arm . . ."

And that's how we end up an hour later at the Plaza Hotel, the most lavish watering hole on the island of Manhattan. The hotel sits proudly at the intersection of Fifth Avenue and Fifty-Ninth Street, at the southeast corner of Central Park. From the resplendent marble steps to the hotel lobby, you can watch horse-drawn carriages trot by. The iconic bar inside is the ultimate spot to celebrate Gloria's life: it's a massive, opulent space with gold inlaid ceilings, a swirling cream and gold marble floor, and more jaw-dropping chandeliers than I can count. Between the marble busts atop fluted columns and elegantly arched mirrors, there are oversized, dark, leafy green plants. A Coco Chanel quote is inscribed on the menu: "I only drink champagne on two occasions, when I am in love and when I am not." With a less skillful decorator, the room's effect could be Mar-a-Lago gaudy, but instead, it's divine. We order a round of three dirty martinis.

"To Gloria," I say, lifting the cocktail.

The surface of the very full drink trembles but doesn't spill as we clink glasses.

"To Gloria," they echo.

After a week of mourning and reminiscing, nothing else needs to be said. The first sip is bracing, sharp and flavorful. Gloria would have loved it. For Rae, apparently it's the liquid courage she needs.

"There's something I need to tell you. Something I could never tell you before, while she was alive."

She typically talks fast, but her words flutter out slowly now, like she's been holding on to them for a long time.

"What do you mean?" I ask.

I'm confused. Rae and I tell each other everything. Always have, always will. Right?

"Oy. What is it?" Mom asks.

Rae runs a finger hesitantly around the rim of her martini glass. The last time she was at a loss for words was sometime during the first Obama administration. She fortifies herself by throwing back half her drink.

"I lied. Years ago. I met Max on September twenty-third, 2011."

I recoil like I've been slapped.

"You met him on September twenty-sixth," I correct her instinctively. The date is seared into my memory.

"No. Gloria predicted I'd meet someone on the twenty-sixth, but then I met Max on the twenty-third."

"I don't understand," Mom interjects, furrowing her brow. "All these years—but you—and he—"

"I fell for him fast," Rae explains.

Her eyes glow the way they always do when she talks about him. She shrugs like this is no big deal, as if the rules of fate simply don't apply to her, as if our family's gift was a meaningless trinket.

"But you'd throw away the chance to meet your person after knowing Max for just three days?" I ask hotly.

"Max *is* my person," she replies just as fervently. Her face softens as she pleads. "I didn't want to admit it at first. You know I didn't even want to meet my match that young, anyway. I spent the entire day on the twenty-sixth scoping out everybody I saw. My eyes were peeled, okay? And there was nobody I met who came even close to the way I felt with Max."

I feel frantic. "But you know that's not how this works. Gloria's never wrong. Never. I mean . . . no offense, Mom, but *look what happened to Mom.*"

She rolls her eyes, not buying into my panic. "I got divorced because I married the wrong guy, not because I defied my mother. He was bad news from the start. I was too young and naïve to see it."

"But then you met Allen exactly when she said you would," I point out.

A waiter comes by to refill our water glasses, and we fall silent, too self-conscious to discuss the prophecy in front of a stranger.

"Think for a second, Rae," I urge, once the waiter has left. "Is there anyone you might have crossed paths with that day? Anyone you remember? Anyone you've wondered about over the years?"

"I've been with Max for more than a decade," she says, like she's explaining basic math to a child. "At this point, I think we're safe."

I'm afraid I'll blurt out something I can't come back from, so I busy myself with my cocktail instead.

Rae looks desperately at Mom. "You're not mad, are you? I mean, you don't think I made a mistake, right?"

"Oh, honey," Mom says. She gives Rae a warm smile. "Not at all. I love Max. He's beyond fantastic—he's family now."

Rae nods. "I know."

I adore Max, but Rae's revelation shakes the foundation I've built my entire life on. I'm not superstitious about anything else, but I've never questioned Gloria's prophetic abilities. Our family has enough examples of people who attempted to forge their own path, only to be thrown exactly back on course: Mom, great-uncle Morris, cousin Roger. This is why I had to walk away from Jonah. I understand why Rae wouldn't want to leave Max once she got attached—I've endured that specific type of heartbreak. It's devastating. But I can't shake the feeling that the future has something—*someone*—else in store for my sister.

"You don't think—" I start.

Rae cuts me off. "Edie."

My name sounds like daggers in her mouth.

"Girls," Mom warns.

"Don't make me regret confiding in you," Rae says.

That shuts me up. There's only one thing more sacred than Gloria's gift—my relationship with Rae.

A few minutes later, I escape to the ladies' room. I sit on the toilet, elbows digging into my knees, face buried in my hands, far longer than necessary. If I go back to the table too soon, there's a decent chance I'll make a bitchy comment I don't mean. All I want is to protect my sister. I love Max like a brother, so my objection isn't anything personal. I only want to protect Rae from getting hurt.

I need to get out of here. Maybe I could go to Theo's. I've barely seen him this week. He came to shiva once, but bowed out of my other invitations. He told me he didn't want to distract from time with my family, and even though I craved more of his support, I was too upset to work up the energy to argue.

Can I come over? I need to get away from my family for a little while.

He replies a minute later.

I know how that goes. I was about to order takeout.
Let me know what you want?

With a firm plan in place, I make it through the rest of my drink without detonating my relationship with Rae.

"I'm going to head out to Theo's," I say.

"You don't want to stay for one more round?" Mom asks.

I hug her goodbye.

"I'm good, but you two have fun."

It's better this way. Otherwise, Rae and I would take the same train back to Brooklyn. For the first time in our lives, I need space from her. I'd rather be alone with my thoughts.

~

When Theo opens the door to his apartment, I greet him with a deep kiss, like we're long-lost lovers reuniting after years apart instead of a newish couple who hasn't seen each other in three days. The door shuts behind me and I back up to it, pulling him toward me. I've had too much time on the train to think; now, all I want to do is clear my mind. I drop my purse to the floor and twist my fingers through his gorgeous hair.

"Hello, indeed," he says.

I slip one hand into his back pocket and the other up his side, under his T-shirt, feeling the warmth of his skin. I urgently need to be as close to him as possible to quiet the roaring storm of thoughts Rae's confession unleashed.

"The delivery guy dropped off our takeout a minute ago," he says between kisses.

"I'm not interested in sushi right now." I curl a finger around his belt loop.

"I see that." He kisses down my jaw, brushes aside my hair, and pulls at the top of my sweater to expose the tender spot where my neck meets my tense shoulder.

His kiss there is more intoxicating than the Plaza's best martini. I can't help but let out a soft moan. "Did I ever tell you I'm glad we met?"

He nods. His lips are momentarily too occupied to speak.

Eventually, he resurfaces. "Yeah, I got that sense."

He is so beautiful. I can't believe he's mine. I take back all the doubts

I've had about him; in the long run, they won't matter. He's fated to be in my life, and so he will be.

"Just checking." I tug off his T-shirt.

I run my hand over his chest, sliding my fingers through the golden hair, scraping my nails lightly across his skin. If I can just get enough confirmation that he wants me, that he'll love me, that he won't ever leave me, that will shut up the deafening questions that force me to wonder what would happen if I veered off course, the way Rae did.

"Are you okay?" he asks quietly, pulling back an inch. "You seem . . ."

He lifts my chin with a finger, searching my expression. Wordlessly, I dare him to finish the sentence. Up close, his eyes are enormous. They could swallow me up. That's exactly what I need.

"I'm fine," I say forcefully.

I close the space between us, savoring the fullness of his lips and the way his hands move under my sweater. He grips my waist and palms my breasts. When his fingers slip into my bra, teasing me, I pull off my sweater to give him better access. I've never wanted him the way I do now.

I nod toward the couch. He gets the message. I straddle his lap, draping my arms over his shoulders, keeping us pressed close. He tugs down the cup of my bra and dips his head over my heart. I grind on top of him, letting sweet friction make my mind go blank.

Theo moves with more urgency now, meeting my frantic pace. He unclasps my bra and I slide his belt through the metal buckle. He strains against the button and fly of his jeans, and I undo those, too. He shifts us smoothly so we're lying across the couch now, and the weight of his body over mine is comforting. But I know if I move even an inch or two, I'm in danger of falling off the edge of the cushions. I need to feel more secure than that.

"Bedroom," I say.

It's all I can get out.

"Yeah."

He sits back and lets me stand. We make it into his dark bedroom, leaving behind a trail of shoes and pants and underwear. His bed frame is low-slung and modern, and I sink onto his mattress. The view out his window is a row of low buildings, a mix of new and old, and leafy trees cast long shadows on the sidewalk. A single street lamp outside the apartment illuminates his room with a soft glow. He lies beside me on the bed, propping his head up, and I wrap my hand around him. He traces the curve from my waist to my hip as I press myself against him, kissing him hungrily.

"Are you sure you're okay? You're not normally like this."

It takes me a moment to catch my breath.

"That's not true," I say, grazing his earlobe.

"You like seduction and taking your time, and preferably opening up a bottle of wine before our clothes come off. Not practically fucking in my doorway."

I love that he can clock me so well. Maybe I've been under-estimating him.

"It's been a really terrible week."

His face scrunches with concern. "I know."

I sigh. "Tonight, all I want is to take my mind off of it."

It's the closest I can come to admitting the truth.

"In that case, I can be an excellent distraction." His voice is husky, tinged with desire.

"Please."

Theo leans in to nip a kiss, then caresses my torso as he makes his way down my body. Now that I've explained myself, he moves with purpose. His mouth skims over where I want him most, languishing attention on my inner thighs instead. My hips pitch toward him. The moment I can't take it anymore, his tongue begins to draw blissful strokes across my skin. My eyes drift closed as Theo loosens the last grips of tension from my body. I relax under his touch, sinking into euphoria until I shudder against him.

He slides up next to me in bed. His lips skim my collarbone for a brief kiss, as if to say, *there*. When I float back down to Earth, I pull him onto me. Tonight, I want him to take control. I need to feel consumed by him wanting me. I can't be the only one steering us, pushing us forward. If I'm going to trust him, I need to know he wants me as badly as I want him.

He props himself up on his elbows and hovers over me for one maddening moment. His fingers twine into mine as he pushes inside. I watch as he bites his lip and his eyes pinch shut in pleasure. His breath is hot on my ear. I savor the way he fills me up, encompasses my field of vision, surrounds me so completely. I can't predict what will happen a year from now, a decade from now. Being with Theo has always meant giving myself up to some higher power pulling our strings like marionettes; it's meant my fate is tied to a man who doesn't believe in the same forces I do. There is so much out of my control, it's terrifying.

But here, now, I'm comforted by the weight of his body moving over mine. I ground myself by focusing on what's solid and real: the brush of his lips across mine, the pulsating pressure from his center, the sheen of sweat I feel at the dip of his spine. He looks down at me with satisfied eyes and a quivering mouth, and brushes my hair back from my forehead with such tenderness. I link my arms around his waist and pull him close, watching him lose himself in me. His fingers dig into my thigh and he buries his face in the pillow. It's almost enough to silence the swirl of thoughts creeping back into my mind.

When he rolls next to me, I lie against his chest. His heartbeat thuds through my cheek. Neither of us speak; we're both out of breath. Maybe that's for the best—it's too soon to share what Rae told me, and that's still all I can think about: how brave she was to take such an irreversible, life-changing risk, and how lonely she must have felt, hiding what she'd done. I think of all the things I haven't yet told Theo, both the secrets, and the things he's never cared to ask. I'm conscious of every single inch of space between us on the bed.

twenty-four

A week later, I'm stifling my feelings with a different vice: this time, drinks with Bennett and Kiara instead of sex with Theo. She's fresh off a town hall meeting with her district's constituents. Bennett texted me earlier today to see how I'm doing, and suggested I join them for drinks tonight at The Crown Inn.

I find them seated on bar stools at the scratched-up wooden bar in the center of the room. This place has the casual, unpretentious vibe of a dive bar, but the chalkboards hanging on the brick walls advertise hard-to-find craft beers and a few patrons sip cocktails in delicate coupe glasses. Bennett leans his elbows on the bar. His sleeves are rolled up and he's focused on Kiara.

"Hey!" I say, grabbing a bar stool on her other side. "How did tonight go?"

"It was all right," she says smoothly, just as he says, "She was excellent."

She makes a face at his praise. "I did fine. We talked about school district funding and policing," she tells me.

"You deserve to be congratulated," he says.

"And I'll accept your congratulations when I win," she insists.

"I'm sure you were great," I tell her. "You *look* amazing."

She runs her hand over the striped blouse I pulled for her. "I don't want to take this off."

I can't help but smile. In my line of work, there's truly no better feeling than making a client feel stylish and comfortable and entirely themselves.

"Have you thought about what you want to wear for election night? Democrat blue? Suffragette white? An amazing Olivia Pope–style coat?"

"I'll try it all on."

When the bartender comes by, on autopilot, I ask for a martini and feel a twinge of sadness. I still see Gloria everywhere: in the vintage *Vogue* covers that hang on my wall, in the mah-jongg card lingering in my purse, in the silhouette of the elderly woman I spotted on the subway. Ordering her signature drink feels like a hug from my grandmother that happens to press on a bruise. I guess that's grief.

"How are you doing with everything?" Bennett asks.

I know he means losing Gloria, but that's only half the reason I feel like I'm falling apart. I've barely spoken to Rae this week. I can't recall a time we've ever talked less in our lives. I guess I heave an enormous sigh, because Kiara laughs.

"Well, *that* says it all," she points out.

"I've been better," I admit. "I still miss Gloria terribly. Do you still have grandparents?"

"No," Bennett responds. "My dad's parents, the ones who came from Mexico, they've been gone since I was a little kid. And on my mom's side, the ones from New York who moved to Illinois, they died a few years ago, just a month apart. It's like they couldn't live without each other."

I don't know if that's heartbreaking or romantic or both.

"Wow."

"I do. One on each side, plus a stepgrandpa," Kiara says, almost like she's apologizing for her good luck.

"Are you sick of people asking you how you're doing yet?" he asks.

"Ha, I don't mind. I know you mean well."

"After Gabe died, it was all people could say to me. I finally snapped and told my school's guidance counselor to shut up and ask me about literally anything else. I remember being a little afraid that I'd get detention for telling her to shut up, but I guess she felt bad enough to let me off easy."

"This is a little different," I say. "Less traumatic."

He shrugs. "Loss is loss."

"You were *such* a teacher's pet, weren't you? Afraid of detention?" Kiara teases.

"I was only trying to keep my school record clean for college applications," he says.

"So, you were a nerd," she says.

"I was one hundred percent the coolest kid on the mock trial team," he fires back.

She smirks. "That's called a nerd."

Bennett and Kiara's phones are faceup on the bar, and they light up at the same time. They both pause to scan the contents of an email.

"I got this one," he tells her, covering her hand with his.

"Thanks." She squeezes his knee.

He shoots off a quick response.

"It's an update from our field director," she explains.

"You must be so excited. How many days out are you?" I ask.

"Twenty-two," they say in unison. Bennett doesn't even lift his eyes from the screen.

"Are you exhausted?"

"A little," Kiara admits, just as Bennett firmly says, "No."

"Babe, you fell asleep at eight p.m. last night."

His fingers stop flying over his phone. He looks up at her with a playful flicker in his eye.

"That was actually a scheduled nap after a jam-packed day of meetings," he says, holding her gaze, daring her to call his bluff.

"*Sure*," she says coolly.

He returns to typing and she shoots me a look full of silent laughter. Moments later, he flips his phone over facedown on the bar. "Done. What were we talking about before?"

"I believe we were discussing how incredibly cool you were in high school," I supply cheerfully.

Kiara's phone lights up with another email. Bennett cranes to look at it.

"I'm on it," she says.

Kiara finishes the email, but a moment later, she gets two more. And then a text. And then a phone call. She answers on the first ring.

"What is it?"

Bennett stopped paying attention to our conversation long ago.

"Mhm. No. Yeah." She pushes her bar stool back and collects her purse. "I'll call you right back."

"What's going on?" Bennett asks.

"I'm going home. It's Nina. She wants to prep me for some events this week."

"Now?" Bennett's face falls. "Stay. You and Nina can work tomorrow."

She kisses him goodbye. "I'll see you in the morning."

Kiara gives me a quick hug, and an apology for cutting our night short, and then she's gone.

Bennett glumly tips back the rest of his beer. He's quiet for a moment.

"You know, the reason I fell asleep so early yesterday is because I was up until three a.m. working the night before," he explains. "I thought if I could get enough done, I'd free up time for her, and then she'd make time to be with me."

"I'm sorry. Twenty-two days, right? There's an end in sight."

He snorts. "Sure."

"You and Kiara seem great together. You two banter. It's adorable. She calls you *babe*. You're both horribly ambitious workaholics, and even if you say you want to date someone who makes more time for you, I think if you actually did, you'd be turned off by their slacker nine-to-five tendencies. Deep down, I know you like the fact that she's such a hard worker."

"I do," he admits. "And she's amazing at what she does."

"See? This is the price you pay to date someone that fabulous. She's extra stressed right now, but it won't always be like this." He looks glum enough that I add, "Anyone would be lucky to date you, you know. The way you cheer her on is really special."

He rolls out a crick in his neck, considering this. "I don't know if I'd go that far to call it 'special.' If you can't root for the person you're with, what's the point? But anyway, thank you."

We order a second round.

"Would you want to run for office yourself someday?" I ask.

"At some point, yeah." He lights up, visibly happier to be discussing this instead of his love life. "I was considering it two years ago, back in Chicago, but then I wound up working in community organizing and I loved it enough that I put off running. And now that I'm here in New York, I think I want to stay. But it takes time to build up credibility as a New Yorker—I'm too fresh. Voters won't trust that. I need to put down roots here first, you know?"

An inappropriate thought takes me by surprise: *if only Theo could talk like that.* It would be so simple if he didn't talk about leaving on tour or recording in LA. I bat away the thought by teasing Bennett with a joke instead.

"Remind me, why should I vote for you?"

He leans forward on the bar, gearing up to give a speech. "Politics aside, because that's 'boring,' right?" He pulls a face.

"Sure." It'll be amusing to see where he goes with this.

"You've seen me organize Max's bachelor trip—so you know I'm detail-oriented, efficient, cost-effective," he says, ticking the items off on his fingers.

"Cost-effective? Bennett, we rented a yacht."

"But it was a *small* yacht," he says earnestly, eyes blazing.

"Your opponent's going to slam you for that during the debate."

He waves his hand. "We were supporting a small business. Stimulating the economy. Moving on! I have the *abuela* vote on lock—they love me. And I'll secure the vote among women ages eighteen to thirty-four because my stylist will make me look extremely good."

"Oh, so you're roping me into this?"

"You want me bringing my business somewhere else?"

I laugh. "No."

"Then it's settled."

"I'll pencil you into my calendar for—what, two, four years from now?"

He bites his lip. "I don't know, we'll see, we'll see. And what about you?"

"What do you mean?"

"Aside from keeping me in great suits, what'll you be doing in a few years?"

I smear the red lipstick print left behind on my glass. If only I had an easy answer for him. I thought I did.

"I want to grow my styling business. The ultimate goal is to land a cover shoot for *Vogue*."

"Well, duh." He looks me straight in the eye like he can see right through me. "And?"

"And what?" I shrink back onto the bar stool.

He spreads out his arms. "What else do you want, Edie? It's a whole big world out there."

The rest of my wish list now seems more fraught than ever before. "I want to be in love," I say quietly. If it sounds frivolous or desperate to admit that out loud, so be it. "Married. With two kids. In Brooklyn. With Rae and Max still close by. And a car to make trips to my parents in Westchester easier."

Bennett is silent for a moment, paying rapt attention. I'm not used to being this vulnerable.

"And if that's too much to ask for, then I'd happily settle for a really great walk-in closet," I joke.

"It'll happen, guaranteed. All of it—though that closet's going to be a tough find in Brooklyn."

"I used to believe in guarantees. Now? Eh, I don't know." I don't like how pessimistic I sound, but I can't force myself to cut through this gloomy mood.

"We'll make it happen. I'd obviously prefer if you had a few political items on your agenda—I'd have more useful connections for you there—but you've got my back, and I've got yours."

[illegible]

Looking [illegible] the [illegible]
[illegible] of his room.

[illegible]
[illegible]

[illegible] the bar [illegible]

[illegible]
[illegible] would get married.

[illegible]

[illegible]

[illegible]
[illegible] Brooklyn.

[illegible]

[illegible]

twenty-five

On Friday night, I'm with Theo and his bandmates at Midway, the dive bar, again. Giancarlo and Ethan are working on my pool skills, and Mika is showing Theo photos of a tour bus she saw on Instagram. The interior is tricked out with a fold-out bar and a mini-fridge.

"It looks sick, but it must be expensive, no?" he asks.

"Actually, if you split it five ways . . ." she begins, walking him through her payment plan.

I focus on my pool game. Their conversation leaves a sour taste in my mouth.

After two rounds of drinks, the bandmates pack up to head out to a friend's party in Ridgewood. They invite us along, but Theo declines.

"I'm not going to make the trek all the way out there when there's a bed with our name on it three blocks away," he points out, like this is the obvious conclusion.

Callum claps Theo on the back as he files past us. "Love makes you lazy, my friend."

I press my lips together, not wanting to touch the L-word. Because despite my best intentions, I still don't feel that way for Theo yet. Not the way I should, according to fate, and not the way I used to feel for Jonah.

Out of the corner of my eye, I catch a familiar face pushing through the doorway. Jonah? No. It can't be. But here he really is, standing fifteen feet away from me. His eyes flicker to mine in a double take, like he can't quite believe it, either. I wonder what he's doing in Brooklyn.

I'm not brave enough to approach him. I broke his heart; the least I can do is give him space. Theo is asking me if I want to stay out for another round or if we should head back to my place, but I hardly register him. The low din of the bar fades out. Instead, all I can process is the sight of Jonah hesitating, then making his way over to me.

"Hi, Edie."

He's in the black cashmere sweater I bought for our first Valentine's Day together. The fabric is starting to pill slightly, like it's been well worn and well loved. Muscle memory prompts me to step into his hug. I'm close enough to detect the musky scent of the shampoo I used to use when I stayed over at his place.

My mind goes blank. My chest tightens. For all the times I panicked about running into him and rehearsing what I'd say, I'm caught off guard.

"Wow, hi," I manage.

Theo looks at me expectantly, pleasantly, like a golden retriever. He has no idea who this is. I've mentioned a long-term relationship in my past, but I've never provided many details. I've always been afraid my voice would crack.

"Jonah, this is Theo. Theo, Jonah—we used to date."

It's a deceptively simple explanation. I hope Jonah isn't offended by it. Theo straightens up and flashes the confident grin he uses onstage. They shake hands. I want to die.

"Pleasure to meet you," Theo says, his voice a touch deeper than usual.

I study Jonah's expression, watching for hints of emotion. But he seems to take this in stride.

"How are you doing? What's new with you?" I ask.

"Everything's fine, good."

I know Jonah well enough to know he's just being polite. He's not normally so tight-lipped. But we aren't close enough anymore that I can call him out on it. How devastating that the most intimate relationships can fray into stiff acquaintances.

"Work is good? You're still living downtown?"

He hesitates. "I just moved to Greenpoint, actually."

I shiver at the thought of him living potentially less than a mile from me.

"I'm surprised you gave up that apartment. You loved it so much."

He looks down to fidget with the band of his watch. "I, uh . . . I moved in with my girlfriend, actually."

A cold wave of shock breaks over me. I can't help but do the math: it's October. We broke up last December. Well, he moved on quickly. When did they meet? When did they fall in love? Did all that happen when I was still mourning what I had given up?

I haven't been in touch with Jonah or his friends since last year. I unfriended and unfollowed him on social media because I knew seeing him online would hurt too much. There's no way I would've known his new girlfriend existed. I have no grounds to be upset by his newfound happiness. I was the one who rejected his idea of living together; I was the one who broke up with him. And now, he finally has what he always wanted: that steady, all-consuming, domestic kind of love I could never give him.

As I rush to compose myself, I feel a bittersweet pang of relief. I didn't irreparably break his heart. I didn't create lasting damage—at least, none that I can see. He moved on, which means I can move on freely, too. Maybe this is the permission I needed all along to let myself fall for Theo.

"Wow, that's a big step." I mean it sincerely.

He gives me a pointed look. "I know."

I probably deserve that one. "Well, congratulations."

"Thank you. And how are you doing?"

"I'm good. Work is great. I'm styling a woman running for Congress, actually. And Rae and Max are engaged." I can't bring myself to tell him Gloria died, especially because I had kept him at a distance from her. Before I lose my nerve, I slip my hand into Theo's, hoping that sends an undeniably clear message summing up the rest of my life. "I'm really happy."

Jonah smiles, but it doesn't quite reach his eyes.

A petite woman in a shearling jacket comes up behind him, tucking her phone in her purse as she approaches. "Babe, thanks for waiting," she says. She stops short when she sees me.

"Oh!" She clearly knows who I am.

Jonah introduces us all. "Divya, this is Edie and her boyfriend, Theo."

I never used that word, but I don't bother pointing that out.

"How nice to meet you." Her voice drips with intrigue.

The tension in the bar is suffocating.

"Well, we were just heading out," I say a notch louder than I need to.

"Good meeting you, man," Theo says.

"You too," Jonah replies tightly. His hand rests casually on the small of Divya's back.

"Bye," she says. There's a playful gleam in her eye, like she's planning to turn to Jonah the moment we're gone and do a full debrief of this awkward encounter.

Outside the bar, I release a breath and run my hands through my hair.

"What a night," I mutter to Theo.

"You okay?"

"Yeah," I say, trying to sound more nonchalant than I feel. "He and I were . . . serious. It didn't end well. And to see him move on and move *in* with someone else so soon . . ."

"Hey." Theo tilts my chin up so we're eye to eye. "You moved on, too."

He kisses me, and when we break away, I summon a smile. Anything less wouldn't be fair to him.

"I sure did," I reply. I slip my hand into his as we set off toward my apartment.

After a beat of silence, he asks, "Do you want to talk about it?"

The last thing I want to do is make Theo worry I still care for Jonah, even—especially—if there might have been a grain of truth to that.

"I'm good. I promise."

twenty-six

Theo stirs in bed beside me the next morning. *Mmrph*, I mumble, wishing I were still asleep. I barely slept last night; I couldn't help but play the encounter with Jonah and Divya over in my head from every angle. Theo rolls toward me, scooping my body closer to his. If I have to be awake, at least I'm cozy.

"D'y'know what time it is?" he slurs in a voice heavy with sleep.

I crack open an eye, taking in the sunlight splashed across my bedroom wall. I feel for my phone on the nightstand and glance at the screen. I have two texts from Shireen.

I have an emergency, she wrote.

Sorry, that sounded worrisome. It's a shopping emergency, she clarified in a second text.

I slump back into bed, too alert now to have a chance at falling back asleep.

"Eight thirty," I tell Theo as I text Shireen back. According to her texts, she's been up since at least 7:45.

What's going on? I ask.

I have an interview on Monday and I hate all my clothes, she says. Are you free to meet up?

Yeah, but when I see you, we're doing a full review of the word "emergency."

We meet at the J.Crew on lower Fifth Avenue, with plans to shop up and down the street if we strike out: there's Aritzia, Banana Republic, H&M, Zara, and plenty of others. I find her clutching a large coffee and flicking through a rack of blouses at a highly caffeinated clip. She's interviewing for a different role within her executive search firm, a big step up in responsibility if she can beat the competition.

"Hi! I'm sorry, thank you for coming," she says. "I know I'm the worst."

"Are you kidding? I love dressing you."

"I'm freaking out because it's a whole day of back-to-back interviews. And because these are people I work with, they've seen everything I own. I want to impress them with something new."

"We can do that. But what about your charcoal Zara dress, the one with the—"

"Pleats? I'm sick of it."

"Or you could do that wrap dress from—"

"The DVF sample sale? Cute but no."

I can envision her whole closet. She has plenty of viable options. But I also know a new outfit can carry transformative powers. So I promise her we'll find something fresh.

As we move through the store, I pull blouses, trousers, and blazers, and drape sheath dresses over my elbow. She tells me more about what's happening at work. By the time we're in line for the dressing room, I catch her up on running into Jonah last night. She goes wide-eyed, freezing with the coffee halfway to her mouth, as I relay every detail.

"I was shocked to see him at all, and then it was another shock to find out he already has a live-in girlfriend. Already!"

Wordlessly, she tilts her head. We knew he wanted that all along.

"It was a relief to see that he's doing okay—I feel less guilty about breaking up with him now—but it also makes me feel kind of weird about Theo." I try to articulate exactly what was bothering me last night. "We still have a lot of growing to do before we're as close as I was with Jonah."

She steps into the dressing room and pulls the curtain shut. "You know, it's normal to date someone for a few months and not instantly know if they're your soulmate?" Her voice gets muffled as she pulls her top over her head, but her point is clear.

"I know. But I never expected to have doubts at this point in my life."

A forty-something shopper snorts as she walks by. "Oh, honey, just wait until you're my age."

I don't have to tell Shireen what I really mean: I didn't think I'd feel this uncertain after the date Gloria predicted for me. I thought with the right person, everything would just fall into place.

Shireen emerges in a red plaid skirt suit and a frown. "I look like the hardworking city girl going home for the holidays in a Hallmark Christmas movie."

"Yeah, next."

She starts to turn back to the dressing room but pauses. "Ignore me if this is a bad idea, but—actually, never mind." She ducks into the changing area and pulls the curtain shut.

"What?"

"No, it's a bad idea, I shouldn't have said anything."

"You've witnessed a lot of my bad ideas. Like that year I was really into vests."

She pulls the curtain open again and gives me a long, hesitant look. "Do you want to be with Theo?" She drops her voice low so only we can hear it. "Forget about fate for a minute. Just focus on how you actually feel when you're with him."

I swallow.

"I know we're going to work out."

But that doesn't answer her question. It ignores plenty of my own: What if I was supposed to meet someone else that day? What if I'd actually be happier alone?

"Sure," she says tentatively, like she isn't quite convinced. "But I just want to remind you that Theo isn't your key to happiness. You can be happy on your own—and that doesn't mean being alone. You have me and Rae to lean on. You've been happy before with someone else, and there's going to be someone else out there who makes you happy, too. I promise that. I know I'm not as compelling as Gloria was, but I hope you believe me."

I think about how much I've given up in service of my family's prophecy, and the solid undercurrent of confidence I've always felt, knowing my match is out there. And I think about Shireen: her romantic future is a question mark, and she's okay with that. I used to secretly feel bad for people outside my family who don't know what's coming to them, but my best friend has never felt weighed down by the uncertainty. Maybe I could learn from that.

"I hear you," I tell her, mulling over her words. "I'm not going to make any rash decisions. And anyway, *you*, mademoiselle, need an outfit." I shoo my friend back into the dressing room.

twenty-seven

On Sunday afternoon, I go to Annabelle Crosby's showroom in SoHo to pull some more suits for Kiara to consider for election night. I've already pulled a half dozen from other brands, but I know Kiara has always felt great in Annabelle's clothes—and on the biggest day of her life, she needs to be comfortable. I have an appointment with DeeDee, and Theo is tagging along because this errand happens to fit neatly between our late, lazy brunch and one of his teaching gigs.

"I've dragged you along to shows, so it's only fair that I see what you do," he says as we take the freight elevator up to the third floor.

"Right, because being serenaded was *such* a drag."

He grins and nuzzles a kiss over the top of my ear, pulling back as the elevator doors slide open. I wouldn't have him join me on a typical work-day, but it's just a quick errand, and besides—it's fun to show him off.

DeeDee rises from behind a desk. She's in a printed jumpsuit I recognize from a past collection. "Hello, hello!"

"Hi!" I introduce her and Theo. "Thanks so much for making this work on such short notice."

"For you? Of course. I've been watching Kiara. She looks fantastic. I put together some options for you in her size." DeeDee points to a rack against one wall. "Feel free to pull whatever you're into."

"Amazing, thank you so much."

I begin to flip through the row of hangers showing off high-waisted flares, slim-cut trousers, sleek jackets with angular lapels and prim buttons. The rack brims with jewel tones I could swim in: sapphire, forest green, eggplant, burgundy. This is suiting at its best; any woman could step into one of these and feel a touch more confident.

Theo rubs the sleeve of a berry-colored suit jacket between his fingers. The luxe fabric shimmers with threads of gold.

"I love it, but she'd fire me on the spot."

He drops the sleeve. "Well, then."

As I work, Theo wanders the showroom and DeeDee chats with him. I hear snippets—my name, small talk about the weather and the election coming up.

And then Theo laughs and says, "That's the tiniest suit I've ever seen."

DeeDee lights up. "Cute, right? We launched mommy-and-me matching outfits last month."

I turn to see Theo holding up a baby-sized sweater in forest-green cotton, not unlike the adult-sized jacket currently draped over my arm. There are teensy matching pants, too. I can't help but let out a soft squeal.

DeeDee shows us some photos of Annabelle Crosby models dressed to match the stylishly-clad infants on their hips.

"Stop it," I say eagerly, as she continues to flip through one adorable shot after the next. "Maybe it's time for me to get into styling kids. How cute."

She swings a playfully accusing finger between me and Theo. "Now, you two would have cute babies."

Theo makes an uncomfortable noise, somewhere between a strangled laugh and a panicked wheeze. "Ha. Riiiight." He looks horrified.

DeeDee flashes me a look, like she understands exactly what I'm thinking. She ever so slightly rolls her eyes, as if to say, *Men.*

"Those are going to sell out so fast," I predict. Anything to fill the strained silence.

I head back to the rack DeeDee put together for Kiara, making my final selections. She gives me some garment bags and we make quick work of zipping everything up. The mommy-and-me outfits catch my eye again. If I were here without Theo, I'd linger over those pieces a little longer. But now is not the time.

Theo and I don't talk much in the elevator or for a half block afterward. I'm working out if or how I can broach the subject of having kids without putting any more pressure on Theo, and I wonder if he's thinking about DeeDee's comment, too. It's not until we're stuck on a street corner, waiting for the walk sign to flash, that I figure now's as good a time as any.

"You seemed kind of freaked out by that baby comment," I observe.

His posture stiffens. It's one of the last warm days of fall, and behind him, a severe blue sky pops between classic wrought-iron lofts. Yellow taxis rumble over cobblestone streets. It's the kind of afternoon you'd typically want to commit to memory to aid you through the worst of winter. But something about Theo is off, and I get a sinking feeling I'll remember this moment for a different reason.

"You want a baby?" he says, squinting a little in the sun.

The walk sign lights up, and I'm grateful that walking side by side means I don't have to face him.

"I mean, not right now, no."

He swallows. "But at some point?"

I shiver at the pained expression on his face. "In the future, yes."

He rakes his fingers through his hair. "I guess I should tell you I don't want kids. Ever. I'm sure of that."

It's funny how you can be working, walking, going about your day like everything is completely normal, and then a single comment can wallop you. A frantic regret washes over me; I want to rewind what happened and push the baby conversation so far down that it never surfaces again.

"I'm sorry?" It's the only thing I can manage to say.

He starts to repeat himself. "I said I—"

"No, I *heard* you," I say forcefully.

The crisp autumn air seeps through my thin sweater. I tense up, overwhelmed. My arms lock tightly across my chest. My jaw is so rigid, my teeth could snap.

"You seem upset," he says gently.

I press my lips together, as if I could physically eat my own words to prevent myself from blurting out the wrong thing. I don't know what's worse—that we have opposite views on an issue that leaves no room for compromise, or that he didn't know me well enough to know that *of course* I want kids. My family is my whole world. There's nothing I'd want more than to pass that love and those traditions down to the next generation. I picture myself with two little girls, who crave deli platters after High Holiday services and hold hands when planes take off and play mah-jongg. One would be named after Gloria. It feels unbearably cruel that the person my own grandmother predicted I'd love is the same person who stands in the way of all those dreams coming true.

"You talk," I say.

It's safer that way.

"Okay." He takes a moment to think. "I've never dreamed of being a dad. My family is . . . you know. We're not that close. Sometimes, I wonder if my parents regretted having me. I don't want to re-create that with a family of my own."

A burst of shame rises up in my chest. I was so quick to judge Theo for not knowing me well enough to innately understand my desires, but I didn't spend a second thinking about his. Of course he doesn't want kids when he spent his own childhood feeling unwanted and unappreciated.

"But what if things were different? You're not going to be your parents. You're nothing like them."

From what I've heard, anyway. He hasn't asked me to meet them yet, and I haven't pressed for an invitation.

"Even so, I like my life as it is," he says, wincing. "I wouldn't want to have to sacrifice any freedom to give kids the life they'd deserve. It wouldn't be fair to them."

An ache builds up behind my eyes. "But we're supposed to be together. There has to be a way for this to work."

Theo is quiet. We both stare at the sidewalk in front of us. My vision swims with tears. I wipe hastily at my eyes, refusing to give in to the flood of sadness that threatens to burst through at any moment.

"We'll figure this out," I say, attempting to sound more confident than I feel. "Right?"

He hesitates. "Edie, I don't want you to bend to fit into my life. If you want kids, then it sounds like we're on two different paths, and—"

"That can't be right," I interrupt him. "People change all the time. Who knows—maybe you'll change your mind, maybe I'll change mine."

I don't want kids right this minute, anyway. Time is on our side. Lots of people compromise in relationships—I can't wrap my head around disappointing Gloria, even if she's gone—but maybe I could give a child-free life a shot.

"I don't think I'm going to change my mind on this," Theo says.

We're descending the subway steps now. I'm not going to let the love of my life break up with me in the Canal Street subway station, among the rusted tiles and trash spilling out of the garbage can in the corner and the hefty rat scurrying past our feet. I can do some real reflection on what I actually want out of life. We could go to couples' therapy. Or maybe he'll surprise me—maybe I can find a way to show Theo how special and fulfilling it could be to create our own little family unit.

I swipe my MetroCard through the scanner and push through the turnstile. He follows me onto the platform just as the train pulls into the station. The prospect of stewing next to him all the way back to Brooklyn is suffocating.

I make a show of patting my pockets and rummaging around in my purse. "I just realized I must have left my phone back there," I lie. "I'm going to run back to grab it."

The subway doors slide open.

"I can go with you," he offers. The words sound half-hearted.

"Don't worry about it," I insist.

It'll be easier for both of us this way. He opens his mouth, as if to say something, but doesn't. Instead, he ducks into the car without hugging me goodbye. The doors glide shut. And the train roars in my ears as it speeds away.

twenty-eight

It's been four weeks since Rae revealed her secret at the Plaza, and we've barely spoken since. Her decision to pursue Max shook up everything I thought I knew about fate, family, and love. I needed some time to process it all. For the past eleven years, I've been looking forward to finding a partner as well suited to me as Max is to Rae—but if my sister strayed from her prophetic match and she's still so damn happy, then what does that mean for me?

But after my conversation with Theo yesterday, I need my sister. Nobody else will do. So, after twenty-four hours of ruminating alone in my apartment, replaying Theo's words on a nauseating loop, I text her.

Can I come over tonight?

It's been a while. Are we good?

She's testing me—she wants to know if I've come around to understand why she ditched her chance at a fated match to pursue Max. I'm still processing how I feel about it, but it's not my place to judge her. Just because we're twins doesn't mean we have to live identical lives.

Absolutely. I miss you.

Same. I'm working tonight—tomorrow night?

That's election night. Let's watch the results come in together?

Great.

During Kiara's last-minute styling session earlier today, the day before the election, she tried on most of my picks and ultimately chose the Democrat blue Annabelle Crosby suit. I layered it with a striped silk blouse underneath, a smattering of delicate gold jewelry, and black leather pumps (for when she's in public—and a cool white sneaker for when she needs to give her feet a break). She looks strong and powerful; I like that the brighter blue serves as a visual cue that she isn't another stuffy old politician in a boring navy suit—she's the next generation's rising star with a bold new vision.

On Tuesday, I steam her suit and help her get dressed. She is unfathomably busy, and so I lint-roll her pants while she's wearing them as she debates edits on her acceptance and concession speech drafts with Bennett. Her publicity director interrupts no fewer than three times with interview requests from various news outlets. When she sneezes, I'm almost afraid it'll put her three-quarters of a second behind schedule.

I work as quickly as I can, then duck out of her apartment so she can move on with her day. I swing by my own polling station in Williamsburg to cast my vote, pack up the remaining Annabelle Crosby samples so I can return them to the showroom later this week, and tackle as many work projects as I can possibly dig up in order to avoid dwelling on Theo.

I can't tell if it's my overly active, overly sensitive imagination out to get me, or if Theo is really pulling back. I haven't seen him since our strained conversation on Sunday afternoon, nor had we texted until I sent him a message this morning.

I don't like feeling like I'm too much for him: too preoccupied with our relationship, too focused on the future, too committed to the idea of fate. It's soul-crushing to know that if I'd played my cards closer to the vest, never telling him how I really felt about having kids someday, I might not have pushed him away. But then again, if I had done that, would I be trapping myself with the wrong person?

I pick up two bottles of Rae's favorite cabernet sauvignon and ring her buzzer at six thirty on the dot. Today is not the day to be late; too much time alone with my own thoughts is proving to be alarmingly morose.

"Come on up!" Rae calls through the speaker.

When she opens the door to her apartment, I squeeze her into a tight hug.

"I know I said it before, but for the record, I apologize for being kind of judgy at the Plaza."

"I mean, we can't *both* be on our best behavior one hundred percent of the time. It's fine. I'm over it. I expected you to take a while to wrap your head around what I did. You've always been so stubborn."

"No, you're the stubborn one," I remind her.

Max joins us in the living room. "I hate to break it to you, but you're both the stubborn one."

I rummage in Rae's kitchen drawer for the rhinestone-encrusted corkscrew she bought as a souvenir in Vegas a few years ago and pour us three glasses of red while she clicks on the TV.

"And just so we're clear, I hope you know I love you," I tell Max. I assume Rae told him about how I reacted to her secret; I need him to know my feelings were nothing personal. "You're like a brother to me. Always have been, always will be, no matter what."

He rubs the back of his neck awkwardly; we've never been openly affectionate like this.

"As long as you don't think I, like, seduced her into a life of bad choices or something."

"Babe, nobody thinks you seduced me," Rae says sweetly.

"Hey!" Max says, blushing a little.

He nudges his glasses down the bridge of his nose and fixes her with what I think might be his best attempt at a smolder. God bless these two. I can't fully shake my curiosity about what would happen if Rae really did pursue whoever caught her eye on the "right" day, but I can't ignore the fact that she and Max have something absurdly special.

"Rae, there's something I want you to have. Consider it my way to show that I have nothing less than full faith in your relationship."

Rae lifts an eyebrow. "Oy, this sounds serious."

"Don't freak out," I implore as I unclasp the chain around my neck with Grandpa Ray's wedding band. "You should have this again."

"Oh, Edie!" She claps a hand to her mouth. "You can't. It's yours now."

"Nope. You gave it to me so I could have good luck and find love, like you did, and who knows what really happened—I have a lot I need to tell you—but I want you to have it again. Now hold up your hair."

She wells up a little as she stops protesting and sweeps her ponytail off the nape of her neck. I fasten it on her.

"Thank you. This really means a lot."

"I know."

We place a delivery order from a nearby pizza place and sprawl out on their sectional and watch the election results roll in. It's not a presidential election year, but the news anchors have plenty of other races to comment on, ranging from the House to the Senate to governors across the country. It's still fairly early, so there isn't much to go off yet, but that doesn't stop the anchors from zooming in and out of different electoral maps, rattling off stats about each county's demographics and voting records. *I'm* stressed—I can't imagine how Kiara could possibly handle this.

"Bennett must be shitting himself," Max says.

"We should book him a massage for when this is all over," Rae suggests. "Would he want a massage?"

"He's physically incapable of relaxing—I think we can save our money," he says.

"I'm going to text him," I announce.

Hi! I just wanted to say that no matter what happens tonight, there's nobody out there who's more hardworking or freakishly efficient than you are. You should be so proud. We're rooting hard for Team Walker tonight!

I take a selfie of us watching the results roll in, with Rae thrusting her wineglass toward the camera, and send it to him. The channel cuts to a commercial break. Rae puts the TV on mute.

"So, wait, what's going on? You sounded pretty ominous earlier."

I glance at the TV. There's no way we can neatly resolve this conversation in the space of a single commercial break, but I can at least start filling her in.

"Well, Theo and I had a . . . I don't want to call it a fight, but maybe it was a fight?"

"Oh, that sucks." Her mouth twists up in sympathy.

"I think this is bigger than just, 'That sucks.' A sucky fight, fine, I could handle. It would blow over. But he told me he doesn't want kids—not that he isn't sure, but that he definitely doesn't want them and doesn't see himself changing his mind."

Rae's face falls. "Edie, I'm so sorry."

I don't have to explain myself any further. She knows how much having my own family someday means to me. My sister scoots closer to me on the couch and wraps me into a hug. She's never been the best at expressing feelings, but now, she takes a stab at whispering soothing words: "It's all right. You're going to be okay. This is hard, but you'll get through it."

Her sympathy is the thing that breaks me. For the first time since Sunday, I let myself cry. She wouldn't sound this somber if there was still a glimmer of hope.

I had been trying to convince myself there was a creative solution right in front of me, and if only I strained hard enough to see it, it would appear. But there's no compromising here. You can't have half a baby.

Max hands me a box of tissues. I take one, dab at my eyes, and blow my nose. I don't care if my makeup runs and smudges here.

"Maybe this is a sign you should reconsider if Theo is really the right person for you," Rae suggests softly.

"Oh, come on," I protest.

Rae and Max exchange glances. I can't keep looking at them. Instead, I fix my gaze on the TV, where the election results roll in with cold, hard precision. Percentages flash on-screen. If only I could quantify my chances of happiness with Theo, or my risk of ruin if I walk away from him.

I know our incompatible views on family doom us. But if I'm truthful with myself, that isn't all. He didn't stand up for me when his friends made fun of the prophecy, and that makes me wonder how else he'll fail to step up to the plate in all of the million little ways that matter over a course of a lifetime. He doesn't yearn to build a life in Brooklyn the way I do. He wants to move The Supersonics out to LA and go on tour. To me, marriage means planting roots, nourishing them; he views it as being tied down too tightly. He doesn't seem ready to commit to anyone long-term.

Maybe he would for the right person—but the longer we're together, the harder it is to believe that his right person is me.

I want to have faith in Gloria's prophecy so badly. I want to summon the blind courage to push forward, knowing that one day, Theo and I will be so impossibly in sync. But I know this isn't what love should feel like; I've experienced it before with Jonah. It felt like the sun warming your back on the first day of spring, and like a sturdy, leather armchair you can curl up in night after night, shaping it to the grooves of your own body. It plugs you in, lights you up as your biggest, best self, rather than illuminating old insecurities and fears for the future. If my relationship with Jonah was the wrong type of love, I can't even begin to fathom what Gloria's brand of one true love feels like. I don't want to walk away from my shot at that. But my faith in it is starting to wear thin.

"How did you do it?" I ask Rae, sounding small.

"Do what?"

"Buck fate. Trust your gut. Weren't you scared of making a life-altering mistake?"

"Absolutely," she says plainly. "Not of messing with our family's tradition, but of what would happen if I ignored the way I felt around Max."

He gives her a private smile as her fingers drift affectionately over his knee.

"Oh?" I furrow my brow, confused. I never thought of it that way.

"I was afraid that following in our family's footsteps meant marrying the wrong person. I kept getting these torturous visions of me years down the road, bored in my marriage to some totally bland guy I was only with out of a sense of duty, sneaking off to see Max. I imagined betraying my husband, giving Max the short end of the stick, and being trapped in a relationship with someone I didn't really love. So, bucking tradition was easy—selfish but easy." She fluffs up her hair. "God, it feels good to finally tell you all that! You have no idea how hard it was to keep it a secret."

"We talked about it all the time," Max says. "For years."

"We call him Mr. Khakis—that's our name for whoever I was probably 'supposed' to wind up with. You know, like some dude in khakis and a vest who works in accounting or something, and his only hobbies are, like, golf or fantasy football."

"I don't know, I sometimes imagine him as more of the bird-watching type who exclusively watches really dull documentaries," Max counters. "His name is probably Paul."

"Or Craig?" Rae suggests.

"Walter?"

"No, no, I got it: *Todd*."

But I'm too distracted to brainstorm with them because Rae's revelation makes the wheels in my head start to turn. This whole time, I've been assuming that pursuing Theo and convincing him that the picturesque life I've been dreaming of is the key to life-long happiness. But what if I had it all wrong?

"Turn it up, turn it up!" Max says. "They're about to call New York."

Rae lunges for the remote as Kiara's headshot fills the upper-right quadrant of the TV. The anchors give a rundown of her background and campaign's history, comparing it with the incumbent Glen Vernon's. I know it's shallow and rude to judge somebody based solely on appearances, but he looks exactly like Mr. Khakis—bland. And from what Bennett has told me of Vernon's politics (he's pro-life and wants to cut federal spending on social programs), I'm not a fan.

"One House race to pay attention to is Vernon versus Walker in New York's ninth congressional district," a reporter explains. "It historically has been represented by Democrats, but changing demographics in the district swung a victory toward Vernon in 2020. It'll be interesting to see what happens here tonight."

Her colleague chimes in, "Let's go to the electoral map—I hear we have results for this district now."

Rae snakes her hand into mine like we're on a flight ready for takeoff. Kiara has poured so much passion and conviction into her campaign; her district's constituents deserve someone who will work hard to represent their best interests in Washington, and she deserves this success. I want her to win for Bennett's sake, too. If they lose, I think there's a fair chance he might actually combust.

Another anchor zooms in on the map. I see the outline of New York City, then Brooklyn, then the borders of the district I've come to recognize in Kiara's office.

"With ninety-nine point five percent of votes in, the Associated Press confirms New York's ninth district goes to Kiara Walker," the anchor announces.

We burst into cheers. Relief washes over me.

"Whoop-whoop!" Rae shouts, squeezing my hand tight.

"Oh my god, she did it," I marvel.

"You're dressing a member of Congress now," Max points out. "That's pretty badass."

I can only imagine what the atmosphere is like wherever Kiara and Bennett are. They must be exploding with excitement. And with her heading to Washington, that means Bennett's vision for a gun-control bill is one step closer to becoming a reality.

"Let's celebrate with shots," Rae says, already scrambling from the couch to the kitchen cabinet.

The anchors move on to share other results, and while I care for the sake of our country, I know nothing else that happens tonight will top this feeling. While my sister debates between tequila and whiskey, and Max selects three shot glasses from their extensive collection, I shoot congratulatory texts off to Kiara and Bennett.

Tonight, I'll celebrate their win. And tomorrow, I'll deal with everything else.

twenty-nine

I arrange for Theo to come over the next night. I take extra care to style myself, as if putting on the armor of Gloria's pearl bracelet and a swipe of red lipstick will fortify me for what's about to happen. I straighten up the garments on the clothing rack in the living room, arranging the pairs of shoes below into neat rows organized by color. I doubt he would care if I summoned him to a pigsty while wearing sweatpants—but I have a gut feeling that both of us will remember tonight in painfully clear detail for a long time.

When Theo arrives at my building, I buzz him upstairs, open the door to my apartment, and wait for him on the threshold. My chest is tight with anticipation.

"Hi," he says, dropping a quick peck on my lips.

"Come on in, make yourself comfortable." I feel oddly stilted in front of him.

He stuffs his hands in his coat pocket and glances past me toward the kitchen, the window—anywhere but at me. He looks as off-kilter as I feel.

I motion for him to sit and join him at the table. The couch would be more comfortable, but that's fraught territory: Would we cuddle? Sit a solid foot apart?

To ease the tension, I ask, "So, how have you been?"

"Fine," he says so tightly I can practically hear the period at the end of his sentence.

"Just fine?" I prod, trying to lighten the mood. "What's new with the band?"

The tactic works.

"Things are actually really looking up for us right now," he says, eyes gleaming bright for the first time since he got here. "One of our songs is doing crazy numbers on Spotify—it's blowing up. I don't want to jinx it, but our manager says this could be our big break."

"Shut up, that's incredible."

For a moment, I forget why I asked him here. I squeal and give him a delighted kiss.

"Is it 'Over the Top'?" That's always been their most popular song at shows.

He laughs.

"No. Your song. 'Soaring.'"

I open my mouth to respond, but I'm speechless.

"It's going to be everywhere, isn't it?"

He knocks on my wooden kitchen table. "Let's hope so."

Dread gnaws at my stomach. I do my best to force a meager smile. I wanted some kind of sign that Theo and I would work out, and this comes close—it really does. It's exciting to imagine hundreds of thousands, maybe millions, of people listening to the lyrics he wrote for me. If I were a different kind of person, that would make me swoon. But I don't want to be a muse—I want to be in love. And despite my best efforts to force those feelings, they're not here. I don't think they ever will be. Not fully. Not the way we both deserve.

"Theo, there's something we need to talk about."

I say it as tenderly as possible, but there's no tone that could mask the significance of those words.

"I haven't been able to stop thinking about what happened this weekend," I continue.

His expression stiffens again. "Me too."

"You and I want different things out of life, and so staying together wouldn't be fair to either one of us."

He gives me a small, pained smile. "I know."

"You do?" I ask, relieved.

"I think I've known for a while," he admits. "But I care about you, and I wanted to give this a shot, because of your grandma's prophecy. I know how much it means to you. I wanted to be the person you needed me to be."

I'm embarrassed that he saw such transparent desperation from me, and still let me drag this out for as many months as I did. Part of me is curious to know exactly when he saw us going off the rails—but part of me is too shy to ask. That's probably another sign we aren't right for each other. I'm not fully myself around him.

"You were. For a while," I say ruefully. "Thank you."

"You don't have to thank me. You know, sometimes I wasn't sure things with the band would work out, and it's not like any of my past relationships—with girls or my family—have been so successful, either. I was wondering if . . . if all that was my fault. But you've always treated me like I was exactly right, just as I am."

I'm touched by his perception of the past few months.

"I hope you know I still think you're amazing."

"I do. That means a lot to me."

He reaches across the table to grasp my hand. The simple gesture is so reassuring—he understands, he sympathizes, and he still cares for me. I look down at his bare fingers; I've never been able to imagine a wedding band resting there. It doesn't fit on him. Not yet, anyway, or maybe not ever.

I take one last look at him, drinking in the hopeful set of his jaw, the shimmer of gold in his dark blond hair, the soft spot beneath his ear where he loves to be kissed.

"I can't believe this is goodbye," I say, struck by the life-changing magnitude of this quiet conversation at my kitchen table.

If Gloria was going to come down and smite me somehow, this—pushing Theo away for good—would be the moment to do it. And yet, I'm still here, still in control. I owe it to myself to discover who else is out there for me, and I know I'll never have the courage to do it if I can fall back on Theo by my side.

My lower lip quivers as my eyes swim with tears. A sob shudders through my rib cage, taking me by surprise. I'm not sad, exactly. Overwhelmed is more like it. For the first time since Gloria predicted my date thirteen years ago, the only roadmap for my future is one I'll have to create for myself.

"I never thought you'd walk away from me," he admits.

"To be honest, I didn't, either."

"I'm so sorry I have to do this."

The lump that's been welling up in my throat finally breaks. I let the tears fall. He hugs me until my breathing steadies, then stands to shrug on his jacket. I watch him blankly, trying to hold on to these last few moments with him before he's gone from my life forever. This feels like a mistake—but I have to trust that it isn't. If I don't love Theo the way I loved Jonah, or the way Rae loves Max, he's not the right person for me. I have to remember that in the months or maybe even years to come, even when I feel lonely, even when I feel weak. Even when I'm afraid I've thrown away my grandmother's legacy. Gloria would never want me to be unhappy.

"So, what are you going to do next?" he asks.

"I don't know. But I have to trust I'll figure it out."

thirty

Ten minutes after Theo leaves, my confidence and optimism curdle into panic. I sink onto my kitchen floor, slumped against the fridge, replaying every detail of the conversation. I didn't think breaking up with him would be this hard. It's not like we were in love. After I left Jonah, my heart felt like a puddle of sewage for months. I couldn't sleep or stop ruminating over painful snippets of memories. I couldn't pass by couples holding hands on the street without rolling my eyes and thinking, *Just you wait.* When I forced myself to go to parties without him by my side, I felt like a baby gazelle barely holding herself upright on wobbly legs. But despite making it through all of that, this experience still frays my nerves. Did I make the right decision? Was I too hasty?

I might have made a huge mistake, I text Rae and Shireen. Is anyone available right this second to cry into a bottle of wine with me?

Yes, be right there. Hold on, Rae shoots back.

Coming ASAP, bringing an extra bottle, Shireen replies.

Just the mere knowledge that they're on their way makes me feel sturdier. This would be worse if I had to go through it alone. I open a bottle of pinot noir, pour a glass, and sip it morosely as I wait for Rae to buzz. When she arrives, she sweeps me into a hug and we retreat to more comfortable territory on my couch.

"When Shireen comes, I can't really explain the full story behind the breakup without telling her about you and Max. Is that okay?"

"Oh, yeah," she says casually, settling back against a throw pillow. "I came clean to her already. It's been a secret for far too long."

"Wow. How'd she take it?"

Rae snorts. "She's not like our family, she's normal. I think she was actually relieved."

That makes me laugh. "I love you."

"Love you, too."

"At least *someone* does." It's a whiny comment, but it's been a hell of a day.

"Hey," she says sharply. "You're more than lovable."

"You have to say that, you're my sister."

The buzzer sounds. "Shut up, Shireen will back me up on this and you know it."

Shireen envelops me in a hug the moment she arrives in my doorway. "Hi, babe." She addresses me cautiously in a soft voice, eyes flicking back to Rae, as if to assess the damage.

I try to reassure her. "Don't look so scared, I'm going to be fine?" But it comes out like a question; my voice breaks as I pour her wine. And then I tell them everything: every concern I had tried to smother over the past few months, how Rae's revelation and Shireen's advice gave me the confidence I needed to leave Theo behind, what it was finally like to tell him goodbye, the surge of fear that makes me wonder if I made an impulsive mistake.

"Edie, I think you did the right thing," Shireen says. "The room you're creating in your life by walking away from him is going to leave space for amazing things to come: more success, more adventures, more happiness. Maybe more men, but they seem like more trouble than they're worth."

"Men are honestly overrated," Rae says. "Gloria was independent by her generation's standards, but even so, she practically raised us since birth to look forward to meeting our husbands."

"Which is an insane amount of pressure to put on yourself," Shireen says. "I mean, no offense."

"None taken," I say glumly.

"Who you're dating, *if* you're dating—that's the least important thing about you," Shireen adds.

"There's so much more to life," Rae promises.

I want to believe them, but Shireen wasn't raised like us, and my sister has never been single like I have. Even without the weight of the prophecy, I'd probably feel pushed to find a partner. The world is built for pairs. The last time I was single, I thought about it constantly: when my groceries were too heavy to carry home from the store by myself, when my bed felt too wide and empty at night, every time Gloria coughed or stumbled and I realized there was no guarantee she'd be around to meet my future husband. And now she's gone.

"You did the right thing," Rae repeats. "You'll thank yourself later."

I have to believe they're right. I've staked everything on that.

"I know, but I'm scared," I admit.

"You took a major risk," Rae says. "It'd be ridiculous if you *weren't* scared."

"Everything heals in time," Shireen adds. "You were devastated after things ended with Jonah, but you put yourself back out there eventually, right?"

"Yeah, but first I went through a *long*, miserable period of crying twenty-four seven and reading way too far into Rupi Kaur's poetry," I recall. "I mean, I wore *sweatpants*. Outside. Multiple times."

"Her one true cry for help," Rae mutters to Shireen, who wrinkles her nose.

"Oh, I know," she says. "Look, things are going to be bleak for a while. But you'll be stronger, more resilient, and more interesting because of the shit."

I have to admit I like the sound of that—the idea that this pain has a purpose to force me to grow into a better woman.

"And fuck it, you need help finding the love of your life?" she continues. "I work in *recruiting*—I can personally put together a pool of qualified candidates and vet them all until we find the most amazing guy for you. We got this."

"We got this," Rae repeats, pressing the wine bottle back into my hands.

I imagine Shireen in a black pencil skirt with a prissy pussy bow blouse, peering over the top of a clipboard at a lineup of eligible bachelors, probing them for answers about why their last relationship ended and what they're looking for in their next one. I saw her grill Theo; I'd trust her to pick out my next boyfriend.

"Thanks for squeezing me in as a client," I joke to Shireen. "I'll swing by your office on Monday."

She offers an encouraging smile, but hesitation flickers across her face.

"What?" I ask.

"It's nothing," she says, grabbing the bottle of wine.

Rae calls her out. "You've always been a terrible liar."

"We can talk about it another time," Shireen insists. "Tonight's about Edie."

"And now I'm curious," I counter. "So spill."

She straightens up and tucks her hair behind her ears. She can't hide the joy that lights up her face.

"Okay, fine. I got the job. I'm going to be a senior associate."

"Hell yeah you did!" Rae says.

"Ah, this is amazing! Congratulations. I knew you'd get it."

Shireen darts her gaze from me to Rae.

"But there's something I didn't tell you earlier. I didn't want to bring it up if it wasn't going to happen. The job is in the Paris office."

I'm so exhausted, the pieces don't click for me right away.

"So, you'll work remotely?"

"I'm moving to France," she says gently.

The significance of her news hits me hard. Chalk it up to the twin thing, but I think Rae must realize I'm too much of an emotional wreck to handle this right now. She does the bulk of the heavy lifting, squealing over Shireen's news, peppering her with questions about her new responsibilities and which neighborhoods she might live in, and starting to plan our first trip to visit her in Paris.

Meanwhile, I'm spiraling. I already lost Theo. I can't lose Shireen, too. Even under the best of circumstances, living with my best friend halfway around the world would be brutal. My feelings have already been through a meat grinder once today. There's no way I'll be able to keep my chin up without her.

But I can't let Shireen know how I really feel. It would be selfish. She worked her ass off for this role. Ever since we flew home from our semester abroad back in college, she's always talked about finding her way back to Paris for good. She feels at home there, the same way I feel most myself right here in New York.

"I'm so happy for you," I blubber, even as I feel lonelier than I ever thought possible.

I sink into hugging her. My tears soak into her dark hair.

"I'm going to miss you so much," she says.

Rae throws her arms around us both and links her fingers through mine. She squeezes them tight, like she's always done to let me know I'm not alone. It's almost enough.

thirty-one

I begged Rae to give me another wedding planning task on Friday night simply so I could have something to do besides sit alone with my own thoughts. She offered up the ultimate busy work: stuffing the save-the-date cards into envelopes and addressing them to guests in neat cursive.

My hand cramps up every time I think about it, she texts. I've been putting it off all week.

Gimme gimme gimme. I got this.

I pick up the supplies from her apartment before she heads off to a night shift at the hospital. The paper goods are adorable: the wedding's color palette takes cues from the hashtag, #MaxsRaeOfSunshine, and accordingly, the save-the-date cards feature pops of sunny yellow along with peaches and corals—perfect for a summer celebration. I have a stack of matching envelopes, a list of names and addresses, and a roll of stamps. If this is what counts as a hot Friday night at this age, so be it.

In the spirit of making this feel like a capital-E Event worth dedicating my evening to, I try to make my night in feel special and cozy. I light a candle, turn on a jazz playlist, and throw on a crisp white pajama set—a boxy men's button-down with matching drawstring pants. The scent of fig, amber, and sandalwood curls through the apartment. I make myself a dirty martini using the fancy olives I splurged on after my breakup, figuring that if I can't have love yet, at least I can have a decent cocktail. I spread the stationery out across my kitchen table and start on the first envelope.

I tuck the save-the-date card inside, faceup, so Rae and Max's engagement photo is the first thing the recipient will see when they open the envelope. They took my suggestion—a photography session on the waterfront in Domino Park, with the full expanse of the Manhattan skyline twinkling behind them. This particular shot is one of my favorites: Rae is as confident as ever, laughing right at the camera, while Max looks tenderly down at her like he can't believe she's really his. They look so giddily in love, so fortified by each other. This is what I'm searching for, isn't it? I even stood there with Theo in that exact same spot after our first date at Sweetwater. That's where he kissed me for the first time. In that moment, I was so sure that the final piece of my life was falling perfectly into place. And now . . .

I shove the card into the envelope, lick the flap, and press it shut. Goodbye. Using my steadiest hand, I write out the recipient's address in the center. I affix a return address to the top left corner, a stamp to the top right corner, and I'm done with the first of a hundred envelopes.

The pajamas, the candle, the jazz, the martini—I'm not fooling myself. I'm alone. I can't do this.

I force myself to start in on the second envelope, but I break halfway through writing out the address. It's one thing to be happy that Rae and Max found each other, but it's no distraction for my heartbreak. I can't muster the energy to do this by myself. I reach for my phone, and pull up Bennett's name.

I know you're probably busy, but any chance you want to come over and help me address Rae and Max's save-the-dates? I text him.

We haven't seen each other since that night before the election at The Crown Inn. I'm sure he's swamped with work, prepping for Kiara's first term as a Congresswoman, but it's worth a shot.

My handwriting is chicken scratch, but I can keep you company, he texts back.

I'm surprised he's free. Deal.

While he's on his way over, I make him a martini to match mine and contemplate changing into real clothes, or at least fastening one more button on my pajama top. But it's just Bennett, right? Outside of work, I haven't had the energy to put together outfits lately. I'm wearing *clean pajamas*—practically my Sunday best.

When Bennett arrives, his cheeks are pink from the late November chill. He unwinds his scarf and hangs up his wool peacoat. His eyes flick over my shirt, catching on the open button. He looks away quickly. Should I have worn something else? I'm not sure which surprises me more: that I suddenly feel underdressed in front of him, or that I don't mind the attention.

"I like your place," he says, taking in the furniture, the art, and my workspace with the rack of clothing. "It's very you."

He doesn't seem to notice that I haven't vacuumed in weeks.

"Thank you. Come here, take a look at what we're working with."

He joins me at the table, examining one of the save-the-dates; his eyes crinkle into a wistful smile.

"Adorable," he says dryly.

"They could model for Hallmark."

He sighs. "Good for them."

I show him how many guests I've crossed off the list and how many more we have to go. He sticks a row of stamps along his pointer finger so I can easily pull them off one by one. We fall into a steady rhythm, a two-person machine, me writing addresses while he stuffs cards into envelopes. Out of all of the groomsmen, I'm glad he's the best man.

When I pause to shake out a cramp in my hand, I rip off the Band-Aid. "I broke up with Theo," I confess.

He chokes on an olive.

"Really?"

I sigh.

"He doesn't ever want kids, and I actually really do. It's not something I'm willing to compromise on."

"Sure, that's really important." He reaches for my arm sympathetically.

I'm hungry for validation that I didn't make a terrible mistake. "It *is*," I agree, feeling vindicated. "We fought, then ended things."

"How are you holding up?" he asks. There's a warmth to his voice that makes me feel like he really cares.

I hesitate. As far as I know, Rae and Max wouldn't have told Bennett about the prophecy.

"I thought he was 'The One,'" I say, making exaggerated air quotes. "So, you know . . . it's just overwhelming, even if I know it was the right choice. Ultimately, we're just not compatible."

"I wondered about that—how much sense you two made as a couple," Bennett admits.

"Was it that obvious?" I ask, cringing a little bit.

He hedges, fiddling with the roll of stamps. "You didn't want to talk about him at all the other night. He didn't seem to know what to do with himself at your grandmother's funeral. You moped around all weekend in Miami waiting for him to text you back."

I snap my gaze up to his. "You noticed that?"

He shrugs. "Yeah. You seemed kind of down."

"Oh."

I'm embarrassed he noticed. I plunk my head into my hands. Was it so obvious that Theo and I were out of sync?

"Hey, hey," Bennett says, gently prying my fingers away from my face. "Don't beat yourself up."

I straighten, busying myself with the task at hand. "I know. I'm trying not to."

I let myself soak up his steady brand of comfort. Bennett has a knack for turning my mood around. It's refreshing, especially after Theo's tendency to say or do exactly the thing that made my down moods worse.

He's quiet for a moment, stuffing cards into envelopes again and sticking stamps in a row down his finger. The stack of finished save-the-dates is now higher than the stack of unfinished ones. I flex my hand and start in on another address. That's when he clears his throat.

"Kiara broke up with me after the election." Disappointment knits his brows together and hardens the set of his jaw.

"Oh, Bennett! I'm so sorry. That's awful. I know how much you liked her."

He shrugs, as if to say, *What can you do?* The tenderness of the gesture makes me fold him into a tight hug. I'm sad for him, but not shocked. Kiara's life is about to get even busier—and she barely had any time for a relationship before. Still, he must be crushed.

"She said she felt we were better off as friends, which I'm going to pretend isn't a massive blow to my ego." He bites his lip and shakes his head, like he can shake off the sting of her words. "But it's fine."

"It's okay to not be fine. I've been a total disaster."

"Somehow, I doubt that."

"A barista casually asked, 'How are you?' while making my coffee the other day, and I almost started to cry. So, yeah, a disaster," I say. I peel a stamp off the tip of his finger and press it to an envelope.

"Well, then we can be disasters together," he says, forcing himself to sound cheerful.

"I like that. Team Breakup reporting for duty," I say, clinking my glass to his.

He cracks a smile—a real one. I've felt lonely since Theo left, but commiserating with Bennett lightens the load.

"We're the saddest, most pathetic wedding-planners Rae and Max could possibly ask for," he observes.

"I feel like that should be a good omen, somehow. Like rain on your wedding day, two newly single disasters leading your wedding party . . . there's something there," I say.

"We'll workshop it," he says.

He riffles through the slim stack of remaining save-the-dates. We'll be done soon, but I don't want him to go.

"What do you think about ordering takeout?" I ask.

Two hours later, the kitchen table is scattered with discarded Chinese take-out boxes. We're full after egg drop soup, scallion pancakes, and beef lo mein. The save-the-dates are completely stuffed, addressed, and ready to go. And Bennett and I have killed most of a bottle of wine while lounging on my couch, talking about anything and everything other than our breakups. He says he wants to adopt a cat, but his roommate is allergic. I help him with crossword clues. ("Wintour's sidekick, ten letters?" "Coddington.") He tells me about his new Saturday morning routine, scouring the *New York Times* real estate pages, which only stokes his desire to buy an apartment here someday, if he can ever save up for it. I didn't realize he has roots in this city, too; his grandmother Maria was a secretary at a Manhattan ad agency just like Gloria was.

She fell in love with one of the accountants. They got married and moved out to Chicago together, where she had family, and the rest is history.

"So, what's your plan?" Bennett asks. "Find a rebound? Swear off dating for a while?"

The question flusters me. For the first time, I'm aware of just how closely Bennett and I are sitting on the couch. I'm leaning against an overstuffed pillow and his socked feet rest on the edge of the coffee table. He had toed off his loafers halfway through the bottle of wine. He looks at ease here, like he's at home. For Bennett, relaxation is reserved for special occasions. With a surge of nervous energy, I get up to sweep the take-out boxes into the trash.

"I'm not exactly rushing to download a bunch of dating apps," I say tightly from across the room.

Which is true. I'm fresh off a jarring breakup. I don't know when I'll feel ready to put myself back out there again. It won't be easy. Attraction and chemistry only go so far, and I'm not willing to settle. I want someone sturdy and dependable, romantic and thoughtful, caring and loyal, sexy and substantial—someone like Bennett, come to think of it. And those kinds of guys are definitely not a dime a dozen on dating apps.

My breath catches with a new realization. I turn my back on Bennett, gathering up our used silverware and washing the forks and knives in the sink. I drizzle lemon-scented dish soap on a sponge as I let the intriguing new thought unfurl in full: What about Bennett himself?

Even at his lowest points tonight, Bennett's supportive warmth has made me see him in a different light. My heart has been so battered over the past year, it should be under glass and lock. Despite that, tonight has sparked a new sense of curiosity in me. I've always liked him as a friend—but could that shift into something else?

I dry my hands on a dish towel, compose myself, and turn to squint at Bennett reclining against a pile of throw pillows. Maybe it's the alcohol, or the heaviness I've felt since Gloria died, or how isolated I feel talking around the breakup without explaining the prophecy, but I make a split-second decision.

"Can I tell you something serious?" I return to the couch, nestling in with my feet tucked beneath me.

This time, I sit close to him on purpose, just to test out how it feels.

He cocks his head. "I'm listening."

"It's kind of a big deal. I've only told two people in my entire life."

The prospect of telling a third doesn't scare me. I'm confident Bennett will listen respectfully, maybe even in awe. I trust him with this private piece of my family's story.

He jolts upright. "Oh, shit. Wow, you weren't kidding, this is serious. Of course."

I tell the story from the beginning, starting with Gloria in the diner in 1958, rolling through her reveal of my date when I was sixteen, and ending with the catastrophic ramifications I could have triggered by breaking up with Theo. This time around, I don't jumble my words. Slack-jawed, he interjects to ask questions, but can't process more than, "What?" and "Whoa, I'm sorry, *what?!*"

Finally, he manages, "So, that's why Max always was so damn smug and assured about his relationship with Rae. I kept telling him—no offense to your sister, she's amazing—but how many people meet their person so young and actually manage to stay together?"

Knowing what I know now, I love to hear that Max has been so on board all along. "Now, *that* is something you'll have to ask them about. It's not my story to tell."

"That sounds dramatic."

"Trust me, it is."

"And growing up, you all believed this?" He sounds curious, not judgmental.

I nod. "Of course. There was proof all around me—my own parents, my aunts and uncles, my cousins. All happily ever after, just like she predicted."

He sputters out facts. "But it shouldn't work. It doesn't make any sense. There's no science behind it."

I've had the same thought myself. We all have. But that's how faith works—you put your trust in a power you can't see and don't fully understand because the infallibility of it resonates deep in your bones.

"You think we don't know that? Look, if your family had a magical shortcut to getting it right, you'd take it, too."

He grins.

"They think they do. Go to church, find a nice girl, marry her. Done."

"Not your style?"

"I haven't been to church regularly since high school. But you never questioned your faith in this?" he asks.

"Not until recently," I say pointedly. "Not until I wanted to fall in love with Theo so badly, and I just couldn't get there."

I feel naked admitting that to Bennett. He gives me a sympathetic look. I wonder how much he cared about Kiara. Did he love her?

I roll off the couch. "Enough of this. Come help me with these boxes."

Mom and Allen dropped them off at my apartment this week, and I haven't had the courage to open them until now. They've been methodically moving through Gloria's apartment, donating what they could (her dog-eared copy of *Valley of the Dolls*, a box set of *All in the Family* on VHS, an old hand mixer), selling off the orange mid-century modern sofa nobody has room for, tossing out the disintegrating linens from her 1958 hope chest. Mom took the pink brocade chair she loved as a girl, and Gloria's mah-jongg set will go to cousin Maya.

"What's in here?" Bennett asks, helping me gingerly move the top box onto the floor.

I rummage in my junk drawer for a pair of scissors to slit open the tape holding it together.

"Some of Gloria's clothes."

"Oh, *wow*." He knows how much this must mean to me.

I pull pieces out one by one, savoring the flood of memories they stir up. When I reach for her pink sequined jacket, a spray of light refracts off the shimmering fabric. She wore this to Mom and Allen's wedding; at the reception, she held hands with me and Rae as we danced in a wild, joyful circle to "Twist and Shout." I finger the long strands of turquoise beads, a souvenir from her Hawaii honeymoon, and remember the way she slipped them around my neck when I was a little girl playing dress-up. There's a 1970s plaid housecoat I've only seen her wear in yellowing pictures tucked into old family photo albums, and a plush sweater that still carries her perfume.

I press the sweater to my nose, closing my eyes and inhaling her familiar scent of Shalimar. My vision brims with tears. I don't mind that Bennett sees. I bet he's had this exact same feeling a hundred times.

"I wish I could tell her I miss her," I say, once I feel steady enough to speak. I dab my eyes.

"You still can. I talk to Gabe sometimes. I give him updates on what's going on with the family. I tell him how the Cubs are doing—he was such a big fan. And when I need advice, I ask him for his input. I don't really believe he can hear me, but it makes me feel like he's still here."

"That sounds comforting."

He nods. "It is."

"I don't know if I believe she's up there. Listening."

I think back to the blunt sound of cold dirt hitting her casket. I can't shake it. It's hard to imagine she's anywhere else but there.

"All the impossible magic she had you believing in, and heaven is where you draw the line?" he asks.

I laugh, seeing his point.

"Fine. It's comforting to imagine her up there."

"She can hang out with my brother. He'll show her the ropes."

"She'll teach him to make martinis."

"And he'll teach her the rules of baseball."

It's a ridiculous scene to imagine. I adore it. I'm grateful for the way he lessens the sting of my grief.

"If she's watching, then she'll know what happens—she'll know I broke up with Theo." With a lift of my eyebrow, I add, "She'll know if I fall in love with someone else."

Bennett starts to cut open another box.

I slump against the wall and drain the last few sips from my wineglass, contemplating the question that's been on my mind ever since I broke up with Theo. I wonder what Gloria would think of my decision. Would she be disappointed in me? Would she understand why I did it?

"She loved you," Bennett says softly, like he can read my mind, as if that explains everything. "No matter what."

I contemplate that as I sift through the items in the second box, garments I've run my fingers over a hundred times as a kid. I want to believe him.

"You said you ask Gabe for advice sometimes?" I ask.

"Yeah."

Then "I'm going to head over to the cemetery this weekend. Gloria and I have a lot to discuss."

thirty-two

I'm on my way to the cemetery to talk to Gloria when the universe gives me a sign. I took the subway into Queens to get as close to the cemetery as I could, then called an Uber for the remainder of the trip. I've been staring out the window of the black sedan—barely registering the sound of the radio or the houses and restaurants whizzing past as I replay every interaction I've had with Bennett in the past six months, straining for any possible hint of his feelings for me—when a familiar set of guitar chords fills the car. And then a deep, gritty voice. It's Theo.

"Thirty thousand feet up / I met this glamour girl / Now I'm living in a whole new world."

I lurch forward.

"Can you turn it up?"

The cab driver indulges me.

"You like this song?"

How unbelievably surreal.

"I, um, sure?"

I peer through my fingers, soaking in the shock of it all, as Theo continues to sing.

"And now I'm soaring, soaring / High-flying with my Brooklyn babe / Feels so right, it has to be fate."

So, The Supersonics are on the radio. Theo is getting what he wanted. I can only imagine what's next for him: a new life in LA, stardom, flocks of women. I have a hunch he'll be all right.

The driver drops me off. It takes me a few minutes to wind through rows of gravestones, some darkened with age, some adorned with small rocks to keep loved ones' memories alive, until I find those of my grandparents. Per Jewish tradition, Gloria's side won't be engraved until next year, when our family will gather here again in her honor.

I don't know exactly how to go about this. All I have are my instincts. I look around in the grass and dirt to find two stones to place atop their gravestone. Two tributes to show I haven't forgotten about them and never will. I sit cross-legged a few feet in front of Grandpa Ray and Gloria's grave, pulling my spine up to be ramrod straight, the way she always wished I would. Cold seeps into my jeans.

Hi Gloria, I think.

The air is still in the cemetery. I don't feel heard. I don't know how this is supposed to work.

"Hi Gloria," I mutter. Maybe that's better. In a louder, clearer voice, I continue. "I miss you so much, you have no idea. We talk about you all the time, me and Rae and Mom. You know, I wanted to play mah-jongg last week, and had nobody to play with?"

A sob slips out. I keep going.

"And I saw this ad on the subway today for Balanchine's *Jewels* at Lincoln Center. I know it's one of your favorites. I thought about going, even though it wouldn't be the same without you. Maybe I'll get two tickets for me and Rae. What do you think about that?"

My face crumples in a way I've grown far too accustomed to over the past few months. I'm so sick of crying. I crunch forward and let the tears fall until my breathing settles into a steady rhythm again.

"Gloria, I don't know if you can hear me. I have to believe that you can. Because I really need your advice."

I tell her everything: how I tried to make it work with Theo, how I knew we could never be truly happy together, how I broke it off. Part of me feels silly, pleading with a slab of stone in a frigid cemetery, with only the faint roar of the nearby highway and a single chirping bird flitting overhead. It's not like Gloria is going to talk back to me. I'm alone here. But part of me needs to believe that I'm not. That she's listening. That she's not gone for good.

It's too easy to imagine her reaction. I can envision her pursing her lips, swirling her martini around in her glass, a judgmental *ha* when she hears I have the chutzpah to walk away from Theo.

Go back to JFK, dollface, she'd say. *Go back to Clifton*, bubbeleh. *Wander around. See if anyone catches your eye. You Millenniums, you think you can do whatever you please? In my day, we listened to our elders. You'd be wise to do so, too.*

Or maybe—no. Would she be more sympathetic?

Well, you sound stressed and exhausted. *Why don't you go book a manicure, hm? I never think straight unless my cuticles are in order.*

Or more maternal?

My poor, beautiful, confused granddaughter. You look like you need a bowl of matzo ball soup. That'll perk you right up.

I strain for her voice, as if hearing her response is merely a matter of listening carefully. But there's nothing. She is gone. And without her, I have to find my own path.

The flare of attraction I felt for Bennett the other night hasn't burned out. Instead, it's only grown. Maybe I'm looking at him through bleary-eyed heartbreak goggles, but even if that's the case, he looks damn good: I like his self-assured posture, his warm brown eyes that blaze whenever he talks about politics or his brother, and his thick, dark hair he tries to comb so carefully. I like the speedy rat-a-tat-tat of his speech, like he's afraid of running out of time to express every last one of his thoughts, and the way he wants to effect real change in our country by keeping its citizens safe. And I'm touched by the way he reacted to the prophecy, respecting it even if he doesn't believe in it himself.

My instincts tell me this is more than just a superficial crush. I was always bothered by how fleeting Theo seemed—ready to go on tour at the drop of the hat, itching at the idea of marriage, uninterested in building a family with me. But Bennett is as sturdy as the earth beneath me. He dreams of putting roots down in New York. He's a family kind of guy, and thanks to Max, he already knows and loves my inner circle. Again and again, he's shown up for me, coming through with just the right words at Gloria's funeral and keeping me company long after Rae and Max's save-the-dates were finished.

I've never let myself dwell on the possibility of anything important happening with anyone other than my fated match. But my sister bucked tradition and found romantic bliss. It's suddenly not so hard to imagine something blooming between me and Bennett. There's already friendship and trust. Care, too. Attraction, at least on my side. I don't know how he feels about me. And he was just so smitten with Kiara. For the first time, that terrifies me.

If Rae and Max can pursue unlikely love, then maybe I can, too. It's romantic as hell. Maybe doomed, who knows. Knowing the obstacles you're up against and choosing to face them together, united as a team—it makes my chest swell with hope.

Gloria was eccentric, sharply particular, and devoted to her intuition. But she also loved her family and wanted us to be happy. I can imagine a world in which she would tell me to forget about the prophecy, if that's I want to do. In Gloria's mind, I think falling in love with the right person was a shortcut to happiness. But maybe there are other ways to finding satisfaction and joy: carving out your own path, learning to trust your gut.

"Hey, Gloria? If you can hear me, remember that I love you. And I hope you understand what I'm going to do next."

thirty-three

On Tuesday morning, I wait until I know Max has left for work, then walk over to Rae's. She thinks I'm swinging by to drop off the save-the-dates—which is true, but that's not the only reason I need to see my sister. My realization has been fluttering in my chest for days, growing stronger with each wild thump of my heart.

As I climb the stairs to Rae and Max's third-floor walk-up, I try to anticipate how my twin might react to what I'm about to tell her. I know her better than anyone else in the world, but this situation is so thorny, it's hard to predict her response. Will she be enthusiastic, excited? Or wary of my crush making uncomfortable waves with her fiancé's best friend and best man in the lead-up to the wedding? I knock on the door and pick at my cuticles while I wait for Rae to let me in.

"Hiii," I trill when she opens up, forcing a normal smile.

Inside the apartment, I present her with two shoeboxes filled with stacks of the neatly addressed envelopes containing her save-the-dates. She opens the lid and examines the paper goods, cooing at the swoops and flourishes of my cursive.

"Thank you so much. They look stunning. These must have taken you hours—I owe you."

I take a seat at her kitchen island, attempting to sound casual. "Actually, it wasn't such an ordeal. Bennett helped me with them."

"Oh, that was sweet of him," she says.

"It was," I say, swallowing hard. Before I lose my nerve, I blurt out, "Do you like him?"

Rae pauses by the coffee maker, where she's measuring out scoops of grounds. "Bennett? Of course, he's Max's best friend."

I perform the world's least casual shrug. "I mean, do you enjoy hanging out with him? Do you think he's a solid guy?"

She narrows her eyes suspiciously. "I think he's fantastic, and also a fantastic candidate for an early heart attack, the way he's addicted to stress and caffeine. Why?"

I slump over the island, mashing the heels of my hands against my cheeks. I look up at her through my eyelashes. My crush feels like a shaken-up can of soda ready to explode.

"When he was at my place the other night, I don't know, there was a . . . a flicker of something new," I say shyly.

Rae rocks forward onto her elbows, sucking in a breath. Her pupils widen, glimmering with something. Excitement? Or alarm?

"We were talking about our breakups, and for the first time, it occurred to me that I could see him as more than a friend," I continue.

Her jaw unhinges for only a moment as she digests my news.

"Whoa, you *like* him."

"I think I really do, yeah," I admit.

"Like how much?"

My words tumble out as fast as Bennett's usually do. Is this how he feels all the time, bursting with too many urgent thoughts?

"I'm not about to run over and propose, but the other day, I was feeling down, and he just turned it all around. He made the night fun, you know? With Theo, so much revolved around huge things, like fate, marriage, him writing music about me—and those are all big, important things, but I also want someone who celebrates the little joys. On Friday, Bennett and I just bummed around my apartment, ordering takeout and splitting a bottle of wine, talking. Nothing fancy, but it was the best."

"And that's how a relationship should be," Rae finishes, lifting one satisfied eyebrow.

"Right? It's the small stuff that counts."

"Did anything . . . happen?"

"No! God, no. I swear."

I'm not blind; this isn't the first time I've noticed he's attractive. But when I was with Theo, it felt wrong to dwell on that.

Rae watches me, thinking.

"I'm into this," Rae announces.

"You are?" I ask, shocked. "But I met him on the wrong day, and we both just went through breakups. He might not even be interested in me and—"

"*And*," Rae interjects pointedly, "I can see it, you two together. It makes sense."

A shaky laugh rises through my chest. "It does?"

So I wasn't just fantasizing. As much as I craved Rae's encouragement, receiving it feels surreal. The part of me shaped by Gloria's prophetic powers had me convinced that seeing Bennett in a romantic light was wrong—but maybe it isn't.

She purses her lips, like she's trying to figure out the best way to articulate it. "Don't you think you two balance each other out? You're the romantic with your head in the clouds, and he's the practical one with the big heart. And you already make a good team. You planned that Miami trip flawlessly."

She's right. I like the way we play off each other, similarly to the way Rae's personality bounces off Max's. I had initially appreciated that Theo and I were both creatives, but there's something satisfying about letting Bennett be the straight man. The more grounded he is, the more vibrant I feel by comparison. And when I was lonely on Friday night, he was the first person I thought of to keep me company.

There's another potential roadblock tripping me up.

"Would it be weird, you and I dating a pair of best friends?" I ask.

"At least they're not twins."

"Thank god for that."

She slides a mug of coffee my way.

"Would you be okay if I maybe talked to Bennett about this?" I ask in a small voice. "Told him how I feel? Or is that too risky right now with the wedding coming up?"

She tilts her head, thinking it over. "I think it'd be worse if you tamped down your feelings, then had to walk down the aisle with him at my wedding, downed champagne from the open bar, and then spilled your guts to him on the dance floor."

"That would be a nightmare," I agree.

"Look, you're adults. I trust you can have a mature conversation about this. If it turns out he feels the same way, amazing—and if not, the wedding isn't until August. There's plenty of time for you to lick your wounds privately and move on."

I take a long slug of coffee as I churn over what to do. Bennett hasn't really shown any romantic interest in me, but on the other hand, he and I have both been dating other people ever since we met. And if it turns out he doesn't see me as more than a friend, I'll be embarrassed, but I trust him to handle my feelings with care. After all, he's just been through that same thing. He's too much of a gentleman to make this painful for me.

Ever since I left the cemetery, I've been straining for signs that Gloria has heard me. I bought a box of apricot and raspberry rugelach with her in mind, but it's not like her approval was spelled out in sugar dust across the pastries. I slipped her strand of turquoise beads under my sweater, pressed close to my chest like a talisman, so I could carry her with me. But I don't feel any more imbued with wisdom. I'm just the same old me.

If I can't get Gloria's approval of pursuing Bennett, then my sister's is the next best thing. We lock eyes. Twin ESP isn't a real thing, but I know she can plainly read the nervous hope dancing in my eyes.

"Please don't say anything to Max about this until I get a chance to talk to Bennett," I ask.

In the past, I might have worried about her bubbling enthusiasm—I'd fear that even with the best of intentions, she'd be too giddy to keep her lips sealed. Now, though, I know she's an old pro at swallowing secrets when it comes to pursuing the person who makes you happy.

"I'll wait for your green light," she promises.

Now I just have to figure out how to tell Bennett what's on my mind. The prospect of confessing my feelings to him is terrifying. But I have to trust I'll be brave enough to try.

thirty-four

I lure Bennett to my apartment that weekend under the pretense of more wedding planning.

"Am I not pulling my weight with best man duties? Why does Rae dump this on you when Max lets me off scot-free?" he asks, hanging up his coat by my door.

While I was dating Theo, I never let myself consider Bennett's looks. But now, I take in his thick hair, dark eyes, and strong chin, and let myself appreciate his handsome features. I get flustered.

"Excellent point. Blame it on the patriarchy, I guess. Men should plan more weddings," I babble. My raw nerves are getting the best of me.

"So, what are we doing, researching caterers? Picking out bridesmaid's dresses? Don't tell me it's already time to do the seating chart," he groans.

"I'm going to research some florists—send some emails about availability and pricing." This is entirely made-up busy work. Rae never asked me to do this. "And you're going to keep me company."

"That's all?" he asks.

"I made you a crossword puzzle," I say, thrusting the piece of paper at him before I lose my courage.

It had taken me all afternoon to write the clues and fit all the words together.

"What?" he looks down, furrowing his brow. "Why?"

"See if you can solve it," I say, dodging his question. "Now. While I work."

He laughs. "This doesn't look too difficult."

"Good." I slide a pen his way. "Or do you work in pencil?"

"I'm feeling confident enough to go pen on this one."

"Impressive. Good luck."

I take the seat next to him at the table, open my laptop and type *Brooklyn florists*—I think. I could have Googled *turkey sandwiches* or *bioluminescent plankton*, for all I'm paying attention. I pretend to read Yelp reviews.

"Some of this seems a little personal, no?" he asks, crossing off a clue.

I suppress a smile. "Hmmm."

"Five across, 'writing utensil,' thirteen letters. It couldn't be my Cross Townsend pen, could it?"

He spins my own cheap Bic around his finger. I never noticed his hands before: supple where Theo's were calloused from playing guitar.

"I haven't the faintest idea."

"And six down, 'vacation spot,' five letters. Miami?"

"That might ring a bell."

"Might?" He raises a thick eyebrow.

I shrug.

"You're distracting me from ranunculus research. Shush."

He gives me a long, steely look like he absolutely knows something is up. I hold his gaze steady for as long as I can bear before blushing and returning to the laptop. I don't have a speech prepared or anything specific to say—I'm hoping that when the right moment comes, the words will click into place.

Because once he finishes the crossword, he'll see the answer to eight across, which spans the center of the puzzle. Clue: "Edie wants to know . . ." Eighteen letters.

I bang out my jitters on my keyboard, typing noisy notes about the benefits of long-stemmed roses versus short. If any of this winds up remotely usable to Rae, I'll be shocked.

Bennett jots down another answer. He wasn't kidding about his handwriting being chicken scratch. He's filled out more than half the puzzle, but eight across is still riddled with blank spaces.

"The answer to thirteen down, 'high school nerds,' appears to be, 'mock trial team.'"

I finally break. A peal of laughter escapes.

He makes a tortured face.

"Highly specific. Feels a little like a jab, if I'm going to be honest."

"I can't confirm or deny if that's the correct answer," I demur.

He rolls his eyes. "Of course you can't."

Thirteen down intersects with eight across. I steal another peek at the grid, watching him mull over the next clue. He fills in another down, scribbles a potential answer in the margins for an across, and solves yet another down that intersects with eight across. He taps his pen over the crossword, silently counting out a guess. I'm too frozen to keep up the ruse of doing any research. Rae can wrangle her own damn bouquet.

Bennett double-checks his guess, dotting his pen over each space on the puzzle. We're just inches apart. He turns to me, looking at me curiously.

"Edie," he says slowly, removing his glasses and running a hand over his eyes, like he's afraid he's seeing things.

"Yes?" My heart rattles against my rib cage.

"Eight across. 'Edie wants to know . . .'"

"It's a question," I say, giving a him a hint.

"I know it's a question. It's eighteen letters. I think it's six words," he ventures.

"Correct."

We lock eyes, each daring the other to make the move. It's far too late for me to back down now. I've practically spelled out his next step for him in black and white.

He rolls his lower lip between his teeth, then grins. Time stretches out like taffy. "'Will you go out with me?'"

Silence hangs between us for a split second, stunned on his end and intoxicatingly hopeful on mine. I feel like I'm ticking up to the very peak of a roller coaster, waiting to free-fall into exhilarating loop-de-loops.

I summon all my courage and flash him a flirtatious smile. "I thought you'd never ask."

He lets out a bark of laughter.

"Oh, that's rich. You're *literally* putting words in my mouth."

"I can say it myself. Bennett, will you go out with me?"

He twists in his seat so he's facing me. The corner of his mouth twitches up skeptically.

"Out with you on a date? Not as friends?"

I push through fluttering nerves to clarify.

"A real date. Nothing platonic about it."

He falters for a half second. My confidence plummets like a roller coaster's sickening drop.

"I don't know if I have a great track record of dating my friends. What, are you going to ask me to run your campaign next?"

He tosses that off casually, like a joke, but I know there's real pain there. Which is why I've waited all week to pull this stunt. I wanted to make sure my feelings for him weren't some desperate whim. I had lain awake late at night, unable to sleep because my thoughts kept circling around this whip-smart, big-hearted guy. I was pleasantly surprised—and terrified—to find that the more I considered a relationship with Bennett, the more hope blossomed in my chest. Spelling out my interest makes me feel uncomfortably vulnerable, but this is too important for me to back down now. I owe it to myself to be honest.

"I'm asking you out because I like you, Bennett. That's all there is to it."

"But the prophecy—"

"Isn't the only thing that matters," I finish firmly. "I took your advice. I talked to Gloria. It helped me make peace with my feelings. I think she'd want me to be happy."

"And you think you'd be happy with me?"

"I'm already happy around you."

A bashful grin lights up his face. I can't believe I can make him smile like that. He anchors one hand on my knee, and then his soft lips are on mine. His kiss feels like the first warm spring afternoon that warrants a breezy little white dress, like the first bite of a molten chocolate lava cake you know you're going to devour until the plate is licked clean. It tastes like a promise. The promise of good things coming soon. It's not a guarantee that we'll be together forever, or even together at all—but we can try. I kiss him back.

thirty-five

By the time Rae and Max's wedding date rolls around in August, Bennett and I are in love. Our relationship bloomed quickly once we gave ourselves permission to explore our feelings for each other. It turned out that he had been intrigued by me, too—only he hadn't been brave enough to make the first move. I'm so thankful I did.

At first, dating him felt like a revelation. When he spoke, I simply listened. I could never truly listen to Theo; instead, I nodded along as my brain whirred to calculate our chances of compatibility, which rose or fell with every new detail he shared about himself. Now that my nerves had quieted down, I could instead pay attention to how I really felt: curious, peaceful, adored, safe.

I learned to appreciate the steady hum of the radio tuned to NPR in Bennett's apartment, and the stack of *New York Times* and *Washington Post* deliveries dropped on his stoop every morning. I discovered he curses in Spanish, cries at sports movies, and goes to church exactly once every year on the anniversary of Gabe's death. I found he has a steel-trap memory, which was adorable when he surprised me with a visit to the Met's Costume Institute exhibit after I offhandedly mentioned wanting to go, and less adorable when I realized he could recall every single instance I've been late for plans due to last-minute outfit changes. I was pleasantly surprised to find that fast-talking, goal-oriented Bennett shuts up and slows down in exactly one place: bed. He leaves languid kisses down the nape of my neck and across the ridge of my hip. He savors undoing me.

This is what love *should* feel like. The first time he saw me with a cold, he got Gloria's matzo ball soup recipe from Max and made me a pot from scratch. Two weeks before our first trip to Chicago, where I met his parents, he gave me a full hour-by-hour itinerary because he knew planning my outfits ahead of time would bolster my confidence. And when I got hit with a burst of inspiration for my first *Vogue* cover, which shot last month, he helped me tack up images on the moodboard on our living room wall. Our love is woven into the fabric of our lives; it's not some puffed-up fantasy built on shaky ground.

He moved into my apartment in June, when his lease was up. We hadn't been together long, but it felt so right. I didn't agonize over giving up half my closet space because the prospect of not waking up to his downy warmth and soft breath tickling my back every morning was even worse. On moving day, he schlepped in boxes of suits, biographies of politicians, and a framed photo of Gabe, age twelve, in a baseball uniform with a bat slung over his shoulder. He bought us a potted plant to see if we could keep it alive. "It's a good litmus test to see if we can manage a cat," he said. "And if we can do *that*, then we can trust ourselves with a little human or two someday."

It's too soon for us to map out our lives together beyond a shared lease and joint custody of a fiddle-leaf fig. We haven't even been dating for a year yet. But I'd be extraordinarily lucky to have him in my life for good, and I know he feels the same way about me. Maybe fate has something else in store—I'm not arrogant enough to definitively say there are no curveballs coming our way. Still, I hope the future is ours to shape and mold together.

Rae and Max's wedding is held at the Brooklyn Botanic Garden on a vibrant day in early August. Sun sparkles across fifty-two acres of lush green grass and fields of magnolias, shrub roses, water-lilies, sacred lotuses. Guests are gathered in rows of white wooden chairs facing a chuppah covered in vines. During the ceremony's procession, Bennett and I walk down the aisle arm in arm. When we reach the end, we split up: I move to my sister's side on the left, he steps next to the groom on the right. Max turns to give him a tiny bemused look as if to say, *You're next?* The moment gives me the best kind of chills.

Watching my sister marry the love of her life would be beautiful no matter what. (And she looks stunning in a minimalist white silk gown with a single row of delicate pearl buttons down the low-cut back.) But knowing what she risked to keep Max in her life, this day feels even more enormously powerful. I choke out a tiny sob when she slides Grandpa Ray's gold wedding band onto Max's ring finger. It fits like it was made for him. When he breaks a glass wrapped in a cloth napkin under his foot, the guests erupt into raucous cheers.

At the reception under the garden's iconic glass dome, every table overflows with a cornucopia of wildflowers. I make a toast to the happy couple, who glow pink-cheeked with radiant smiles. Bennett helps lift Rae's and Max's chairs during the hora. Olivia shows Shireen—jet-lagged from Paris but still more than ready to celebrate—adorable photos of her infant. Alana and Trevor slow-dance. There's no bouquet toss because the last thing Rae wants to do is put unreasonable pressure on anyone.

Annette Lyons, Gloria's oldest friend from the ad agency and a friend of our family for decades, waves me and Bennett over to her chair. She's remarkably sharp for ninety; Rae says she RSVPed with a promise to make it to the dance floor. Enormous clip-on earrings and a swipe of coral lipstick brighten up her deeply lined face.

"Hi, Annette." I greet her with a hug and make introductions. "This is my boyfriend, Bennett."

"I remember you," she tells him. "I saw you at the funeral. You looked awfully familiar."

"How are you doing?" I ask.

She scowls. "My daughter is making me move into some godforsaken assisted living home. Not that I need that. But she's been packing up my things, going through decades of belongings and tchotchkes and dusty photo albums. And that's where she found something I think you should see."

She reaches one shaky hand for her purse, fumbles with the clasp for a moment, and produces a black-and-white photograph. The edges curl and ripple with age. There are six twenty-something couples in formalwear seated at a round table covered in a white tablecloth. The bottom right corner is scrawled with "1957" in faded black pen.

"That was the ad agency's holiday party. Secretaries, accountants, ad men. You recognize anyone?" Annette asks.

I peer at it closely. A familiar face catches my eye.

"That's Gloria."

"And?" Annette prompts.

I scan the other faces. "Is that you?" I ask, indicating the young woman in a bouffant and glittering earrings next to my grandmother.

"That was me."

"Beautiful. Thank you for showing this to me," I say, handing it back to her. "This is so lovely."

"No, take another look," she insists. "You, too, mister."

Bennett cranes his neck. As I point out Gloria and Annette to him, his jaw goes slack. He stares at the couple seated next to my grandmother.

"Those are my grandparents," he marvels.

Annette slaps the table.

"I knew it. You look exactly like your grandfather."

"You knew them? How?" I ask, baffled.

He figures it out before I do.

"They met at an ad agency in New York. I didn't realize it was the same one Gloria worked at."

"She set them up!" Annette supplies. "They were her first match."

I can't believe it. I take a closer look at the picture. It's like seeing Bennett transported back in time. He and his grandfather share the same warm, crinkling eyes, the same lock of dark hair that springs forward over their forehead, the same strong chin. His grandfather is in a white dinner jacket and black bow tie, like a crisp James Bond. His grandmother has cat-eye glasses, short curls that show off her features, and a familiar smile—the same one spreading across Bennett's face right now.

"She would have loved to see this," Annette says. "I know she'd be so happy. So proud."

"I wish she could be here with us," Bennett says.

I press the photo to my chest. "I know she is."

acknowledgments

Whew—writing a novel during a pandemic is not easy! I was in the earliest stages of working on another idea when Covid-19 upended our lives, but as the news turned bleak and tragic, I wanted to switch gears. So, in April 2020, I set out to write something vibrant and full of all the things I missed: bustling streets, restaurants, bars, live music, travel, flirting, wearing real clothes, hugging my grandparents, and the characters who make New York such a memorable city. Escaping into Edie's world sustained me through a strange year. I hope her story brought you a little slice of joy, the same way it did for me.

My agent, Allison Hunter, is spectacular. Her enthusiasm and passion for this book made 2020 a little brighter—a true feat. I adore having Allison as my guide, cheerleader, collaborator, and friend. It's always a pleasure working with Natalie Edwards, an excellent sounding board who kept us organized every step of the way, and I'm thankful for everyone's support at Janklow & Nesbit.

My editor, Kaitlin Olson, challenges me to become a stronger writer with each draft and each book. She has an incredible knack for distilling a manuscript to its heart and finding ways to make it sing. Her wise editorial feedback (how is she *always* right?) is such a gift. Jade Hui ensured we were running smoothly on track. Tamara Arellano and Lisa Nicholas lent their eagle eyes to this manuscript, and Vi-An Nguyen created this knockout cover. Without Megan Rudloff's savvy public relations skills and Katelyn Phillips's and Karlyn Hixson's top-notch marketing expertise, this book would likely not be in anyone's hands right now. Many thanks to Lindsay Sagnette, Suzanne Donahue, Jimmy Iacobelli, Libby McGuire, and Dana Trocker at Atria Books for their continued faith in me.

At UTA, Mary Pender-Coplan is a true wonder, and I'm glad to have Orly Greenberg's assistance. Special thanks to Kylie McConville, Emma Rosenblum, and Bryan Goldberg at BDG for letting me balance both sides of my career.

The book community continues to blow me away every day. I'm particularly honored to have support from indie bookstores, including some local gems—McNally Jackson, WORD, and The Strand—as well as Porter Square Books and The Ripped Bodice. Magic happens between these shelves; it feels very special to play a tiny part in that. Many thanks to #bookstagram for spreading the word about my novels. And most important, to each of my readers: thank you. Your ongoing support means I can live my biggest dream. It is the ultimate gift.

Many people were kind enough to let me grill them on various subjects to ensure *Meant to Be Mine* would feel as authentic as possible. Audree Kate López provided insight into her work as a stylist so I could paint an accurate picture of Edie's career. Morgan Sperry broke down the wild world of political campaigns to add color to Kiara's and Bennett's work. Roshan Berentes graciously let me borrow details of her life to flesh out Shireen's character. Kelsey Mulvey shared her knowledge of Westchester, and Veronica Lopez helped me craft a fabulous Miami itinerary. Dr. Emma Albert-Stone and Dr. Julian Bruce Orenstein taught me about heart attacks, Xander and Zoe Orenstein walked me through the finer points of Jewish burials, and Julia Orenstein taught me a thing or two about indie rock bands.

To all my friends, you know who you are! From sending bottles of bubbly when I finish drafts to cheering me on at book signings (even virtual ones!), I'm the luckiest to have you in my life. There's a reason I've never written a book without an A+ best friend character—you're it.

My grandparents were endless sources of inspiration for this novel. To create a beloved New York icon like Gloria, I turned to my memories of Rose Orenstein time and time again. I was delighted to include a nod to Fred Orenstein's lifelong disdain for Barbra Streisand, which extends beyond the grave. Jerry Hart's colorful vocabulary inspired Gloria's use of "*bubbeleh*," "dollface," "Millenniums," and so much more. Eleanor Hart passed down her mastery of mah-jongg and her matzo ball soup recipe (try it—you'll love it). Given their influence, I knew from the start that *Meant to Be Mine* would be dedicated to my grandparents. What I didn't know was that during the months I spent writing the first draft, our family would lose both Jerry and Eleanor within just twenty-seven days. I didn't get a chance to share the dedication with her before she passed, but I'm so enormously grateful I was able to tell him. They were the best book publicists Boynton Beach, Florida, has ever seen, and I am so happy to have had nearly three decades with them.

Nearly every fated date in this book corresponds with a significant day in my own family's history. At its core, this story is about love and family, and I've been surrounded by the best examples of both. To Jack, Audrey, and Julia Orenstein, I love you. Julia, nothing can top the way your face lights up when you read my early drafts—thank you. Mom and Dad, you were my first favorite love story. Your extraordinary support and unshakable belief in me make all of this possible. The Meyers have nothing on us.

GLORIA MEYER'S MATZO BALL SOUP

. . . which is really my grandma Eleanor Hart's recipe for matzo ball soup. The golden broth is filmy, rich with flavor, and serves as a home to matzo balls (although it's just as delicious on its own). This "Jewish penicillin" is a holiday dinner staple, but it's also perfect for the cold winter months or when you're sick. Each spoonful warms you up and tastes like a hug. Forget your Bat Mitzvah—mastering this soup is the true sign you've become a Jewish woman.

When I asked my grandma to teach me the recipe a few years ago, she said, "Well, it's not a real recipe. My mother made it this way. Everyone makes it this way." And now you can, too.

As is the case with many family recipes that get passed down through the generations, the measurements aren't exact. Women like Gloria cooked by instinct. I've provided my grandma's suggestions verbatim, as well as an approximation based on my own experiences making this soup.

Serves 6 to 8

For the broth

1 whole chicken

1 yellow onion, skin on

"lots of celery, cut into pieces" (2 stalks)

"lots of carrot, cut into pieces" (2 large carrots, peeled)

"some parsnip, a piece or two, nothing much" (a two-inch piece)

kosher salt, to taste

pepper, to taste

1. Clean the chicken.
2. Place the chicken, onion, celery, carrot, and parsnip, and salt and pepper, to taste, in a large pot with enough water to cover the ingredients, and bring to a boil over high heat.
3. Once boiling, remove the scum that comes off the chicken.
4. Turn the heat to low and let it cook for 90 minutes. Every 30 minutes or so, remove the scum and (if needed) add salt and pepper. If the soup's flavor isn't strong enough after 90 minutes, continue cooking it.

For the matzo balls

Follow the directions on the Manischewitz Matzo Ball Mix box.

about the author

Hannah Orenstein is the author of *Playing with Matches, Love at First Like*, and *Head Over Heels*, and is the deputy editor of dating at *Elite Daily*. Previously, she was a writer and editor at Seventeen.com. She lives in Brooklyn.